SECOTAN

AN ALTERNATIVE ENERGY NOVEL

Alset Publishing

ISBN: 0615434924
ISBN-13: 9780615434926

SECOTAN

AN ALTERNATIVE ENERGY NOVEL

– HENRY GORHAM –

Colonial North Carolina 1714

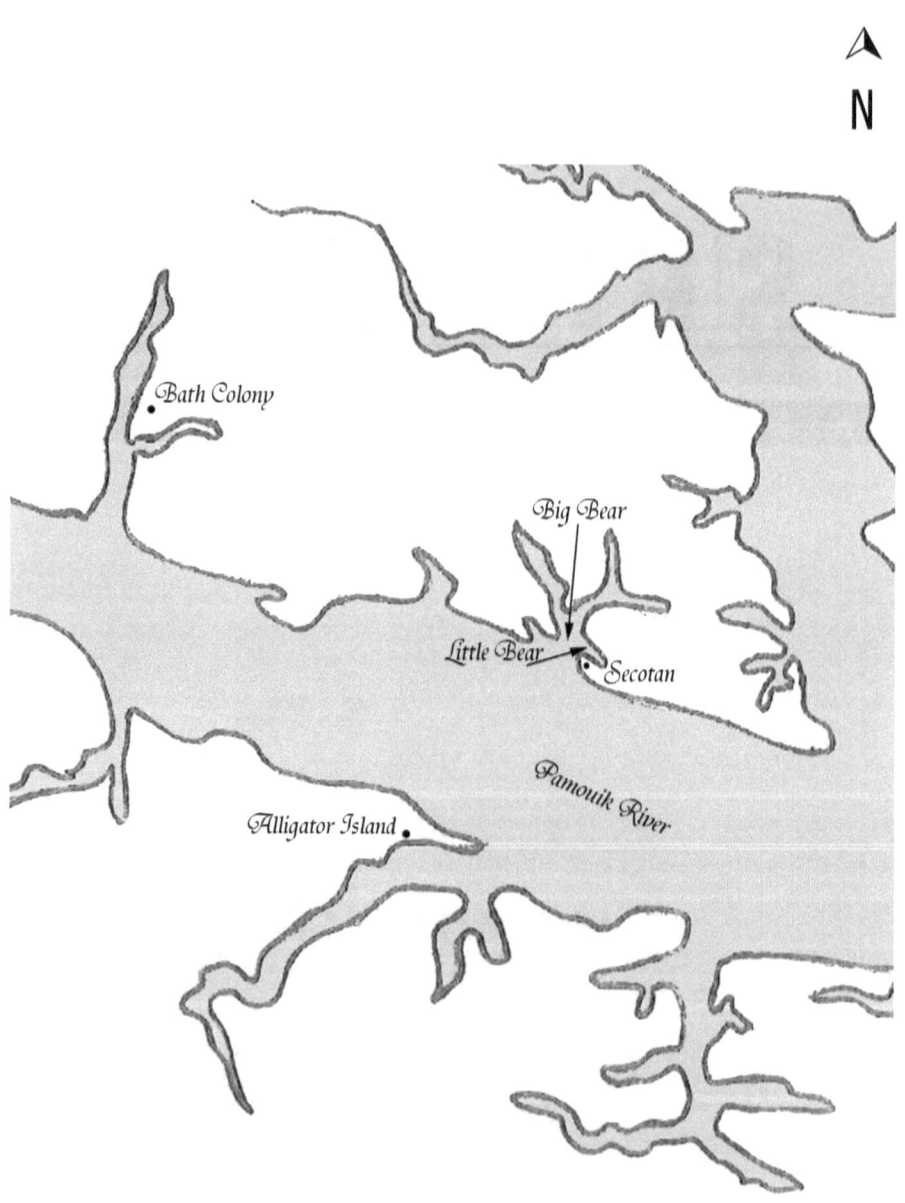

North Carolina 2008

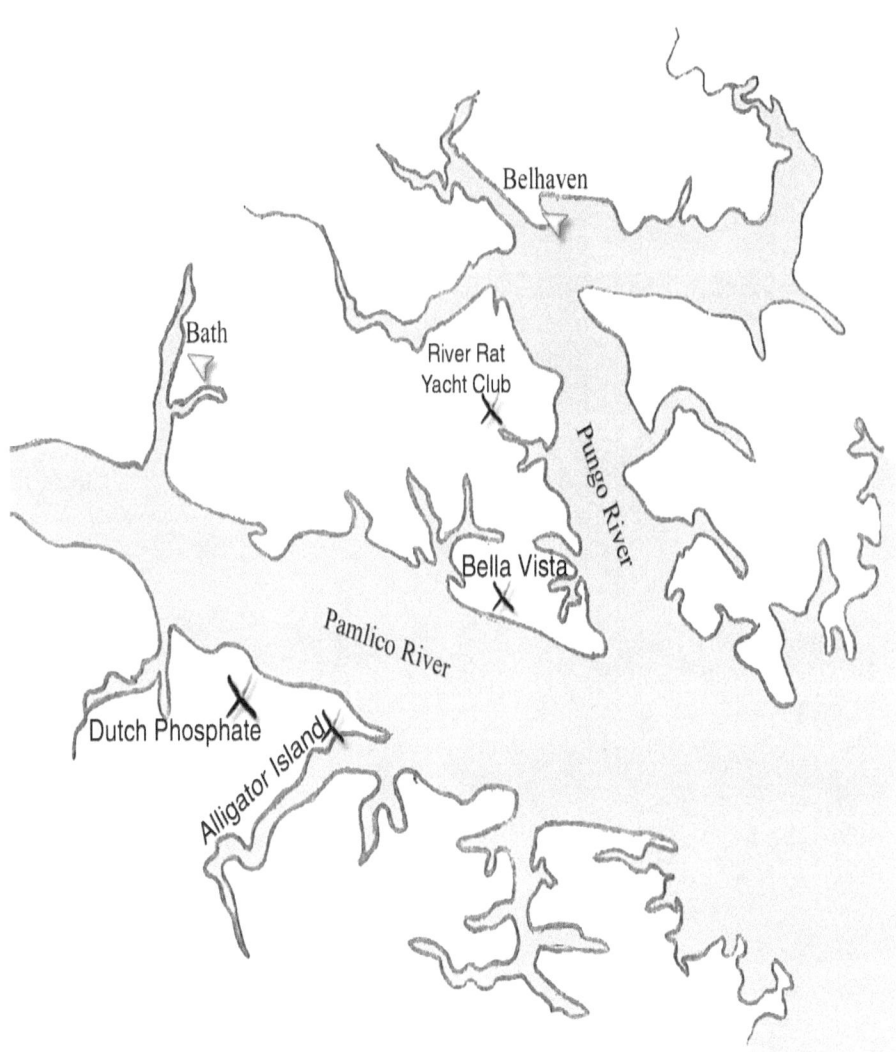

PART I

CHAPTER

1

Hatteras studied the approaching shoreline closely as the giant canoe rose and fell with the rhythm of the waves of the Pamouik River. With powerful, synchronized paddle strokes, the six young amber-skinned men in front of him propelled the old canoe through the river's steep chop. Many years ago, this thirty-foot-long canoe had been expertly burned and carved out with oyster shells from a massive old cypress tree by the ancestors of these young Algonquin Indian men. With crisp commands, Hatteras directed them toward a large osprey nest perched high in the top of a gnarled old loblolly pine that stood like a sentinel at the east entrance to Big Bear Creek.

On this return trip to their village from the swamps on the south side of the Pamouik, the canoe carried four large clay urns containing Hatteras's treasured pocosin. Being the medicine man and shaman, Hatteras felt relieved to have completed the important task of gathering the swamp's mysterious green that he would use to provide the village with medicine and heating oil for the upcoming winter. Fortunately, there had been no sign of the white man.

As the old pine slid past them to their right, Hatteras barked the Algonquian command for a hard right turn. The paddlers on his right dug their paddles into the water, while the three on the left continued their pace. In unison, the men leaned to the right side of the canoe, sending it smoothly to the east and into the entrance to Little Bear, a narrow creek that led to their village. Ahead of them, hidden in the trees on the north bank of the Pamouik River lay their home, the village of Secotan. Their pace now slowed, the canoe ghosted gracefully up the still waters of Little Bear, surrounded by thick underbrush and tall reeds on either side. Putting both hands to his mouth, Hatteras released three wolf howls that echoed across the water and into the woods ahead, signaling their return. A few moments later, the canoe slid onto a sandy beach under a stand of ancient cypress and live oak trees. Hatteras was the first to step onto the shore. Although seventy years old, he moved with the agility of a man much younger. Only his long gray hair and deeply wrinkled face gave away his age.

Strapped securely to the bow of the canoe with strips of deer hide were four large clay urns. Each had been filled with what the Secotan called pocosin, which the young men had collected under Hatteras's careful direction during their trip to the southern shores of the Pamouik River. Two more amber-skinned young men appeared from the woods and joined the paddlers in lifting the urns from the canoe. The eight young men carrying the urns followed Hatteras down the winding path that led to the village. Moments later, the pathway ended at a large clearing, with an open, side-less, thatched-roof structure in the middle. They had reached the center of Secotan.

Sitting on a high knoll, the village had a commanding view of the three-mile expanse across the Pamouik River to the south, and the entrance of Big Bear, a half-mile-wide creek, to the west. The waters around Secotan teemed with fish, crabs, and oysters. The low ground to the east was rich in nutrients from centuries of decaying plant matter. On this fertile patch of ground, the Secotan grew their fruits, vegetables, and tobacco. Farther to the east and beyond the village garden stood a dense forest, providing an abundance of deer, rabbit, turkey, and black bear. Across Little Bear Creek to the north, a densely wooded knoll dropped off into thousands of acres of low country interspersed with forbidding swamps, marshes, and maritime forests. The southerly breezes of summer flowing across the Pamouik cooled Secotan and pushed menacing mosquitoes inland and away from the village. In winter, the woodlands across Little Bear shielded the village from the prevailing cold north winds. With its isolated location, few white men had dared venture to it. As a result, Secotan had been mostly spared the ravages of smallpox that had decimated other Pamouik tribes in more accessible villages along the river. Their harmonious and peaceful coexistence with the world around them had served them well. The

Secotan believed, and with good reason, that they received special favor from the benevolent Mother Earth and Father Sky.

The men carrying the large urns followed closely behind Hatteras through the village center. Only young children, their mothers, and elderly villagers were present at this time of day. The children played happily as the women, both young and old, ground maize from the village's communal vegetable garden into the flour used to bake their bread. The elderly men seated nearby nodded with respect as Hatteras and his procession passed in front of them.

After crossing the village center, Hatteras stepped briskly onto a wider pathway on the opposite side of the clearing, with homes of the villagers interspersed among the trees along the way. Moments later, they turned left onto a narrow lane that led past Hatteras's home to an outbuilding directly behind it. Under his direction, the tanned men, now glistening with sweat, carefully placed the urns on the ground near the outbuilding. Hatteras nodded to them and stepped inside. In the middle of the room he saw a bed of hot coals that would soon be shimmering around the massive orange clay pot in the center. Three tubes made from shoots of bamboo descended from the pot to a smaller one sunk in the ground a few feet away. Nodding with approval, Hatteras stepped back outside.

Next to where the men had placed the urns, a large circular vat made of animal hides sat in an excavated pit twelve inches deep and twenty feet in diameter. Still under Hatteras's careful direction, the men tilted the tops of the urns one by one, pouring the thick emerald green liquid slowly into the vat. Once the last urn was emptied, Hatteras dismissed the young men and they headed back to the village. Along the way, they passed by a group of women and three men with drums headed for the outbuilding behind Hatteras's home. At the front of the procession was a tall, stately, gray-haired woman who was clearly the leader.

Upon their arrival, the women formed a circle around the vat, removed their moccasins and stepped into it. With a glance to the drummers, the gray-headed woman signaled them to begin a rhythmic cadence with their drums. With graceful, fluid movements the women began what they knew reverently as the pocosin fire dance. As the women danced, they and the drummers chanted to the Great

Spirit, to summon its help in transforming the thick green vegetation under their feet into the magic oil that the village used for healing and illumination. With each footstep, the thick green soup lost some of its texture.

As the women continued their dance, Hatteras walked back inside the building, where he found his daughter, Selu, busily chopping herbs on a table near the giant orange clay pot. Picking up a stone mallet, he joined Selu in preparing the herbs needed for the healing potions and salves. Meanwhile, his thoughts drifted to how his once little girl had grown up and now knew the secrets of a medicine man and shaman. It was with great pride that he watched her expertly performing the tasks needed to make the special potions and heating oil from the swamp's green pocosin. But it troubled him that she paid little attention to the young men of the tribe who had expressed an interest in her. Instead, she seemed content to spend her time and energy learning the secrets of a shaman.

His thoughts drifted to his wife, Wahnenauhi, who had crossed over to the spirit world the year before. She was one of the few residents of Secotan to be lost to the white man's smallpox. While Selu had also caught the illness, she had been strong enough to defeat it and survive.

Hatteras worried about the fate of Secotan, with the ever-encroaching white man moving east toward their village. He remembered the time when there had been many tribes along the Pamouik. Now there was only one, the Secotan. He often thought about how the village could preserve its special way of life in the future, and how his understanding of the magical powers of the swamp green could be passed to the generations to follow. He was painfully aware that other tribes along the Pamouik had fled to the west, only to face an enemy even worse than the white man, the Tuscarora Indians. The brutal Tuscarora tribe had killed many of the fleeing Pamouik and had made slaves of the ones they did not.

Hatteras was especially concerned about the future for his daughter. She would have been described as a beautiful woman in any era or culture. Having inherited her tall, statuesque figure and deep-set, inquisitive brown eyes from her mother, she was a desirable woman in the eyes of any man. Hatteras remembered how, from the time she was a young girl, she had expressed little interest in conforming to the traditional role of a woman in the village's tribal society. Instead, she preferred to spend time with him, rummaging through the forest to collect herbs and assisting in creating his potions. As she grew older, she had begun to learn and understand the unique and special gifts of a shaman. She often told Hatteras that, more than anything else, she wanted to learn how he connected with the spirits of the earth and sky, air and water, and with their ancestors for his visions that foretold of things to come.

⊕ ⊕ ⊕

Hatteras occasionally went outside to inspect the vat and check the consistency of the emerald liquid being mashed under the women's feet. The process continued for several hours. After studying the mixture in the vat one last time, Hatteras raised his right hand, palm down, to signal to the tall gray leader that they were done. The drumming and dancing slowly ceased. As the drummers and dancers returned to the village, Hatteras heard their voices and laughter fading away as they walked down the pathway that led back to the village center.

Selu appeared shortly after from the brew house with several quart-sized clay vessels. They both knelt beside the vat to examine its contents. The pocosin from across the Pamouik was now a thick emerald-colored paste. After kneading its velvet texture between their fingers, they exchanged nods of approval. With a wooden ladle, Selu filled several quart-sized urns with the green paste. Returning to the outbuilding, she placed them on a table in a corner, away from the heat of the coals around the huge orange pot in the room's center. Then, with a large clay vessel she began transferring the vat's remaining paste to the magic orange pot, surrounded by a now red-hot bed of coals built from her carefully nurtured fire.

"I will leave now to gather the remaining ingredients," Hatteras said in his low baritone voice. "The fire must stay hot. I will return before the sun leaves us."

"Yes, Father," she said absently, absorbed in her task.

Picking up a large deer-hide sack, Hatteras left through the doorway of the outbuilding and walked briskly past their home on the pathway that led out of the village. The home of Hatteras and Selu was a long rectangular structure known to the Indians as a longhouse. The sides were made with river cane woven between small vertically aligned saplings. The domed roof was formed by lashing the sapling tops together with strands made from animal hides. An elaborate tapestry of birch bark and animal hides was used for the roof. Inside, thick mats made from woven deer hides divided the longhouse into four separate rooms. Behind the structure was a sunny half-acre plot where Hatteras grew his special herbs and his corn, tomatoes, squash, and tobacco. In a back corner of the plot was the outbuilding, where Selu remained to oversee the magic green that was now brewing. The outbuilding stood in the shade of an old oak tree and was made of materials similar to those used to construct the longhouse, but was much smaller in size.

As Hatteras walked down the shaded village path, he looked toward the sun in the west to insure that enough light remained for his quest on this late-fall day. He passed a dozen neatly kept homes constructed much like his, but they were smaller and had thatched roofs made from marsh grass instead of birch bark and animal hides, which were valuable to the Indians and were only available to a tribe's leaders. As the village's medicine man and shaman, Hatteras was among this honored group. To the Secotan, Hatteras was more than just a healer. He had a connection with the spirits, who spoke to him of the future and gifted him to make the magic green pocosin that healed wounds and gave light and warmth in the cold months of winter.

As Hatteras walked past the homes of the village, he noticed how eerily quiet they were at this time of day. The men were hunting, and the women were either tending crops in the fields on the outskirts of the village, or were with their very young at the village center.

The footpath out of the village soon narrowed and began weaving its way into a lush maritime forest. The medley of a mockingbird followed Hatteras as he walked along the shaded trail through giant oaks, gum trees, and the few remaining pines that had not yet been crowded out by the evolving hardwood forest. The occasional burst of a pileated woodpecker's staccato *ta-ta-ta-ta-ta* call came deep from the forest ahead.

Hatteras slowed his pace and studied the forest around him. The aroma of honeysuckle now permeated the air. Stepping quietly off the path, he followed the sweet scent through the underbrush to an opening surrounded by a thick drapery of honeysuckle growing abundantly in the trees on the edge of the clearing. Hatteras picked several handfuls of the honeysuckle blooms and placed them in his pouch. Thick clusters of sassafras sprouts grew in the clearing's shaded border. After inspecting them carefully, he pulled up several small saplings by their roots, folded the pliable young stems reverently, and pushed them down into his sack, thanking Mother Earth for each of the sacred and bountiful ingredients as he went. The small opening was now filled with the blended bittersweet fragrances of sassafras roots and honeysuckle. Hatteras stepped quietly back to the pathway and followed it deeper into the forest. Through the trees ahead were revealed two more of his secret ingredients, mushrooms and tree moss. The mushrooms grew in abundance in the moist soil shaded by the towering oaks above. After selecting several large mushrooms, he picked up a long dead tree limb and studied the patches of tree moss in the limbs overhead. Having made his selection, he used the dead limb to remove several clumps of the tangled gray webs from the branches.

With his sack now full of the necessary herbs and ingredients for his special medicines, Hatteras began to retrace his steps back to Secotan. As he walked through the shadows cast by the late afternoon sun filtering through the trees, he reverently thanked the forest spirits for their bounty. An hour later, he was back on the main path that led to the village. The dwellings he passed were filled with voices. Walking along the path, he heard the laughter of children and the occasional clatter of clay pots and utensils as preparations were made for the evening meal. Smoke from cook fires wafted upward through the thick oaks that canopied the village. Men sat outside their homes, talking, laughing, and smoking tobacco from long clay pipes. They all nodded with respect as their revered medicine man and shaman walked past.

Arriving at his home, he walked to the outbuilding and entered. The magic orange brew pot dominated the room. As he set down his deer-hide sack, Selu looked up and exchanged a warm smile with her father. The small room was still very hot. Selu was kneeling between the brew pot and the sunken collection urn, gently stirring the oily contents of the buried urn with a narrow wooden ladle. A green liquid dripped steadily down the bamboo tubes from the enormous central brew pot to the collection pot being stirred by Selu.

"How is it?" asked Hatteras.

"Come see, Father," said Selu, as she handed him the ladle.

Hatteras peered down at the emerald green liquid in the urn that was now almost full.

"This is good, Selu. The spirits have favored you with their knowledge. You too are now gifted with the knowing. Respect and guard it well."

Selu nodded. "Thank you, Father, but I have a wise teacher." Obviously glowing from her father's words, she ladled the oil into gallon-sized clay urns, placing them in rows in a corner of the room.

"That is enough for now," announced Hatteras. "We are done for today."

CHAPTER

2

As Tobias Knight walked down the hall leading to Governor Eden's office, the sound of his boots on its heart pine floor echoed ahead of him. After giving the colonial governor's door two hard raps, he heard the governor's singsong voice respond, "Come in, Tobias."

As Tobias opened the door and stepped inside, he saw the governor seated behind his expansive, ornate oak desk. In front of him sat Captain John Blount, a well-known trader in the colony. Behind them, the orange glow of the setting sun filtered through the west window that overlooked Bath Creek and the merchant ships docked below. On the desk in front of them, Tobias noticed two crystal goblets filled with what he knew to be the governor's favorite English brandy.

Tobias hesitated for a brief moment to summon a look of pleasant surprise. Although Tobias had no respect for Blount and how he had amassed his wealth, he understood the politics of the colony well enough to keep his feelings hidden.

"Well, well, Captain, it's good to see you," said Tobias. He crossed the room and embraced Blount as if he were an old friend.

"It's good to see you, Tobias. You look well."

"I am, thank you, as do you. How was your trip from England?"

"Not too bad. As I was just telling the governor, we had one storm, but I have seen worse. Fortunately, we lost only five of the thirty head we were bringing over."

Tobias almost winced at these words, knowing the "head" to which Captain Blount referred were actually people, who were known as indentured servants. He also knew that the trip across the ocean was a horrid experience for these people. They were crowded in a small hold below the deck for over two months during the passage. There was no place for human waste, no light, and only small rations of food and water. The lone requirement for the sea captain was to deliver his cargo alive. In payment, the captain received a land grant from the king of fifty acres for each person delivered.

As secretary to the colonial council, Tobias had records of Blount completing eight round-trips across the Atlantic in the past five years. From the colonies, his ship transported a lucrative hold full of Carolina leaf tobacco. On his return from England he brought an even more valuable cargo, people. Desperate to escape the miserable living conditions of eighteenth-century England, the poor clamored to be one of the fortunate few of the king's subjects to escape to the promise of a better life in the New World. They had little information about what might lie ahead for them across the Atlantic, but it had to be better than what they then endured.

Tobias had always suspected that Captain Blount had ambitions far beyond those of a sea captain. He had amassed a small fortune from his previous profitable slave trade with the colonies. To Tobias, it was now apparent that Blount's attention was devoted to the accumulation of land in the new colony and to becoming a rich planter. During the five years in which Blount had been delivering indentured servants, Tobias had observed him accumulating, through land grants, thousands of acres that could grow tobacco and produce a great fortune. To Tobias, it was obvious that Blount yearned to be part of the colony's landed gentry.

"Twenty-five head," commented Governor Eden thoughtfully. "That should provide you with another twelve hundred and fifty acres of land. You will soon be one of the largest landowners around here. How many acres do you now have, John?"

"Close to six thousand is my guess. But I'm weary from these ocean crossings. It's time for me to turn my ship over to a younger captain and start clearing fields and planting tobacco."

As the discussion continued about Captain Blount's plans, Tobias stood at the west window, eyeing the dock activity below. His long, thick auburn hair glowed slightly in the last rays of fading sunlight. Suddenly, it occurred to him that Blount might be overlooking one of the provisions in his deeds. From having prepared all the king's Bath colony deeds for the governor's signature, Tobias was very familiar with their standard provisions.

"When did you receive your first deed from the king?" asked Tobias, as he turned toward Blount.

"It was about a year and a half ago. Why do you ask?"

Tobias crossed the room to a bookcase against the wall behind the governor's desk and pulled down a large, dark, canvas-covered book with the words *King's Deeds* on the front cover. Walking back to where Blount was seated, Tobias set the book down on the front edge of the governor's desk and opened it. Turning to one of Blount's deeds, Tobias pointed to a paragraph, and in his baritone voice began to read out loud.

"As a condition to this deed, Grantee shall commence the clearing and cultivation of the lands so granted herein within two years of the date of this grant. If this condition is not met, the lands so granted shall revert back to His Majesty the King."

Finished with his reading, Tobias struggled not to smirk. "Captain Blount, are you going to be able to meet this condition?" he asked with passive resolve. Watching Blount frown, then squirm slightly as he pondered the question, Tobias knew he had struck a nerve.

"I have actually found the perfect spot to do as the king requires," Blount finally replied. "It has excellent soil for tobacco. But there's a problem."

"What is that?" asked Tobias.

"An Indian village is sitting in the middle of the best high ground on the property."

"Where is it?" asked the governor.

"It is on the north shore of the Pamouik, about twenty miles due east of here."

Captain Blount stood and walked over to a map hanging on the wall beside the governor's west window. Pointing to the location of the village, he continued, "Here are at least three hundred acres of rich bottomland that would be excellent for tobacco." Moving his finger to the southwest on the map, he continued, "This is a high knoll, overlooking the river to the south. Big Bear Creek, as the savages call it, is just to the west, and meanders to the north and through the property. It has enough depth for a small ship to navigate. It's perfect for off-loading supplies and on-loading tobacco."

"That must be the Secotan," commented Governor Eden. He stood and crossed the room for a closer look at the map. "They are the last of the Pamouiks. Most of them were killed by smallpox a few years ago, except for the ones at the village of Secotan. They somehow survived it. What remained of the other Pamouik tribes moved to the west and joined with the Tuscarora. But not to worry, we've about had it with these savages. Only last month, a bunch of Indians raided a farmstead just north of us. The man, his wife, and two children were asleep when the savages attacked. They set fire to the house and the barn, destroyed the crops, and stole all the livestock. The family, fortunately, got out with their lives, but that was all. Everything they had worked hard to create over the years was gone."

"Why do we tolerate that?" fumed Blount. "We must far outnumber them by now."

"We aren't going to tolerate it, and we are going to do something about it," the governor said emphatically. "The council met last week on this very problem. The vote was six to one that, with one more incident like that, the militia will be sent down to the Secotan village and finish them for good."

Tobias had been standing and looking out the window at the dock activity below to hide his growing discomfort and agitation as this conversation progressed. When the governor was finished, Tobias turned quickly to face the captain and the governor.

"With all due respect, gentlemen, we have no proof that the Secotan were responsible for last month's raid. It could easily have been done by a rogue band of Tuscarora Indians to our west. They are still very angry about being driven from their homeland over the past twenty years."

"That doesn't matter," replied the governor angrily. "They're all savages. The sooner they're gone, the better." Standing quickly, he poured the men another round of brandy.

As the last rays of sunlight faded through the west window, Eden, still agitated, stood and lit a glass lantern on his desk. With the thick smell of burning whale oil filling the room, Tobias gulped down his brandy, walked across the room, and threw another log into the office fireplace. Returning to his seat beside Blount in front of the governor's desk, Tobias listened patiently as Blount adroitly turned the discussion to the politics of the colony and his request to be considered for membership on the council. Knowing the governor and the politics of the colony as he did, Tobias had no doubt that the governor was receptive to this proposal. The taxes from a thriving plantation like Blount's would provide much-needed revenue for the governor and his colony. But also knowing the governor's penchant for keeping his cards close to his vest, Tobias was not surprised to hear him simply assure Blount that his request would receive careful and fair consideration by the members of the council. Believing their business concluded, Tobias Knight bid the governor and Captain Blount a good evening and quickly departed.

After Tobias left the governor's office, he walked down Main Street toward his home several blocks to the south. The conversation he had just heard troubled him greatly. He understood the politics of the colony all too well. If Blount could build his plantation, it would provide the colony with tax revenue it desperately needed. It was not going to take much provocation from the Indians for the council to feel justified in ransacking the Secotan village. He cursed himself for mentioning the time condition in Blount's deeds.

Tobias's conscience was haunted by his experience with the village of Secotan the year before, which now seemed like only yesterday. He had been hunting alone, as was his preference. Venturing farther east from the Bath colony than he ever had been, he pressed through miles of lowlands until he reached a maritime forest just north of the village.

The forest was eerily quiet. Suddenly, a large bobcat perched overhead in an old oak tree growled its presence. Spooked by it, Tobias's horse threw him violently to the ground. His left leg immediately exploded in pain. After regaining his senses, Tobias looked down to see his left femur protruding through the fabric of his wool trousers. Each time he attempted to move, he was overwhelmed by excruciating pain and fell back to the ground. His last conscious memories were of buzzards circling overhead, and finally of the bobcat lurking nearby, awaiting the death of its victim.

After two days of helplessness and agonizing pain, hunters from Secotan found him and brought him to Hatteras, their medicine man. By the time he reached the village, he was delirious with fever from a serious infection raging in his leg.

Tobias regained consciousness several days later. He was lying on a mat in a strange room. Through a blurred vision, he could see a domed roof, fashioned with what looked like animal hide. Even though it was the middle of January, the room was comfortably warm.

Hearing movement to his right, Tobias looked across the room to see a shapely young woman and an old man grinding some sort of vegetable matter on a table which appeared to have been made from a tree trunk. In front of them was a large clay urn burning oil that strangely had no scent.

As he stirred, the young woman turned her head to face him.

The older man also looked at him. "Ah, you awake," he said.

"Where am I?" asked Tobias groggily.

"You in Secotan," the old olive-skinned man replied. "You fall from horse and break leg bad. The spirits favored you, for we find you. Their magic making you better."

The two Indians got up and knelt over Tobias. The young woman gently lifted the blanket that covered his legs and examined the wound. "Infection start to leave you a day ago," she said. "You much better now."

Tobias knew the chances of recovering from a serious infection were often slim. He looked down and saw a ten-inch gash in his left leg, covered in a mysterious green substance. There were also wooden braces on each side of his leg made from carved tree limbs woven tightly together by some sort of vine. He watched as the young woman patted a thick green paste onto the wound.

"What is that?" Tobias asked guardedly, but with no energy to protest.

The old man smiled faintly and said, "It heals bad wounds."

"But what is it?"

There was no response.

"So you are a medicine man?"

"I am Hatteras. With guidance from the spirits, I hope to soon make you well."

Being too weak to continue the conversation, Tobias fell back into a deep sleep.

For the next month, Tobias remained under the care of Hatteras and Selu. Each day he grew stronger. Selu fed him and Hatteras well. At first, the villagers watched Tobias from a distance with curiosity, but as they continued to observe their revered shaman's kind treatment of this stranger, they assumed they should do the same.

During this time, Tobias had many discussions with Hatteras about the history and the culture of the Secotan. As he watched the villagers in their day-to-day lives, he was struck by their reverence for and harmonious existence with the land and water around them. Contrary to their reputation in Bath, they were gentle people who lived their lives in harmony with what Mother Nature had provided them. However, while Hatteras would speak freely about almost any subject, whenever Tobias tried to turn the discussion to Hatteras's healing paste and the oil that lit and heated his home, he became elusive.

"How do you make this oil?"

"It is very old and has been passed down to me by the ancestors."

"Who knows how to make it?"

"Selu and I are the only ones left who know."

"From what is it made?"

Hatteras said nothing more in reply to the questions of his inquisitive guest. This went on until Tobias finally quit asking. Instead, he began to watch silently as Hatteras and Selu went about preparing their brew. Tobias thought it was strange that while Hatteras would not disclose the ingredients and process, he went about making his magic oil knowing that Tobias was watching intently.

By late February, Tobias had regained enough strength to begin walking with the assistance of Selu. Their walks were short at first, but became longer as Tobias's strength returned. During these walks, he was struck by her bright questions about the colony, his position as secretary, and a world that was unknown to her. Somehow, he was oblivious to their slow but simmering romantic bond.

Soon it was April, and Tobias and Selu were now taking longer walks together alone. With spring plants emerging, Hatteras was spending most of the day foraging for the herbs and emerging plants he used for his healing ingredients. The rest of the time, Hatteras tended to the usual medical needs of the villagers or crossed the Pamouik to obtain the green swamp growth needed for his mysterious lamp oil and healing potions.

During the days that Hatteras was away, Selu and Tobias spent many hours together. The warm bond between them continued to grow. With spring's rising temperatures, Selu had replaced her heavy winter attire with a deerskin top and short skirt that barely hid her slender hips and full, round breasts. One afternoon in late April, they set out on another of their routine walks. As they reached a secluded sandy beach next to the river, Selu stopped and turned away from Tobias to face the water. Slowly, she removed her top, letting it fall silently to the ground. She stepped out of her deerskin skirt and waded into the river. Tobias watched breathlessly as Selu's shapely, amber-skinned body began to disappear into the water. When she was waist-deep, she glanced back over her shoulder at Tobias, smiled shyly, and said, "Let's bath. You join me?"

Selu turned and dove into the river, out of sight. Tobias quickly removed his clothes and followed her. After playfully frolicking in the warm water of the Pamouik, Tobias caught Selu's hand in his and pulled her gently to within inches of his body. Facing one another in waist-deep water, their eyes locked as if in a trance. Tobias slowly kissed Selu's lips. His left hand moved gently over her firm body, and she responded by tilting her head back and arching her hips toward him. As his right hand slid down onto her firm buttocks, he felt a strong rush of passion welling up in his body. After several long, sensuous kisses, Selu began clutching Tobias's body. Selu's moans were deepening as their tongues met playfully and teasingly. Tobias put his arm around her waist and pulled her athletic body toward his. Selu surprised him by lithely wrapping her legs around his waist. Tobias immediately felt an increase in his physical response as she pressed against him. Selu let out a brief scream and sank her teeth into his shoulder. It suddenly dawned on Tobias that Selu was a virgin. Overwhelmed with passion, he thrust his way into her inner depths. Selu responded by digging her nails into his back. Totally consumed, they lost themselves together. Moments later, Tobias exploded uncontrollably inside her.

As the wave of passion faded, Tobias held Selu's hands in his while softly kissing her lips and finely chiseled cheeks. Lifting her gently in his arms, he carried her to the water's edge and lowered her onto the warm sand of the beach. Lying by her side and peering into her dark brown eyes, he moved his hands slowly over her beautiful body with long, languid strokes of his hand. His lips began exploring the amber skin he had come to adore. They lay in the sunshine exploring each other's bodies for what seemed liked hours. Tobias's hand eventually began moving over Selu's breasts and thighs. He soon found her warm wetness, and she began moving rhythmically under his touch. Tobias's own arousal returned, and they were soon entangled on the beach as if drawn together by forces beyond their control. The sounds of their mutual pleasure escalated and floated into the forest behind them. As their rhythmic coupling intensified, they reached a plateau of ecstasy for several minutes before coming together in a crescendo of passion. Later, as if awakening from a dream, they found themselves lying next to one another on the secluded beach as the sun began its descent in the western sky above the Pamouik. They had no way of knowing that this was a turning point not only in their lives, but also for those of generations to come. From this day forward, their passion grew to consume them in escalating levels of pleasure neither had ever experienced or imagined. For Selu and Tobias, it was a time of ecstasy that few couples ever knew.

As their days together passed, Tobias tried to come to grips with the fact that he was hopelessly in love with this beautiful Indian woman. He tried to reconcile his feelings for her with the reality of his position, and he began the painful process of considering his options. He was the secretary of the council that governed the Bath colony of North Carolina. He was also one of its wealthiest inhabitants. He could return to the colony with Selu as his wife, but most of the colonists believed all Indians were nothing more than wild savages. Bringing Selu back with him would never be accepted. Could she ever be happy living among his people? He would probably lose his position as secretary of the council and be shunned by the entire colony. Regardless of what he ultimately did, he knew he needed to get back to the colony. Once there, he would sort this out and come up with a solution.

A few days later, after the evening meal, Hatteras left to attend a meeting with the tribe's chief and elders. Tobias swallowed hard and took this occasion to tell Selu what he dreaded to say. "I must return to Bath for a short while. There is business that needs my attention. I will return when I have found a way for us to be together."

A wave of guilt flooded over Tobias as Selu began to weep softly. Gently, Tobias reached over and pulled her into his arms. A lone clay lamp burned faintly, providing an eerie illumination.

When Hatteras returned, Selu jumped up, ran across the room, and tearfully flung her arms around him. After several moments, Hatteras spoke softly. "Selu, you knew this time would come. Tobias must leave us for now."

Early the next morning, Tobias mounted his horse and rode quietly out of the village, unnoticed by its sleeping inhabitants.

⊕ ⊕ ⊕

In the months that followed, Tobias never spoke to anyone of his experience with the Secotan. It would not have been politically wise for him to speak well of Indians when the colonists viewed all of them as savages and a nuisance. However, when alone, he quietly grieved the loss of Selu. Not a day passed that he didn't think about her, Hatteras, and the kind and generous treatment he had received while recuperating in their village. Most importantly, he would never forget how these people could have left him to die, but did not. Given the way the white man had robbed them of their land, decimated their population with smallpox, and made some of them slaves, he would not have been a bit surprised if they had killed him or left him for dead. Instead, they had treated him with kindness and respect, as they would have done had he been one of their own.

The plodding hoofbeats of horses pulling a carriage on the brick street outside jolted Tobias back to the present. He knew this would be a night of restless sleep.

CHAPTER

3

Tobias was quietly working on monetary issues of the colony when Governor Eden suddenly bounded through the doorway of his office. It was almost with glee that the governor announced there had been an Indian raid on a farmstead several miles to the east of Bath. The closest Indian village was Secotan. The Tuscarora Indians to the west were not the likely culprits. Although there were no injuries, the resident family had been terrorized. Their home was burned to the ground, and all their livestock were stolen.

Governor Eden quickly called an emergency session of the council. The only issue on the agenda for this meeting was the attack. As secretary, Tobias was the first to arrive at the Council Room, which was on the same floor as and across the hall from the office of the governor. Shortly after, the council's newest member, Captain John Blount, arrived with council members Joshua Durham and David Perkins. Tobias had noticed that since Blount's recent appointment to the council, he had gone out of his way to cultivate the friendship and favor of these two influential members. The trio's quiet aloofness this afternoon gave Tobias the impression that they had already discussed the meeting's agenda.

Moments later, the door to the governor's office opened and he strode into the Council Room, followed by one of the council's most vocal anti-Indian members, Joseph Waters. As Governor Eden called the meeting to order, Tobias noticed that Captain Blount was seated at the far end of the table, with his new cronies Durham and Perkins seated on either side of him.

Councilman Joshua Durham was the first to speak. "It happened two miles from my home. I have a wife and three young children to think about. It could have been my family that was wiped out, or it could have been yours."

There was a loud chorus of "Hear, hear!" around the room.

John Bunting, the commander of the colony's militia, then took the floor. "We all know the only village close to where this raid occurred is Secotan. It had to be them. We should burn them out of here, once and for all."

There was another chorus of "Hear, hear!"

Tobias could not help but notice the wry smile on Captain Blount's face as he sat listening silently to the proceedings. There was no discussion of evidence that would prove the raid was the work of the Secotan. The tribe was simply being presumed guilty by the council.

Tobias had listened in disbelief to the unreasoned discussion. Unable to sit silently any longer, he stood and addressed the council.

"I, like the rest of you, wish to protect our people, livelihoods, and livestock, but how do we know this raid was carried out by the Secotan? Unlike the Tuscarora, they have never been known to attack anyone. We know the Tuscarora have been responsible for many bloody escapades. What evidence do we have that the Secotan had anything to do with this raid? If anyone here has evidence that it was the Secotan, let's hear it."

"We don't need evidence!" shouted Councilman Perkins, jumping to his feet. "They're all savages. Even if the Secotan haven't attacked us yet, it's just a matter of time before they do. I say let's run them off now before it's too late."

Tobias watched in disbelief as the motion carried. His vote was the solitary dissent. He could not help but notice the smirk that now appeared on Blount's face.

"Very well, gentlemen, we have reached a verdict," pronounced the governor. "Mr. Bunting, as commander of the militia, you are to assemble your men, proceed to the village, attack and destroy it."

Tobias left the meeting in a state of shock and turmoil, pondering his options. He finally concluded that there was only one: he must go to Secotan. Upon returning to his office, he summoned his clerk. "I will be leaving tomorrow for several days of hunting. If anyone asks, that is where I have gone."

Tobias slept little that night, his thoughts constantly straying to Selu and her village. Before first light, Tobias found his way in the darkness to the barn, saddled his horse, and was soon galloping east. The farther he went, the more the trail deteriorated, slowing his progress. As he reached the tributaries flowing into Big Bear Creek, he pushed his horse to trudge through miles of narrow foot trails and swampy slush. Once around the northern fingers of the creek, he headed south toward the high ground of Secotan.

When he reached the village, the early afternoon sun was still high in the sky. At the edge of the village, he stopped, dismounted, and led his horse slowly down the main street of Secotan. At first, all he received were stares from the villagers. Then a few of them began to recognize him. By the time he reached the home of Hatteras, word of his arrival had preceded him. Hatteras was out front to greet him.

"Welcome, good friend Tobias. You must be tired and hungry. We have plenty food for you here."

"Thank you, Hatteras. I gratefully accept." Once inside the main living area, Tobias quickly turned to Hatteras. "We must talk."

"It can wait. Sit down, and let us enjoy some food. Then we discuss it."

"How is Selu?"

At that moment, Selu stepped into the room. In her arms was a sleeping infant. Looking at Tobias with a proud smile, she said, "Tobias, meet your daughter. She has your eyes. I named her after you and my mother. Her name is Wahnenauhi Knight."

Moving to Tobias, she kissed his lips softly and gently put the baby, bundled in a soft, furry bear hide, into his arms. Although in shock, Tobias beamed as he held his daughter, while trying to process the meaning of being a father.

"Selu, she is beautiful," he said proudly.

Nodding with approval, Selu replied, "I need a little time to finish meal." Gingerly, Selu took the sleeping infant from Tobias and quietly left of the room.

Hatteras motioned for Tobias to sit, and the two settled onto soft floor mats made from deer hides. As Tobias was trying to come to grips with the realization that he was father to Selu's child, Hatteras spoke happily of the full moon ceremony he would perform the following night and how pleased he was that Tobias would be there for it. He then turned to the recent hunting successes of the tribe. Tobias listened quietly, nodding occasionally but saying nothing. His thoughts were elsewhere. He was haunted by the realization that this extraordinary place and its inhabitants would soon disappear in a sad and violent end, and that he now had a daughter among them. Even sadder was the fact that his ties to Bath meant there was little he could do to save them. Even if he tried, he would be defeated along with the Secotan.

After a few moments, Hatteras stopped talking and looked at Tobias. "You are very quiet, Tobias. What troubles you?"

Tobias sat quietly, trying to decide how to deliver the doomsday message for the village. He finally spoke. "The people of Secotan are in grave danger. There have been some attacks recently on farmsteads around Bath. The Secotan are being blamed. The council voted yesterday to send the militia to destroy Secotan."

Hatteras looked at him blankly. "That cannot be. You know that we live in harmony with all living things around us. We attack no other man. This is our home. We will not be driven from it. What have we done to harm the white man? Do you believe we have attacked the white man?"

"No, I do not believe that. I know your ways. Your people have done nothing to harm the white man. I agree and understand, but these raids have made the people of the Bath colony very angry. They want to blame someone. I tried to convince them that it could be the Tuscarora, or, as I have suspected, some Tuscarora who were paid by some bad white men to do these raids. I believe it is these greedy men who want to take the lands where you live, raise your crops, and hunt and fish for themselves. They will stop at nothing to take these lands away from you. They do not want to listen to reason. They do not want to know you are peaceful. Truth means nothing to them. They want the land, and they want it now. A militia on horseback will soon attack Secotan. Its members will destroy your homes and kill any villagers who are still here when they arrive. You are in grave danger."

Hatteras sat quietly for a few moments. "You are at great risk for coming here. If these men learn that you have been here to warn us, they will kill you, too."

"I could not let you, Selu, and the villagers be slaughtered. This is the least that I could do. I tried to reason with the people who are sending the militia to attack you. They would not listen to me. You saved my life. Your people were kind to me. I wish I could do more. Now that my daughter is among you, I feel an even deeper need to help. I have missed Selu terribly, and I would like to take her and my daughter with me, but I am afraid that would be unfair to them. The Bath colonists would never accept them and would treat them badly."

Selu entered the room to find the two men sitting in silence. "Our meal is ready," she announced.

Their dinner was a combination of oysters, flounder, and sweet potatoes steamed in wet seaweed on top of coals from Selu's cook fire. Selu placed the sleeping Wahnenauhi on a bearskin blanket between her and Tobias. They sat thoughtfully, saying and eating little, until Hatteras finally spoke.

"Selu, Tobias has brought bad news to us. He has learned that the white men from Bath believe our village is responsible for recent raids on their homes. They will soon come here to try to destroy our village. Tobias knows we are a peaceful people and tried to reason with them, but they are angry and believe we are responsible. Tobias has wisely counseled that one cannot reason with unreasonable people."

Selu asked softly, "Father, what shall we do?"

"I know not. I must seek guidance from the Great Spirit. I will tell the elders of this and have them summoned to the sacred circle, and ask the Great Spirit what we must do. We will know the answer as the sun drops below the sky."

Hatteras stood slowly and stepped outside into the light of the late afternoon sun. Moments later, the deep, ominous cadence of a drum could be heard from the center of the village.

"What is that?" Tobias asked.

"It is a summons. The elders are being called to assemble at the sacred place. From there, Father will conduct ceremony and seek guidance from our ancestors and the Great Spirit."

⊕ ⊕ ⊕

The location of the sacred ceremony was at the southern edge of the village on a bluff overlooking the Pamouik. Being the first to arrive, Hatteras walked to the edge of the stone circle and looked out over the river. Rippled reflections of the setting sun, stirred by a gentle southerly breeze, danced across the surface of the water in front of him. Hearing quiet footsteps approaching, Hatteras turned and studied the elders who were now gathering around the outside of the stone circle's perimeter. Stepping into the circle, Hatteras methodically went about preparations for the ceremony as he had learned them from his shaman father. First, he removed white sage from one of his rabbit-skin pouches, placed it into a large clamshell, and lit it with a small swamp-green lamp he had brought with him from the village. It was soon giving off a thick gray smoke. Holding the shell of smoldering sage in his right hand, he moved slowly around the large circle of stones and walked through its interior carefully, letting the smoke of the sage cleanse the inside of the circle. He then stepped outside and cleansed the circle's perimeter and the elders standing around it with the smoke from the smoldering sage. He next sprinkled blue cornmeal throughout the interior of the circle to ground the elders and their sacred ceremony to Mother Earth.

The shaman resumed his spot outside the southern perimeter of stones. Turning to face the circle, he looked skyward and asked, "May we enter?"

Hatteras stood motionless for several moments, continuing to look skyward. Turning, he nodded to the chief, a tall, stately, gray-haired woman with deep-set dark brown eyes and high cheekbones. Reverently, she stepped into the circle and sat cross-legged on the north side of the circle. Hatteras nodded to the remaining elders, and they moved quietly into the circle. After all were seated, Hatteras, their shaman, moved reverently to the circle's center. After placing a large black bear hide in the center of the circle, Hatteras knelt, opened his ceremonial pouch, and with his left hand removed a long clay pipe stem. It would symbolize the male, to be joined with the female later in the ceremony.

With his right hand he picked up the clamshell of still-smoldering sage and circled the pipe stem, letting the smoke envelop and cleanse it. This was a repetition of the cleansing techniques that had been passed down to shamans for countless generations before him. Once it was cleansed, he placed the pipe stem gently on the far south edge of the bear hide. The next item from his pouch was the pipe's wooden bowl. It symbolized the female that would join with the male pipe stem. With the sage smoke wafting from the shell, he cleansed it and placed it on the altar.

Hatteras removed a large bear paw that symbolized Big Bear Creek to the west. After cleansing it with the smoke of the smoldering sage, he placed it on the west side of the bear skin. He removed a small bear claw symbolizing Little Bear Creek to the south, cleansed it with the sage smoke, and placed it on the south side of the altar, a few inches to the north of where he had placed the pipe. The last item from the pouch was a dried kernel of corn from the harvest of the previous summer. After cleansing it, he placed it on the altar.

Walking to the edge of the circle, Hatteras leaned down and picked up the lamp, which was still burning with a bright blue and orange flame. After carefully cleansing it with the sage smoke, he placed it upon the center of the altar. The last item to cleanse was his drum, which he then placed reverently between the burning urn and the bear paw.

Having completed the cleansing process, the shaman stood and walked quietly to the south side of the circle. Facing the setting sun to the west, he closed his eyes and stood motionless. The steady southerly breeze flowing across the river danced through the long, thinning gray hair of the man the villagers revered.

Several minutes later, he opened his eyes, took a seat on the south side of the bearskin across from the chief, and began the ceremony. Reaching down with his left hand, he lifted the pipe stem from the altar. With his right hand, he picked up the wooden bowl. Symbolizing the joining of male and female, he slowly inserted the stem into the bowl of the pipe. Holding it by its bowl in his left hand with its stem pointing outward, he turned to face the east. Lifting the pipe slightly above eye level, he placed a small pinch of tobacco into the bowl while spilling some onto the ground below. The tobacco that reached the ground was a symbolic gesture, in which part of the tobacco was returned to Mother Earth in gratitude for what they had harvested from her. The old shaman then spoke in a clear, strong voice.

"From the east we receive our rising sun. It brings us new days and new opportunities that follow them. We give thanks to the Great Spirit for each new day that we live upon our Mother Earth."

Hatteras then turned to the south; with the pipe still elevated, he pushed another pinch of tobacco into the bowl, again spilling some to the ground below.

"From the south, Mother Earth provides us with spring and the warm winds of summer that will follow. It provides us crops to nourish us."

Turning to the west, with the pipe still slightly above eye level and the stem pointed outward, he pushed more tobacco into its bowl and again spilled some on the ground.

"To the west where our sun goes down, we receive darkness, and with it our spirit beings. The spirits of darkness protect us and foretell our future. The darkness of the west reminds us that we will all someday reenter the world of spirits. It reminds us to honor, respect, and care for one another and our Mother Earth while we are here."

Hatteras turned to the north, the last of the four directions. After pushing more tobacco into the pipe's bowl and again spilling some as a symbolic offering to Mother Earth, he continued.

"From the north we receive the cold, short days of winter. It is a time to contemplate the richness of our experience here on Mother Earth and to consider how well we have honored, protected, and cared for it and one another."

Having acknowledged the four directions, Hatteras knelt and touched the bowl of the pipe to the ground. "We acknowledge our Mother Earth. It is she who nourishes the crops that feed us. And like the crops, we all come from seeds that flourish because of her generous nourishment."

Hatteras turned the stem of the pipe upward to the sky. Carefully loading and spilling another pinch of tobacco, he proceeded to acknowledge Father Sky.

"From Father Sky and his limitless stars, we receive our direction to make the pocosin that gives us light and warmth. Daily he joins with Mother Earth to give us our energy, wisdom, and strength."

Hatteras then held the pipe over his head, pointing it straight into the sky.

"Oh, Great Spirit, we seek your wisdom and guidance at this defining moment for our village."

The shaman lifted the pipe to his mouth, lit it with flame from the urn, and took three long draws, releasing each exhalation of smoke to seek the Great Spirit. He handed it, bowl first, to the right hand of the elder on his left. After receiving the pipe, the elder slowly turned the pipe 270 degrees counterclockwise and then spoke.

"Great Spirit, our village has received the blessing of your bounty for many moons. We seek your wisdom. Do we fight the white man who would take your bounty from us?"

Lifting the pipe to his mouth, he took three long draws and passed it, bowl first, to the right hand of the elder on his left. After a quiet few moments, the elder spoke.

"Great Spirit, our harvests are plentiful. Your woods and waters are filled with food for our people. Do we fight to protect it, or flee once again and give to the white man what is not his to take?"

After taking three draws on the pipe, he passed it to the elder on his left. This continued until the pipe had been around the circle and returned to the shaman. Hatteras thanked the ancestors, the spirits of the directions, Mother Earth, Father Sky, and the Great Spirit for their many blessings and guidance; then, he took another three long draws and returned the pipe to the altar.

Looking to the now red and orange sunset sky, Hatteras continued the sacred ceremony.

"We gather here seeking the guidance of Great Spirit. We ask for guidance that will honor our ancestors, the seven generations who came before us and the seven generations who will walk Mother Earth after us. Oh, Great Spirit, we ask for your wisdom today as our tribe faces a great crossroads. We ask that our decision today bring no harm to any living thing. We seek to honor and protect Mother Earth and the bounty that she provides to our people, and to our people who will walk with Mother Earth in the generations to come."

Hatteras picked up his drum from the altar and began moving his fingers gently across its surface. As his ancestors before him, he knew a drum should be awakened in this fashion before its use in a ceremony. He began drumming a rhythmic call to summon the Great Spirit into their sacred circle.

Following the cadence of the drum, the chief began a low, slow, melodic chant. As the elders joined in, Hatteras began to increase the rhythm and intensity of his drumming. The chanting escalated into a loud chorus of male and female voices in eerie minor chords. The drum seemed to lead them toward a crescendo as Hatteras pounded it violently. With no sense of time or place, he found himself ascending into another dimension. Images of the past and future flowed as waves through a vortex that engulfed him. To the elders around him, their shaman seemed a man possessed. Although an eternity had rushed through the vortex summoned by Hatteras, it lasted only moments, and left its message for him as the shaman. Hatteras's hands slowed, and the intensity of his drumming began to subside. The chanting of the elders subsided as if following the direction of the drum. As the drum beat softly for a few moments, the elders' chants became an earthy flow coming from deep in their throats.

With the sun setting below the Pamouik, Hatteras placed the drum onto the bearskin, picked up the burning urn, and raised it slightly above his head.

"The Great Spirit has spoken. The message is clear. We are not to fight those who will surely come. We are to seek a peaceful existence, as has always been our destiny. If we go west, we face more white men. We are few, and the Great Spirit says the day will come when there will be more white men than there are stars in the sky."

Hatteras lowered the urn to chest level and sighed.

"Mother Earth has given us great bounty here. She is pleased that we have honored her. She has now shown us the place where we must go to find safety and where we may continue to enjoy her bounty. We are to go south across the great Pamouik to the high ground that lies above the source of this fire. This land will be protected by the spirits and the giant alligators of the swamp that surrounds it. No white man will dare try to find us there."

All eyes turned to the stately woman chief seated across from Hatteras. After contemplating his words for several long moments, she finally nodded and spoke.

"We shall follow the guidance of the Great Spirit. Tomorrow at first light, we begin. The message must go throughout Secotan tonight."

The elders sat reverently around the circle in the enveloping darkness as Hatteras carefully wrapped and returned each item on the altar to his deer-hide pouch. He rolled up the bear-hide altar, stood, turned to the chief, and nodded. She stood and led the elders silently out of the circle and back down the path to their village.

After the elders were gone, Hatteras sat in the fading light from the west, watching the small flame flickering in the urn. His thoughts were now with the rest of the message from the Great Spirit, which he had not shared with the elders. Hatteras had sought guidance for Selu, Tobias, and their young child. He also had sought direction for preserving and protecting the knowledge that only he and Selu had of the magic of pocosin. His heart was saddened by the reality that the bountiful life they had known in Secotan was over. The Great Spirit had spoken. As always, they would follow its wise guidance.

There was only a glimmer of orange in the western sky when Hatteras stood and left the sacred circle. Retracing his steps back to the village, he arrived at his home to find Tobias holding Wahnenauhi, with Selu looking on adoringly. Seeing her grandfather, Wahnenauhi wiggled her arms and legs joyfully. Walking over to her, Hatteras lifted his granddaughter into his arms and quietly caressed her.

After a few moments, Selu spoke. "Tell us, Father. What direction did we receive from the Great Spirit?"

Hatteras gently lowered his granddaughter into Selu's arms and walked across the room to a bench full of clay urns. Pushing the urns aside, he reached for an urn hidden behind them. Retracing his steps across the room, he placed the urn on a table in front of Selu and Tobias. He carefully removed a leather pouch from the urn and looked directly into the eyes of Tobias.

"Here are the ingredients for making our pocosin. The Great Spirit guided me to write down what I know of this oil because there could come a day when it might be lost. If what Selu and I know does not survive us, it will still be preserved with this writing. Secotan will soon die, but this knowing must not. When Selu and I someday join our ancestors, it must be preserved. Tobias, you are to take this with you. At all costs, guard and protect it. Selu and I will soon cross the Pamouik where no white man can find us. Only you will know where we go. You will always be one of us, and you must return to walk often among us in our new village. But you cannot speak of us or our secret to anyone. It must remain known only to the three of us."

Hatteras studied Tobias closely, measuring whether he realized the importance of what the shaman had just requested.

"If I am to tell no one of this, then what shall I do with this writing?" asked Tobias.

"The Great Spirit came to me as the sun was falling below us. A descendant daughter of you and Selu will someday come forward. She will come to know it is time to open the urn. Only the Great Spirit knows who she is. It will make known to the descendant daughter when she is to open the urn. You must ensure that the urn is entrusted to the hands of the oldest daughter of you and Selu. If she has joined the spirits before you do, then to her oldest daughter. You must ensure before you leave this earth that the urn is protected through the coming generations of descendant daughters in this way. The instructions to Wahnenauhi and her daughters will be the same. With each generation, this urn with its knowing must pass to the oldest daughter." Still studying Tobias closely, Hatteras continued, "Can you promise the Great Spirit that you will make this happen?"

Tobias nodded solemnly. "It will be my honor to follow the instructions of your Great Spirit."

Hatteras returned Tobias's nod, replaced the pouch in the urn, and handed it to Tobias. Placing both of his hands on Tobias's shoulders, Hatteras said, "My son, I am confident you will. The Great Spirit will always be with you."

With preparations to make, Hatteras turned and quickly stepped out into the night. Selu and Tobias stood silently, looking at the urn.

"We must seal this in a way that it will be preserved for a very long time," said Tobias. He watched Selu consider what he had said.

"I know what we should do," she said, motioning for him to take Wahnenauhi. After setting the urn on the table, Tobias reached out to take his daughter in his arms. Selu turned and stepped outside.

After several moments, she returned with a handful of moist clay left over from when she had molded a new cook pot earlier in the day. While holding Wahnenauhi, Tobias watched Selu carefully pick up the urn with the writing inside. After replacing the lid, she methodically encircled the joint between the urn and its lid with a layer of soft clay. Soon the lid was indistinguishable from the urn. Tobias followed Selu as she stepped back into the night and walked over to the red-hot coals of the cook fire. After wrapping the urn in layers of wet seaweed, she placed it carefully among the coals. Selu looked up at Tobias and he nodded approvingly. After Selu rearranged the coals to ensure an even heat, she followed Tobias as he stepped back inside, with Wahnenauhi now fast asleep in his arms.

A few moments later, the pounding of deep drums echoed from the center of the village. The footsteps of villagers soon could be heard as they began running down the main pathway outside of Selu's home toward the village center.

Seeing Tobias's puzzled look, Selu explained, "They go for instructions from the chief. We will all be very busy tomorrow." Putting her arms gently around his neck, she looked into his eyes and whispered softly, "But tonight, we are together."

The next morning, Tobias awoke to the sound of activity he had never before heard in the village. Stepping out into the bright morning sun, he saw villagers busily dismantling their homes and packing their possessions. In Little Bear, the three large canoes of the village were being loaded for the first of many deliveries across the three-mile expanse of the river to the new location of Secotan.

Seeing Hatteras and Selu busily dismantling what could be removed from the outbuilding, Tobias walked over to lend a hand. For the remainder of the day, Tobias worked nonstop to assist Hatteras, Selu, and the other villagers in dismantling their homes and helped with moving them and their possessions into the big canoes that would transport them across the river. By the end of the day, the village looked like a ghost town. What was once a vibrant community was now nothing more than mounds of discarded clay pots and dying coals left from the last of the cook fires.

Selu and Hatteras waited until the last canoe was prepared to depart before saying their farewell to Tobias. Tearfully, Tobias and Selu embraced for what they feared could be the last time. After holding his daughter close in his arms a few moments, he passed her gently back to Selu. Standing in front of Hatteras, Tobias spoke reverently. "You have great wisdom. I wish to have more time to learn of it."

Hatteras studied Tobias for a moment before responding, "My son, you will always be one of us and welcome in our home."

As the sun set over the Pamouik, Tobias watched as the giant canoe ghosted quietly down Little Bear, until it disappeared behind the tall water grass and into the mouth of Big Bear for its journey across the Pamouik.

After several moments of sad reflection, Tobias mounted his horse and slowly rode back to the village. All that remained were the remnants of abandoned homes and the smoldering ashes of dying cook fires. Waves of fond memories of his time in this once vibrant village swept over him. A full orange moon had begun its ascent above the trees in the eastern evening sky. Once out of the village, he began the slow trek through the moonlit swamps and maritime forests of the low country that had become familiar to him. Hours later, as the sun rose, he guided his horse onto the well-traveled path that led back to Bath. He stopped at the edge of an upland tributary of upper Big Bear to give his horse a chance to rest and drink. As Tobias waited, he heard the unmistakable sound of riders on horseback galloping toward him from the direction of Bath. He quickly led his horse away from the trail and into the woods. Moments later, thirty or more riders with muskets and cutlasses thundered past, heading east. Tobias sighed, thankful that the Secotan had safely made their escape.

Once the militia passed, Tobias led his horse from their hiding place in the woods and returned to the trail. An hour later, he arrived at his home overlooking Bath Creek. Opening the door to the barn, he led his tired horse into his stall and brought him hay and water. Looking his horse in the eyes, Tobias gave him a good pat on the neck and said, "Well done, my friend. Thank you."

Tobias picked up the deerskin satchel that held the urn from Secotan, strung it gently over his shoulder, and walked slowly out of the barn. Entering the back door of his house, he found his servants beginning their daily duties. Seeing their tired master, they welcomed him into the kitchen for a hearty breakfast of ham, eggs, and corn bread. At this early hour, his clerk was still asleep in one of the upstairs bedrooms.

After a hearty breakfast, Tobias felt exhaustion overtaking him and walked quietly up the stairs to his bedroom. He placed the urn carefully in a secret compartment underneath a floorboard beside the room's fireplace. Collapsing on his bed, he pulled the covers over him and soon succumbed to a tired but troubled sleep.

PART II

CHAPTER

4

Kurt Benjamin frowned as he studied the computer screen in front of him. When he was hired six months ago as the new director of Alternative Energy Operations for the United States Oil Company (USOCO), Jeffrey Morton promised him full access to all the company's past research projects. While he had reviewed many, he recently discovered a well-disguised file called the Enhanced Maize Project that was locked. Using computer skills learned during his stint with the CIA, Kurt had followed the trail of this project back to its origins at the USOCO Department of Alternative Energy. *Why is this project disguised, and why am I not allowed access to it?* he asked himself. Running his fingers thoughtfully through his thick wavy brown hair, he leaned forward to make another attempt at access. He heard footsteps in the hallway outside his office door, and a familiar voice soon followed.

"Good morning, Kurt," came the cheerful greeting of Omar Rashid. Kurt quickly minimized his search screen and opened one depicting current research projects at the lab.

"And good morning to you, Omar," Kurt said, as he turned his chair to see his new friend and boss standing in the doorway to his office. Both Kurt and Omar liked to arrive early at the USOCO Laboratory for Alternative Energy Research. By doing so, they avoided Houston's morning rush-hour traffic and enjoyed some productive quiet time before the arrival of their co-workers at eight a.m. They found that they had many common interests and had hit it off from the beginning. Both men were nice-looking, smart, and single. They moved in some of the same social circles and had little difficulty attracting female companionship.

"So, Kurt, what have we here?" asked Omar, looking over Kurt's shoulder at the multicolored graphs and charts on the computer screen.

"This shows the results of some experiments we're doing with combinations of naturally occurring compounds," Kurt replied.

"Anything caught your eye?"

"Not really. We're doing some broad-ranged screening, with a few long shots thrown in just for fun."

Omar smiled. "Why am I not surprised?"

"Nothing ventured, nothing gained," Kurt retorted. He studied the computer screen for a few seconds before turning his chair around to face Omar. "Hey, changing the subject, the weather on Saturday is for highs in the upper seventies with winds ten to fifteen from the southeast. I'm thinking about doing some sailing. Care to join me?"

Omar's perceptive brown eyes studied Kurt inquisitively.

"Oops, I guess I should have asked if you're a sailor," continued Kurt.

"Actually, I used to sail frequently, but it's been a long time."

"What did you sail?" asked Kurt.

"Dhows."

"Dhows," repeated Kurt, squinting slightly and trying to recall where he had seen one. "Oh yes, I saw them on a dive trip in the Persian Gulf." Kurt thought a few seconds more. "And in high school, I remember reading in the book *The Sons of Sinbad*, by Villiers, about dhows and their pearl divers. Omar, if you can sail one of those things, you can sail anything. So, do you want to get those sea legs back?"

Omar responded with a big grin. "You bet. What time and where?"

"How about ten thirty Saturday morning?"

"Great," said Omar. "Where is your boat docked?"

"It's at the Houston Yacht Club, thirty minutes south of here. I'll e-mail you directions."

"Thanks, Captain," replied Omar, giving Kurt a quick salute with his right hand. "I'll see you Saturday morning," he said, and he turned and stepped briskly out the doorway.

Back in his office, Omar wondered what his new friend Kurt was doing mixed up with these eccentric scientists in the USOCO Laboratory for Alternative Energy Research. From reviewing Kurt's work over the past six months, he had no doubt about his management skills and intellect. He was a problem-solver with a positive attitude, unlike most of the directionless scientists around him. Omar had learned from their frequent early morning chats that Kurt owned a forty-nine-foot Hylas sailboat, and now he knew that it was docked at the Houston Yacht Club. Kurt was an avid scuba diver with a master diver certification. Fluent in Spanish, he often spoke of his favorite dive spot, the second-largest barrier reef in the world, off Ambergris Cay, Belize. These were not the sorts of activities his lab mates would ever dream of undertaking.

Sitting at his desk, Omar's thoughts turned to how events could have brought both him and Kurt to the USOCO lab six months before. Omar's title was vice president of Alternative Energy Resources. His responsibilities included oversight of Kurt, the new director of Alternative Energy Operations, and its day-to-day research activities. Both Kurt and Omar had been drafted by Jeffrey Morton, the chief of operations of USOCO, for their new assignments. They had been assured that this would be a two-year stint, and that it would be a very beneficial step in their future advancement up the USOCO ladder.

Morton had emphasized to them that the team lacked focus and direction, and they were to provide it. The team's mission was to think outside the box to find any and every conceivable energy alternative to oil and gas. Each came away impressed that USOCO was devoted to finding affordable alternative energy sources that could supplement or replace the world's dwindling reserves of oil and gas. Both men had read *Twilight in the Desert: The Coming Saudi Oil Shock and the World Economy*, by Matt Simmons. In his book, Simmons departed from his conservative Republican banker background to detail why world oil production of eighty-six million barrels per day had peaked. With exhaustive research, he set forth how the world's oil-producing companies had overstated their reserves for years, leading an ever more oil-thirsty world into a false sense of complacency. Both men believed that Simmons's research was correct, and that USOCO needed to find an alternative energy source to oil as soon as possible.

Omar opened the folder in his computer that held Kurt's résumé. His education included a bachelor's from the University of Florida—double major in chemistry and geology—and a master's degree in geology from the University of Virginia. His résumé also listed a four-year stint with the U.S. Department of State as an overseas attaché.

Omar wondered why Kurt never discussed his time with the State Department. Whenever this period in his life came up, Kurt had always found a way to carefully redirect the conversation. Knowing that such assignments were sometimes a cover for CIA operatives, Omar had not pushed the issue.

During Kurt's time at USOCO, he had been given assignments to direct a variety of oil and gas exploration project teams all over the world. His teams' uncanny successes at finding productive oil and gas fields did not go unnoticed by his superiors. Like Omar, he was on the radar of the upper-management echelon of the United States Oil Company.

It was just past nine a.m. when Kurt pulled his Range Rover into a parking space near the pier where his sailboat was docked. Moments later Kurt stepped on the stern deck of his sleek Hylas 49 sailboat. He immediately began tuning the rigging by tightening the stern stays' turnbuckle. With Kurt's meticulous maintenance, the varnished teak handrails looked factory-fresh, and the stainless steel winches sparkled in the light of the mid-morning sun. On the stern transom, the name *Carpe Diem* was emblazoned in bold blue letters highlighted in red. Kurt was adjusting one of the yacht's stanchions when he heard footsteps coming down the pier.

He looked up to see Omar approaching. "Good morning, Omar. You're just in time. Could you hold this stanchion in place while I tighten up this snap shackle?"

Omar stepped forward, needing no further instruction. Afterward, Kurt gave him a short course in the yacht's rigging. Omar had a few questions about handling the sails and their furling and reefing systems.

After clearing the breakwater to the marina, Kurt motored to the southeast and out into Galveston Bay. As Kurt brought *Carpe Diem*'s bow into the wind, Omar released the roller furling main with several strong pulls on the halyard. With the yacht's bow now over to port, Kurt watched the mainsail fill with the steady southwesterly breeze. Nodding with approval, Kurt said, "Okay, Omar, let's release the headsail."

"Aye-aye, Captain," replied Omar, as he pulled on the headsail halyard.

Seconds later, with both sails full, Kurt felt the yacht surge forward on a brisk starboard tack. As they reached hull speed, the splashing sound of waves being cut away by the yacht's bow filled the cockpit.

As Kurt studied the sail settings, he said, "You're very comfortable on a sailboat."

"It's like riding a bike," Omar replied, as he watched the sails for any sign of a luff. "Some things you just don't forget."

During the next few minutes, both men busied themselves adjusting the lines that controlled the sails. Finally satisfied with what he saw, Kurt asked, "Want to take the helm?"

"Sure," said Omar, as he stepped behind the yacht's large stainless steel wheel.

Kurt disappeared down the companionway to the galley. A few minutes later he returned with two bottles of water. Tossing one to Omar, he settled onto a cushion on the port lazarette. After taking a sip of water, Kurt asked, "So tell me, Omar, what's it like to sail one of those dhows?"

"Not much to it," replied Omar.

"But they are ancient vessels," Kurt said. "I'm interested."

Omar unscrewed the top of the water bottle and took a long swig. He closed his eyes and felt the comfortable motion of the boat briskly cutting its way through the waters of Galveston Bay. In his mind he returned to his homeland of Sharjah, a small emirate of the United Arab Emirates.

"Kurt, let's start with my great-grandfather. In his younger days, he had a fleet of dhows in the Persian Gulf to support his prosperous pearling business. By the time I was born, my great-grandfather had passed away and the pearling business was about over. As pearling declined, oil was being discovered. Work in the oil fields was much easier, much safer, and certainly paid better than diving for pearls. As the pearling business waned, my grandfather got rid of most of his fleet of dhows. But he kept his favorite and refurbished it. With her mahogany hull and decks, she was a beauty. As a child, I loved nothing better than to sail with him. They were simple boats, nothing like this. Wooden hulls, canvas sails, and Manila halyards and sheets. That was it."

"So how did you get from there halfway around the world to here?"

Omar had come to appreciate Kurt's genuine interest in people and was not at all uncomfortable with the directness of the question.

"Well," he said, "it's a story you may have trouble understanding, being from the West. I will be happy to tell you, but it is a bit involved."

"We have all day. I'd like to hear it. But before you start, let's make a tack and head over toward the west side of the bay."

Kurt uncleated the jib's port sheet and gave the starboard jib sheet a few wraps around the starboard winch. At Omar's command of "ready about," Kurt responded, "Ready." Omar then gave the final command of "hard alee" and pushed the wheel over to starboard. As the bow pointed up into the wind, the sails flogged gently and soon filled again as the bow nosed down to starboard. With several quick turns of the winch handle, Kurt tightened the starboard sheet, and they were off on a brisk port tack to the west.

"Okay, let's hear the story," said Kurt.

Omar began searching his mind for where to begin. "What do you know about the history of the United Arab Emirates?" he asked.

"Very little," replied Kurt. It was a careful answer. One of Kurt's undercover CIA assignments had been in Saudi Arabia, where he had interacted with agents in Abu Dhabi who were trying to determine the political stability of the recently formed federation called the United Arab Emirates. He knew the information he had received about their enormous oil and gas reserves was still technically classified, so he could not be too forthcoming in his answer to Omar's question.

"Then let's start there. Of course you know that the United Arab Emirates is a collection of different emirates, with each one governed by an emir. You may know from your USOCO assignments that the United Arab Emirates has one of the largest reserves of oil and gas on the planet."

"Yes, I do," replied Kurt.

"My family owns very productive oil fields in the emirate known today as Sharjah. When my father was a child, no one in my family dreamed of such a thing, nor could they imagine the changes this discovery would bring to them and my country. Because my great-grandfather had done well in the pearling trade, he was able to acquire several large tracts of land on the coast of the Persian Gulf. He basically bought the vast majority of the land in the emirate of Sharjah, and with it, the title of emir. At the time, most of it was considered worthless desert, just miles and miles of hot, dry sand. You couldn't farm it, you couldn't graze cattle on it, and there was very little fresh water. My great-grandfather bought it anyway." Omar paused, glanced at the sails, and continued, "Today, this sandy wasteland produces slightly over a million barrels of oil per day. With the price of oil at over one hundred and twenty-five dollars a barrel, many oil experts project that within a year it will be over a hundred and fifty."

"When I was in the field," commented Kurt, as he made an adjustment to the mainsail, "we expected to spend about twenty-five dollars per barrel to get it out of the ground and delivered to the tanker."

"It now costs us about twenty-eight dollars to produce a barrel for shipment to the refinery."

Kurt looked out over the bay as he mentally did the math and tried to make sense of why Omar was working for USOCO. He knew Omar held an undergraduate degree in mechanical engineering from North Carolina State University in Raleigh, with honors, and was a member of Phi Beta Kappa. He also knew that Omar had later earned an MBA from the Wharton School at the University of Pennsylvania.

Kurt thought about the prejudices often suffered by Arab nationals in the United States. With his charm and grace, however, Omar had risen above the prejudices of narrow minds that knew nothing about his country and its rich cultural and religious traditions. Omar had quickly advanced through the ranks of junior executives at USOCO. He was smart, smooth, and produced results, the exact criteria for advancement in corporate America. But after going through all this in his mind, Kurt could make no sense of Omar's involvement with USOCO.

He turned and looked directly at Omar, who was obviously enjoying himself at the helm. "Okay, Omar, I have a question, and you certainly don't have to answer it."

"Ask it."

"So, why are you still here working for USOCO when you could be home running your own oil company?"

Omar thought about it for a while before responding. "That is a fair question. There is much that you, having grown up in the West, could not understand about the world I come from. By the time I was a teenager, my family had learned the hard way that the world they had known for centuries was changing rapidly and forever. The major oil companies were coming in like vultures for a feast. We were simple, uneducated people and unsophisticated about the ways of the West. I was determined to study and work in the Western culture, and eventually return to my country with the knowledge that we needed."

"And all this time I thought you came over here on a scholarship and a student visa and now have a green card."

They both had a good chuckle.

Stating the obvious, Kurt said, "That is information that certainly will not go off this boat. Imagine the reaction of Jeffrey Morton, the guy who hired us, if he knew that you were the son of an emir from one of the United Arab Emirates."

"Absolutely. And, Kurt, I tell you this because my father and brother are having increasing difficulty managing the growing complexity of the family's business operations in Sharjah. While my father has not yet asked me to return home to help, I expect that call will come very soon. It could be a month or several months. But, my friend, I do not want you to be surprised when it happens. Responsibility for managing the Department of Alternative Energy will then likely fall directly into your lap."

Kurt pondered the implications of Omar's last words but decided not to respond. Instead, he wanted to hear more of Omar's story. "I don't understand, Omar. Sending you off to the United States seems to be a pretty radical thing for a family to do to its oldest son, the heir apparent to the title of emir, and the one who will eventually control the family's oil fortune. Your family could have contracted with Western oil companies to manage their oil wealth."

"That is true, Kurt." Omar thought for a moment, wanting to choose his words carefully before continuing. "To understand the path chosen by my family, you need to hear a story that was relayed to me by my grandfather on my sixteenth birthday. You may then be able to view things through the eyes of an Arab and in the context of past treatment by the West. Let's take ourselves back many years to an experience that my family had with a large American oil company."

46

Omar paused for a moment, looking at a heeled sailboat on a windward tack several hundred feet to the west. He turned back to Kurt, whose intelligent blue eyes were studying him intently, waiting for him to continue. "Perhaps the best way to understand this is for me to tell you that story told to me by my grandfather. There was a beautiful silver sword that he kept in a glass-doored cabinet in his living room. I had admired it since I was a very young child. When I would ask him about it, he would say, 'The sword has a story that will be told to you when you are older.'

"As I grew older, I would often ask, 'Am I old enough now to hear the story?'

"His reply was always, 'I will tell you when you are older.'

"In the meantime, with my childhood imagination and the help of a plastic toy sword, I made up any number of gallant adventures for me and my grandfather's mysterious sword.

"On my sixteenth birthday, he brought me into his living room, removed the sword from the cabinet, and sat down on a cushion with it placed across his lap. Motioning for me to sit on a cushion in front of him, he pulled the sparkling sword from its sheath and held it out for me to take. As I held the sword on my lap, my grandfather said to me, 'Omar, this sword has an important story for you to know and remember, so listen carefully.'"

Omar paused for a moment. "Kurt, to appreciate this story, we must go back many years and try to imagine ourselves in the deserts of Sharjah before oil had been discovered. My country was very poor. Schools were almost nonexistent. Very few in my country could read Arabic, much less English. My grandfather had inherited the title of emir and ruled Sharjah. My father, Kareem, was a young teenager. His brother, my Uncle Habib, was several years older than he.

"One day, two men from a big American oil company came to the home of my grandfather, the emir of Sharjah. The year before, he had given this oil company permission to do test drilling on one of his family's remote tracts of land in the desert. It had all been agreed upon with a handshake. However, on this day, after a year of exploration and test drilling, these two men brought papers with them. My father and Uncle Habib were also present. It soon became obvious to my father and uncle that these oilmen were trying to get the emir to sign these papers right away.

"Kurt, you need to understand that, at the time, my family's years of good fortune from pearling were over. The combination of over-harvesting and the introduction of cheap cultured pearls from Japan had resulted in the demise of the pearling industry. With the loss of its pearling business revenues, my family needed a new source of cash flow to support the lifestyle to which they had become accustomed.

"One of the Americans was quite tall and did most of the talking. Addressing the emir, he said, 'These papers just allow us the rights to a small percentage of what we might someday find. It is a big gamble for our company. As we all know, the chances of actually finding a productive oil field are always small. But this contract will help our company pay its expenses if we do. As you can imagine, what we are doing out there in the desert is very expensive.'

"The emir and his sons said nothing, and simply listened. The contract sat on the table in front of them. Habib and the emir could speak and understand some English, but could not read it. My father, however, had learned not only to speak good English, but to read it as well.

"After listening intently a while, Habib said, 'We appreciate your visit today. We will consider what you have said and will review your papers, but we are not in a position to sign today.'

"The tall American smiled and said, 'Well, you have nothing to worry about here. These papers will reward you generously if we do find oil. To encourage you to go ahead and sign today, we are prepared to make a significant good faith down payment immediately.'

"'And what would that be?' asked the emir.

"The tall American leaned toward the emir and said in a low voice, 'We are prepared to deposit one million dollars into your bank account today. These papers just allow us to recover our investment and have some amount of profit if we are lucky enough to find oil. If we do, you will be rich beyond your wildest dreams. Just sign this, and we will transfer the one million dollars to your account. In what bank would you like us to make the deposit?'

"The emir responded, 'We bank with the Abu Dhabi Commercial Bank.'

"Habib immediately interjected, speaking firmly, 'He will not sign anything today. Come back in a week. By then we will have discussed it and my father will have made his decision.' The emir nodded in agreement.

"The two Americans sat motionless and stunned. It was obvious to them that the deal would not be struck that day.

"The emir nodded graciously and said, 'We will be pleased to see you in one week. Will next Tuesday at three o'clock suit you?'

"The Americans exchanged disappointed glances, but nodded in agreement.

"'Very well,' replied the tall American. 'We will return next Tuesday. I am confident that, as businessmen, you will find this contract fair and reasonable.'

"Habib escorted them to the door and bid them a good day. After they departed, the three of them began an earnest discussion of the Americans' offer. As they talked, my father took the document from the table and walked over to a window where he had enough light to read it.

"When my father and uncle were young children, the emir had hired a tutor to come to their home once a week to teach his sons what was not available to them in their school. While Habib had little interest in learning English, my father absorbed it like a sponge. At the time of the Americans' visit, he could read and speak English fluently. As it turned out, making the tutor available to teach Kareem English would soon bring the emir's family great fortune. Many others in the Arab world were less fortunate because they could not read and did not understand the contracts they signed with the oil companies from the West.

"As the emir and Habib discussed the proposal of the oilmen, Kareem stood quietly at the window, absorbed by the Americans' document. He finally returned to where his father and brother were seated and said, 'I have read this. It is a contract.'

"'What does it say?' asked Habib.

"Kareem proceeded to read the contract slowly, translating as he went. He first read a long string of 'whereas this' and 'whereas that.' He then read several paragraphs that began with 'It is therefore agreed that.' At one point, Kareem stopped reading and looked up at the other two men. They were listening to him intently.

"'Please continue,' said the emir.

"'Article III. B. 2.07. REVENUES. After costs as defined herein are subtracted, revenues shall be apportioned eighty percent to operator and twenty percent to owner.'

"'Stop,' ordered the emir. 'Go back and read that again.' Which he did, more slowly than before. When he finished the second reading, Habib jumped to his feet.

"'They are trying to cheat us! Eighty percent of net proceeds? They want to steal from us. I knew we could not trust those infidel Americans.'

"My father then added, 'Why would they give us a million dollars now? Have they found oil and did not tell us?'

"'We don't know that,' replied Habib. 'They have the area closely guarded.'

"'We'd know,' said the emir. 'Our cousins who work there would have told us if they had struck oil.'

"Habib responded, 'They might not know, because none of our people are there at night. Our people are only there to do the work of animals during the heat of the day. The Americans often run their drilling rigs while our people are at home in their beds. We do not know what happens there at night.'

"There was a long pause before the emir spoke. 'We must learn. We will watch them ourselves while they think we are sleeping. But we must be very cautious. No one outside this room can know what we are doing. We will meet tonight at ten o'clock at the stables. I will select our best camels. That is the only way.'

"Before leaving the house that night, the emir went to the cabinet and removed the sword that I held in my lap as I listened to this story. When the emir removed it from its sheath, it sparkled even in the dim light of the room's lanterns. He confidently slid the blade back into its sheath, slung its harness over his shoulder, and joined his sons at the stable. They tried to talk their father out of going with them, but he would hear nothing of it. Although he was no longer a young man, he knew the desert far better than his sons, and was not about to let them go into it at night alone.

"After the saddles were securely strapped to the camels, they climbed up onto them and rode off into the blackness of the desert night.

"'Why didn't you take a jeep?' I asked my grandfather. 'Wouldn't that have been much faster?'

"'Good question,' he replied, 'but had we done so, the outcome of this story would have been far different. I would not be here today to tell you this story. We needed to approach the drilling site undetected. Not only would the jeep's noise have given us away, the desert holds many unforgiving surprises. The reliable, silent camel was the only way to cross the open desert this night and arrive at our destination unobserved.'

"Now, with a bitter edge to his voice, my grandfather continued, 'With no moon, the stars were brilliant and gave us clear guidance. The desert gave up little sound except for the swishing of the hooves of the camels as they moved across the sand. Our progress was slow but steady. But most importantly, it was quiet. After two hours, a glow of light appeared on the horizon ahead of us, confirming that we were approaching our destination. Thirty minutes later, we halted and dismounted the camels. We were at the base of a large dune that was no more than fifty yards from the drilling operation. After securing the camels there, out of earshot of the site, we trudged soundlessly up to the top of a dune. We moved quietly and spoke not at all. Lying on our stomachs at the top, we watched the brightly lit beehive of activity below. The sounds of men and machinery drifted up to us.'

"My grandfather told me that, as my father studied the scene below with his binoculars, he soon recognized the two Americans who had been at our house that day. The tall one was issuing orders to several men who surrounded him. After these men nodded and walked away, he turned and motioned to a man in a black uniform with a rifle who had been standing behind the others. When the rifleman stepped forward, the tall American began giving him orders, gesturing to the rifle and then pointing in a circle to the high dunes of the desert surrounding them. The gunman nodded and walked away.

"Moments later, the drilling rig came to life. The quiet of the desert was replaced by the loud pounding of the diesel engine driving the drill into the bowels of the desert. For the next hour, the drilling went on uneventfully. The drilling rig crew continued to move about busily, replacing pipe on top of pipe. Suddenly, there was a swarm of activity. The tall one, who had disappeared into a tent, must have been summoned on his portable radio, because he rushed from the tent with a camera.

"From the top of the dune, they watched as a black, bubbling goop percolated up from the crust of the earth and then suddenly became a roaring hundred-foot geyser. The tall man was now at the scene taking pictures. The men around him were jubilantly jumping up and down and slapping each other on the back.

"They were too busy celebrating to hear the low roar of an approaching sandstorm moving across the desert in their direction. Even if they had heard it, they would not have known what was coming. But the emir and my father and uncle on the dune above them immediately recognized the sound.

"'Stay here,' the emir commanded. 'Watch them for as long as you can still see them.'

"The emir slid quickly down the dune into the darkness to get the camels. The two brothers were too entranced with the scene below to notice the approach of the rifleman. They were both startled when they heard a voice behind them asking, 'Why are you here?'

"They turned to see a figure dressed in black and the barrel of a rifle pointed directly at them. They studied the dark man in silence.

"'You must tell me why you are here,' ordered the gunman.

"Finally, Kareem responded, 'We are simple fishermen returning from a pilgrimage. We were on our way back to our village when we saw the light. What is all this?'

"'You cannot live to know,' replied the gunman. As the man in black was preparing to squeeze off the shots that would have been their end, a flash of silver struck the right side of his neck. His head, disconnected from his body, fell to the sand at his feet and rolled down the dune. As if in slow motion, his knees buckled and he fell forward into a lifeless heap in front of them.

"The emir stepped forward from the darkness, wiped the blood from his sword, and pushed it expertly back into its sheath. Standing over the rifleman, he said sadly, 'This did not have to happen to you. May Allah preserve your soul.'

"The sandstorm was now descending upon the scene below. The emir and his sons watched the bedlam for a few minutes, until the swirling sand shrouded the drilling site from view. My grandfather, father, and uncle mounted their camels and disappeared into the desert behind a wall of windblown sand. Within an hour, the shifting sands from the storm swallowed the rifleman forever into the bowels of the desert."

Omar paused for a moment. Kurt had been listening intently.

"My grandfather then said to me, 'Omar, this is the lesson you are to take with you forever. We are to control our destiny. This is our country and our heritage. The infidels of the West must be under our control. If not, we will be under theirs. Never, ever forget that.'"

Several minutes passed in silence before Omar continued. "This episode my family had with the oilmen from the West is why I am here. You are now the second person in the United States that knows who I am. No one else needs to know, especially at USOCO."

"Your secret will stay on this boat," replied Kurt solemnly.

With a series of tacks, they sailed south to Redfish Island and anchored. Over a lunch of fruit and sandwiches that Kurt had purchased from the Houston Yacht Club deli before their departure, Omar continued the story of his circuitous route to the United States Oil Company. Kurt was totally fascinated, and with skillful questioning learned from his training with the CIA, he gained enough information to have completed a briefing on the emirs of the United Arab Emirates and the economies of this loosely knit federation. At Kurt's encouragement, Omar had detailed the years since that fateful night in the desert. Omar's family was now fabulously rich, but without their revered son. It was obvious to Kurt that Omar was not long for his position at USOCO.

By the time they weighed anchor for the return to port, the breeze had picked up to a brisk eighteen knots. Omar set the whisker pole on the jib while Kurt connected the jibe protector to the main. *Carpe Diem* immediately leapt forward on a wing-on-wing downwind gallop across the bay.

The sun was setting as they completed the last leg of a broad-reach through the entrance markers to the breakwater that led into the basin of the Houston Yacht Club. Omar had been at the helm for most of the run north. As he headed the bow into the wind, Kurt hauled in the roller furling headsail and then the main. Kurt took the helm, steered the *Carpe Diem* to its slip, and backed it flawlessly into its berth as Omar secured the dock lines.

After washing down the deck and tidying the boat, the two friends walked up the pier to the parking lot beside the club. Along the way, they agreed to meet later at the Village for dinner.

Driving back on Highway 225 to Houston, Kurt's thoughts turned to Omar's story. From his Middle East CIA assignment several years ago, he remembered that the emirate of Sharjah had some limited oil resources, but they were dwarfed by those of its sister emirate, Abu Dhabi. *What will Sharjah do for revenue once its oil is depleted?* He had considered asking this question as Omar told his story, but decided against it. Kurt had learned to listen to his hunches, and this one told him loud and clear that more pieces to this puzzle were yet to appear.

CHAPTER

5

It was two thirty p.m. Kurt, Omar, and the two people they considered the brightest members of the research team, Jennifer and George Batts, rode the elevator from the USOCO cafeteria back to their seventh-floor laboratory. They had spent the last hour in a secluded corner of the cafeteria discussing the research project on which Jennifer and George had been working for the last three months. Without speaking, they stepped off the elevator and walked briskly to the lab conference room.

After Kurt closed the door, he turned to Jennifer. "So where do we go next with this project?"

Jennifer ran her hand through her shoulder-length silver hair as she sat down next to her husband, George. After pushing her reading glasses on top of her head, she focused her hazel eyes directly on Kurt and continued their lunchtime discussion.

"It may be a long shot for large-volume energy production, but we have made great progress with it on a small scale here in the lab. The generator is something George came up with from studying some of Tesla's work from the early 1900s. The idea is to run a generator with permanent magnets that do not require the energy that we are currently using with our electromagnetic generators. With just a little electricity from a battery going into this generator, we have produced three times the electricity going out using these permanent magnets. We think we can create generators the size of window air-conditioning units that could produce enough power to run the average household and would require little if any maintenance. What makes it really exciting is that it should produce excess power that could be fed back into the grid, giving the users credits from their electric company. They use no fossil fuels and thus create no pollutants. We could finally gain our independence from oil, gas, and coal."

While Jennifer had been presenting the concept, Kurt noticed that George, with a scowl on his face, had been busily scribbling formulas on a notepad in front of him. With his long graying black hair in a pigtail and his piercing black eyes behind wire-rimmed glasses, he looked every bit the brilliant scientist that he was. Kurt watched George, who eventually quit scribbling and looked up from his notepad to interject.

"That's true, but a number of big hurdles remain. This project will require a one-hundred-eighty-degree turn in USOCO's focus on oil and gas for its revenues. If my preliminary research is correct, this could eventually make power production from fossil fuels obsolete. To develop this project will require an enormous investment from USOCO." A sneer appeared on George's face. "But given USOCO's response to other promising ideas from our lab, this project too will probably be dead on arrival when it reaches the management level of Jeffrey Morton."

Kurt looked at George inquisitively and asked, "What do you mean?"

George continued with a bitter edge in his voice. "Jennifer and I have been here for more years than I want to admit. And yes, we have seen many ideas come through. Some had no promise, but others did. We have seen concepts developed here in the lab by some very bright, capable people that disappeared into oblivion when they reached the upper-management level. I fear that sending this revolutionary idea up the chain of command to request the kind of funding we need for it will doom it forever."

After listening quietly, Omar spoke. "I'm willing to do whatever I can within my power to secure approval for this project. It really looks like it has merit. Let's not be so pessimistic."

George sighed and tossed his pencil on the pad of paper in front of him. "We were involved in another promising project a few years ago. Months of long days and late nights were spent on it. But to go to the next level of research to prove our findings economically viable required investment capital by USOCO that would have been a pittance compared to its net annual revenues. What did we get for it? A congratulatory-sounding thank-you-but-no-thank-you from the very man you report to, Omar—Jeffrey Morton himself. Forgive me if I sound bitter, but I have reached my limit of tolerance with USOCO's upper management. I'm beginning to believe we're wasting our time sending our findings to the shortsighted people who are running this company."

⊕ ⊕ ⊕

At that moment, Omar's cell phone vibrated, and he glanced at the number. It was a call from Sharjah.

"I am so sorry," he said. "I must take this call." He stepped into the hallway. "Hello, this is Omar speaking."

"Hello, Omar, my son. How are you?"

"I am doing very well, Father. And you?"

"I am fine, but your grandfather is very sick."

There was a moment of silence. "I am so sorry, Father. How bad is it?"

"It is bad. He will not be with us much longer. He has turned the duties of the emir of Sharjah over to me. I love your brother, Naji, but he is limited in what he can do for us. The emirate of Sharjah has now reached the point where we need your help. It is time for you to return."

Although Omar had known he would eventually receive this call, he was still unprepared all the same. "Father, may I call you back within the hour? I am in the middle of a meeting."

"Yes. I will await your call."

As Omar stepped back in the room, the other three were sitting in silence. Kurt spoke first. "Let's think about this for a few days. I suggest we continue the work on it and meet again for lunch on Thursday." Everyone agreed, and George and Jennifer departed, leaving Omar and Kurt in the conference room alone.

"Kurt, I just received a call from my father in Sharjah. My grandfather is quite ill and has turned the duties of emir over to my father. He has asked me to come home to run the family's business interests."

"You look somewhat shocked, Omar. You knew the call had to come eventually."

"Yes, Kurt, you are correct. The reason for my being here was to prepare me for when this time came. And the time has now come, but it's hard to digest."

"When will you need to leave?"

"I don't know. I must call my father back within the hour. I suspect it will be soon, probably less than a month."

After a few moments of silence, Kurt released a long sigh. "Well, if you leave, I will, too."

Omar looked at his friend curiously. "Why would you do that, Kurt? You've only been here a little over six months. Besides, my job as vice president of Alternative Energy will be yours for the asking."

"Maybe so, but something just doesn't feel right about what we're doing here at USOCO."

Omar studied Kurt closely and asked, "What does that mean?"

"I don't know. I can't quite put my finger on it yet."

"Don't be too hasty, my friend. You should at least give it another six months."

"We'll see," Kurt responded skeptically.

⊕ ⊕ ⊕

Several days later, Kurt was driving his Range Rover down Buffalo Speedway on his way home from a long, frustrating day at USOCO. Nagging concerns of why the Enhanced Maize Project was a locked directory still resonated in his mind. But the thought of spending time with Jennifer and George Batts, who had recently begun inviting him for dinner on Thursday evenings, lifted his spirits.

Living only four blocks from Buffalo Speedway, he had less than a ten-minute drive from the lab to his house, which was tucked in the middle of the upscale neighborhood in Houston known as West University. He drove along its quiet streets, shaded with thick canopies of ancient live oaks, and turned into his driveway. In West University parlance, Kurt's home was politely referred to as a bungalow. Small by West U standards and one of the few that remained from the flurry of post-World War II construction, many of these functional little houses had been torn down or hauled off to make room for the stately structures that now dominated the neighborhood. Kurt preferred the quaintness of the bungalow and the easy care of a smaller space. Just east of West U, between Kirby Boulevard and Rice University, was the Village, an eclectic collection of restaurants, bars, and shops. Since it was just a short walk from his home, Kurt found the Village convenient and occasionally spent evenings there with Omar and some of their friends.

Many of the streets in the unique enclave of West U were named after American universities. Kurt's house on Fordham was two blocks east of the home of his two favorite employees, Jennifer and George Batts. Kurt had hit it off with the Battses, especially Jennifer. Soon after meeting them at the lab, Jennifer had invited him to their home for dinner. The Battses were a couple in their late fifties with no children, and they found the company of the younger Kurt Benjamin to be delightful. He eventually became an expected Thursday evening dinner guest.

Although it was still the middle of February, Kurt knew that winter in Houston would soon be over. However, on this night, temperatures were expected to dip below freezing for one of the few times all winter. As Kurt walked down the sidewalk on Fordham, the low streetlights illuminated a canopy of live oaks above him. Along the way, he passed one neatly manicured lawn after another in front of a variety of residential architectures. Many of the homes had the trademark West U gas lanterns lighting their front stoops and porches.

It was just past seven o'clock when Kurt walked up the front walkway that led to the Battses' home. Standing on the porch, he heard the door chimes in the foyer announce his arrival. The door opened, and a smiling Jennifer Batts stood in front of him. Fitting for this cool late-winter night, Jennifer wore a blue cashmere turtleneck sweater with her trademark faded blue jeans. "Come in, Kurt," she said cheerfully.

As Kurt followed her into the den, he immediately detected a pleasing aroma coming from the kitchen. "Hmm, something really smells good. What is it?"

"George is making a pot roast for us. It just needs to cook a little longer. We're working on a bottle of zinfandel from our last trip to Napa Valley. Want to try it?"

"Sure. What is it?"

"It's produced by a little winery called Benessere, at the northern end of the valley."

George soon entered the room with three glasses and an opened bottle of wine, and gave a hearty, "Evening, Kurt. Cold enough for you?"

"Sure is, George. We need to be in Belize."

The Battses had heard stories of Kurt's scuba-diving adventures on the world's second-longest barrier reef, just offshore from the island of Ambergris, Belize. George filled the three large glasses to the appropriate one-third level, and handed one to Jennifer and one to Kurt.

"Here's to our slave-driving lab master," George said sarcastically, as he raised his glass for a toast. All three had a good chuckle, and their usual lively Thursday evening was under way.

"This is one fine zinfandel, George," said Kurt. "How did you find this winery?"

"We were traveling north on Highway 29 and had gotten up to St. Helena. We were about to turn around when we noticed a small sign beside a driveway for the Benessere Winery. Something about it just caught our eye. Although it was getting late in the day, we decided to give it a try. It's a small family-run operation, and the wine tasting was actually being conducted by one of the proprietor's sons, a nice lad named Jonathan. After we had tasted their Sangiovese, we tried this zin and immediately fell in love with it. It's a very versatile wine and should be perfect for tonight's pot roast."

"I can see why," agreed Kurt.

George continued, "Anyway, as we were sipping this zin, this big, black, wooly animal lumbered into the room. It had huge, brown, bloodshot eyes and was drooling profusely. It had to have weighed a hundred and fifty pounds. Before I knew it, it was two feet from me and growling ferociously. I was convinced that a black bear had somehow found its way into the winery, and we were about to be mauled. Can you imagine the headline, 'Tourists in Local Winery Mauled by Rabid Bear'? At that moment, Jonathan looked over at this thing and in a commanding voice bellowed, 'Down, Stormy!' Like a hundred and fifty pounds of blubber, the black bear collapsed on the cool concrete floor. 'Good girl,' he said, and a large dog treat flew through the air, which the bear expertly snatched without getting up from the floor. Seeing the look on our faces, Jonathan laughed and said, 'No reason to be alarmed. She's just a big old friendly Newfoundland that mysteriously showed up at the winery a few months back. I've never seen her act aggressive like that. Anyway, this big girl seems to love the cool temperatures in the winery. And she especially likes all the attention she receives from our guests. Our only problem with her is that she's a little too friendly. Our wine-tasting guests sometimes don't know what to think when this big bear-looking thing comes up and starts licking them in the face.' I have to admit that I was getting ready to run for the door when I first saw the thing."

"But enough of our story. Let's go enjoy George's pot roast," said Jennifer, and she motioned Kurt toward the dining room.

The conversation over dinner was light and lively. However, at one point, Jennifer noticed that Kurt had gotten quiet and asked, "Is something bothering you, Kurt?"

"Well, I have been wondering about something," replied Kurt, as he set down his fork. "I've been studying USOCO computer files on some of the projects that the lab has undertaken over the past few years. In doing that, I've seen some very interesting ideas explored. However, I stumbled on one file that was not actually in the lab's directory, and for some strange reason it was password protected. I was unable to access it."

"What was the file name?" asked Jennifer.

"It was called the Enhanced Maize Project." Kurt saw George and Jennifer exchange glances and asked, "You know the project?"

Jennifer took a good sip of wine before responding. "George and I spent most of our time on nothing but that project for the better part of a year. It was the same project we talked to you and Omar about at lunch this week."

"Maize is the Indian word for corn," commented Kurt, "so I'm guessing it was an ethanol project."

Jennifer shook her head and replied, "Actually, it was an algae project that had been deliberately misnamed because of security concerns. Our research led us to suspect that genetically altered algae could be developed and grown under certain restrictive conditions using specific enhanced nutrients to produce a variety of algae that would double in size every seventy-two hours. We believed that it could be refined efficiently into a biodiesel that would be an economically viable alternative to oil. At the same time, it would, like other ethanol products, produce very little in CO_2 emissions. As you know, CO_2 emissions are depleting our protective ozone shield, which many believe will ultimately cause dramatic climate changes with catastrophic worldwide consequences."

"From our experiments," George interrupted, an agitated edge to his voice, "we really thought we had stumbled onto something huge. Unfortunately, once the proposal reached the policy-making levels of upper management, it disappeared into oblivion. Some six months after the proposal was submitted, we were called into your predecessor's office and told that the trials in the field with our proposal had proved to be economically unfeasible."

Kurt sat uncomfortably as he felt George's piercing black eyes burning at him through his thick wire-rimmed glasses. *This is one bitter man,* Kurt thought, and he phrased his next question carefully. "Do we know where, how, or who conducted these trials?"

"No," replied George bitterly. "When we asked, the response was, in effect, 'You don't need to know.' I can't tell you how demoralizing it is to have a project you believe in sabotaged for no rational reason."

"But you have moved on to the project we discussed at lunch this week," Kurt offered, in an effort to defuse George's obvious anger. "It's the one that you explained was a continuation of work by Nicola Tesla. That research sounds like it could really set the oil, gas, and coal industries on their heads."

His agitation having subsided, George responded, "It's a complicated project and will be a long shot. But if we are right, yes, it could indeed set the fossil fuel industries upside down."

"Enough talk about work. Let's have dessert," Jennifer interjected cheerfully. She rose from her chair and stepped into the kitchen. Moments later, she appeared with three plates of hot brownies topped with vanilla ice cream and set them on the table in front of them.

"Will you look at that," Kurt said enthusiastically, and immediately plunged a fork into his brownie. After savoring the first bite, he turned to George. "This is delicious. Not only are you a wizard in the lab, but in the kitchen as well."

The conversation turned to the Houston Texans' lackluster season, and they all agreed that next year had to be better. As they finished dessert, Kurt glanced at his watch and noticed it was ten thirty. After thanking his hosts for another delicious dinner and a delightful evening, he bid them good night and stepped into the crisp, cool air of one of Houston's final nights of winter. As he walked back to his house on Fordham, he hardly noticed anything along the way. His thoughts were totally focused on the Battses' account of the strange abandonment by USOCO of what seemed to be a very promising alternative energy source to oil. *Why would they not have pursued something as simple as algae as a potential biofuel? Why is this project locked so that I, the director of Alternative Energy Operations, cannot access it?*

Kurt slept fitfully that night. Finally, at four a.m., he got up, showered, dressed, and drove his Range Rover to his favorite breakfast spot, the Buffalo Grill. It opened at four a.m., which suited his usual early morning schedule perfectly. The service was fast, the servings were ample, and it had the best omelets in town. Before going in, he dropped two quarters in the newspaper box and pulled out the morning's edition of the *Houston Chronicle*. He was intrigued that the feature headline was "Ethanol: An Economically Viable Alternative?"

As usual, he walked across the large room of tables to a counter to place his order. Mounted prominently on one of the walls was an enormous buffalo head that appeared to be leering at the patrons no matter where they sat in the restaurant. He poured himself a large coffee from a dispenser on a counter to his left and selected a booth to the right of the entrance, beside a front window. A few minutes later, he heard his order called and went to a counter on the other side of the restaurant to retrieve his breakfast. Returning to his booth, he picked up the *Houston Chronicle* and quickly turned to the article by David Ivanovich of the *Chronicle*'s Washington Bureau. He began reading Ivanovich's interview with the vice chairman of Chevron Corp., Peter Robertson:

Q: You've raised concerns about President Bush's call to slash gasoline consumption by 20 percent by 2017 and use more alternative fuels. What's the problem?

A: Today we're at about 3 or 4 percent ethanol in the gasoline, and that's using a fair amount of the corn crop. There's an additional ethanol capacity being built in the country right now. I think there's every expectation the farmers are going to continue to grow more corn, and we're going to get up to E-10 (10 percent ethanol). When you get up to 10 percent ethanol in gasoline, you have a bit of a problem with cars. To go over 10 percent requires a different car fleet. And by the time you get to E-10, you're kind of straining the corn crop. My guess is that somewhere in that time frame, we're going to crack the code on this cellulose conversion (making ethanol from switch grass, cornstalks, wood chips and other plant waste). We've got a lot of projects in that area. We're going to move forward from 10 percent to 12 percent to 15. By that time, hopefully, we'll have a bunch of new vehicles in the mix. My only concern is whether we can get there in the time frame that's been advertised.

Q: Policymakers want to encourage construction of new refineries, but you've argued the emphasis on renewables could hamper that effort. How so?

A: We are working hard to substitute up to 20 percent of the U.S. gasoline consumption with ethanol or with some alternate fuel. That's going to reduce the need for traditional refining capacity. We just completed an expansion at Pascagoula. So, we're continuing to do refinery capacity expansion. But going forward, if we're in a market that grows at 1 percent a year and we've got a serious set of proposals and the probability of substituting 10 to 20 percent of the fuel, then you've got to say, "Why would I invest in additional gasoline refining until I understand a little bit more what's happening in the market?"

Q: Let's talk about climate change. Does Chevron support mandatory caps on greenhouse gas emissions?

A: Chevron has been very vocal in saying we believe that we need a U.S. framework for dealing with the issue of climate change. Today, we have 18 different blends of gasoline around the country. And under the Clean Air Act, different cities, different metropolitan areas have different standards. On top of that now, all kinds of states and municipalities are putting in ethanol mandates. That adds complexity to the gasoline supply system. If on top of that we have a state-by-state climate change set of frameworks, then I think we're going to make our whole system far more complex than it needs to be, with the result when you have interruptions in any particular area—whether it be a hurricane or a refinery shutdown—moving this stuff becomes very, very complicated and, frankly, increases cost to the consumer and increases volatility. We want a national framework on CO_2.

Q: Pump prices are again pushing $3 a gallon. Do you anticipate uproar on Capitol Hill?

A: I really don't. The last time was after hurricanes Katrina and Rita, and we went a long way toward explaining what it is that drives the price of gasoline. And I think a lot of people have accepted that the biggest single driver of gasoline prices is crude oil prices.

Kurt put the newspaper down and finished his breakfast. Fifteen minutes later, he was back on Buffalo Speedway heading for the lab. The article in the *Chronicle*, combined with what he had learned at dinner the previous night, swirled through his mind raising troubling issues. *The major oil companies are clearly aware of the implications that ethanol could mean to their bottom line. What if a process could be developed that would efficiently mass produce ethanol that could mix with gasoline or diesel fuel at levels above the 10 to 15 percent discussed in the article? Would that significantly affect bottom-line profits of the world's oil-producing countries? Why would USOCO lock the Enhanced Maize Project?*

Moments later, he pulled into the empty USOCO parking lot and selected a spot directly in front of the building. Slamming the door of the Range Rover, he jogged to the entrance door and raced inside. Jesse, the lobby security guard, perked up and smiled broadly at seeing his usual first early arrival. "Good morning, Kurt."

"Good morning to you, Jesse," replied Kurt hastily, and he disappeared into the elevator.

An hour later, Kurt had a program running a random series of codes in an attempt to access the Enhanced Maize Project file that he had been locked out of previously. His prior CIA training was at work. He had been one of the best computer hackers in the agency several years ago, but the technology had moved rapidly forward in the years Kurt since. He tried half a dozen configurations with no success, but kept experimenting. His experience had taught him that creativity and persistence were the keys to getting past a computer's security code. It was six thirty a.m. when he finally found the code breaker. The dizzying flashes on his computer screen suddenly stopped, and the file opened in front of him. Kurt was about to begin reading when there was a knock at the doorway. Instinctively, he minimized the file and opened a current project file for work being done by the lab. Glancing up, he saw at the door his good friend Omar, who, smiling as usual, said, "Good morning, Kurt."

CHAPTER
6

MARCH 14, 2008 — DUTCH PHOSPHATE CORPORATION HEADQUARTERS, NEW YORK CITY

When Sarah Carpenter answered the call on her direct line, she was pleasantly surprised to hear the voice of her friend and classmate from the Wharton School. "Omar, I am so pleased to hear from you. How are you?"

"I am doing very well, and you?"

"I am, but I've been immersed in a major project for the company lately. It's kept me in the office far more than I would like, but it's exciting."

"Sounds like you need to take a break and get back for some sailing on the Pamlico."

"I'd like to, but that will have to wait for a while."

"How is your Uncle Jason? Is he still teaching at East Carolina University?"

"He is, but now only part-time. He still loves it, but he decided to give up his full-time teaching position to devote time to some research projects he always wanted to pursue. How is the job going with USOCO? And how is your family, Omar? What do you hear from them?"

"The answer to both questions is rather involved, Sarah, and would take a while to explain. How about this? I plan to be in New York next week on business. Why don't we meet for lunch? What are you doing next Wednesday?"

"Well, let me check my calendar." After a brief pause, she responded, "Hmm, nothing I can't rearrange. Where shall I meet you?"

"How about that Italian place on Pine Street, the one that's two blocks down from you? Is it Antonio's?"

"It is, and that sounds great. Is eleven thirty too early?"

"No. That's perfect," said Omar.

"Your timing is excellent, Omar. I have something I'd like to run by you."

"Yes," said Omar, "and I have something I need your thoughts on as well."

"I'm intrigued. See you next Wednesday."

After hanging up, Sarah looked out the windows of her corner office overlooking the New York skyline and wondered what her friend might want to talk about. It obviously had something to do with his family and his position at USOCO, but was not something he wanted to discuss on the phone. *Omar always was a bit mysterious,* she thought. *I'll just have to wait until next Wednesday.*

When Sarah was six years old, she and her parents were in a head-on collision with a drunk driver. While her parents were both killed, Sarah had managed to escape with only minor injuries. She was taken in by her Uncle Jason and Aunt Alice and reared in the small college town of Greenville, North Carolina. A third of the town's population was composed of students at East Carolina University, where Jason was a professor, teaching courses in chemistry and geology. Two years after Sarah moved to Greenville, her Aunt Alice became a victim of breast cancer and passed away six months later.

Sarah's introduction to the Dutch Phosphate Corporation came early in her life. She and her Uncle Jason spent many of their weekends and most of their summers at the family's cottage on the north shore of the Pamlico River. One summer while at the river cottage, Uncle Jason and Sarah had gone for a ride on the ferry to enjoy the beautiful day and just for something to do. Not in any hurry, they drove around and ended up on the main street of Aurora, where they discovered the Dutch Phosphate Corporation's fossil museum. They spent a couple of hours there, viewing a movie about how phosphates were created in the area over several million years ago and looking at the museum's many displays of fossils of land and sea creatures. When they made their way back to the entrance to leave, the curator directed them to one of the mine's discard piles across the street and told them to have a go at finding their own fossils. Hours later, it was all Uncle Jason could do to pull Sarah away to catch the ferry. A passion for hunting for fossils was ignited in Sarah that day. With Jason's academic credentials, he was able to obtain from the Dutch Phosphate Corporation almost unlimited access to the recently mined pits, and he and Sarah became frequent visitors in search of ancient fossils. By age eleven, Sarah had won her first science fair project with a presentation of shark and whale teeth from her digs at the mine.

She stumbled into the chance to work at the mine's museum in Aurora between her freshman and sophomore years at the University of North Carolina at Chapel Hill. There, she was able to meet a number of the management-level personnel at that mine, including Jim Clark. It was not just her striking good looks that caught Jim's attention. He realized that Sarah was also very knowledgeable about how phosphates were created, and the dinosaur, shark, and whale remains that were left when the seas had receded fifteen million years ago, and she was very comfortable speaking to groups of visitors about them. During the remaining summers of undergraduate school, she worked as an intern for various department managers at the mine. At the time of her graduation from UNC, she knew and was comfortable with all phases of the fertilizer production process. After graduation, Jim persuaded her to work as his administrative assistant in his new job as chief operating officer at the company's headquarters on Pine Street in New York City. After a year, she took a leave of absence to attend the Wharton School at Penn. When she received her MBA two years later, she returned to the Dutch Phosphate Corporation. While she had other tempting offers, Jim persuaded her that Dutch Phosphate had a home for her and she had a bright future ahead of her there. During the four years after her return, she had had a number of special assignments to the company's fertilizer production plants around the world. When Jim was promoted to chief executive officer, the board of directors offered Sarah his old position of chief operating officer, and she had jumped at the opportunity.

Five days later, as Omar stepped from the yellow cab onto the sidewalk of Pine Street in New York City, the cold winds funneling through the tall buildings hit him like a brick. Having lived the past few months in the warm Houston winter, he had forgotten to bring an overcoat. Fortunately, Antonio's was only a few steps away.

Upon entering the restaurant, Omar was greeted by the maitre d'. "Welcome to Antonio's. Do you have a reservation?"

Omar glanced around the restaurant and saw Sarah, who was waving at him from a table in a back corner.

"My friend is already seated over there."

"Very well. I will send your waiter over to assist you."

"Thank you," replied Omar, and he walked briskly toward Sarah's table.

As Omar approached, Sarah stood and opened her arms to greet him. She was every bit as attractive as he remembered. Her auburn hair was in a tight bun instead of flowing over her shoulders or in a ponytail like it had been in their school days. *This is the necessary business look*, he thought. Her five-foot-eight-inch frame was still shapely. After a long, warm hug, she stood back, smiling and observing him closely with her penetrating sky blue eyes.

"Omar, you look as handsome as ever."

"Thank you. And you look fabulous."

"Shush, Omar. Sit down and talk with me."

Sarah resumed her seat, with Omar to her immediate right, and fired off several questions. "Why are you in New York? How is your family? How are things at your new position at USOCO?" She paused and laughed. "I've just asked you several questions at once. I am so sorry. Please, catch me up. It truly is good to see you again."

Omar smiled. While their relationship had always been platonic, Omar could not have felt closer to her had she been his own sister. They had always confided openly with one another. Their meeting today would be no exception.

"I am here on some business for my family, and will have to return to Houston later today." Omar then carried her through the previous six months at USOCO, including his new friendship with Kurt. "He is bright, insightful, knows how to motivate people, and gets things done. Most importantly, I trust him completely. Besides you, he is the only person who knows my background."

"Wow," said Sarah. "You are fortunate to have someone in charge with that level of talent."

"I truly am. It certainly makes my job easier."

"Changing the subject, Omar, you mentioned on the phone that something is going on with you, USOCO, and your family. What is it?"

"Yes, things are happening quickly for me. I received a call from my father. He has asked me to return to Sharjah to take charge of running the family's business operations."

"And how do you feel about that?"

"I have very mixed feelings," responded Omar. "My family sent me here to prepare me for the time when I was to return. They believe that time is now. I am needed at home. The family interests have become too big and too complex for my father and younger brother to handle."

"You have been in the United States for, what, twelve years now? Four years at NC State, two years at Wharton, and six years at USOCO?"

"Yes, Sarah. One part of me does not want to leave. I will truly miss you and the good friends I have here."

"I understand," said Sarah. "This is what you must do. Your family is very fortunate to have a son like you. But do you really have to leave so quickly?"

"My family's business interests have expanded far beyond their original roots in oil production. Our oil production has created the revenue we needed in order to invest in other business opportunities. We have made huge investments in commercial construction and real estate development in the past few years and continue to do so. We are now the largest construction and real estate development company in Sharjah. These two areas alone accounted for over eighteen percent of our net income in 2007, up from about ten percent in 2002. Real estate values have increased at a dizzying three hundred percent in the past five years. There has been an enormous influx of foreigners to supply the demand for engineers, construction personnel, and laborers. This in turn has created a shortage of affordable housing. In my emirate, Sharjah, the annual inflation rate is now running at ten percent and could go higher. This, combined with sometimes harsh working conditions, is sparking labor unrest. Just last year we had a riot where fifteen hundred workers burned or destroyed cars, buses, and just about anything else they could get their hands on. On top of all that, our currency, the *dirham*, is pegged to the U.S. dollar. We have all watched the dollar's value plunge in the past couple of years. Our *dirham* has consequently fallen with it. Finally, and most significantly, as to why I must now return to Sharjah, we have a worldwide economic contraction looming. The supply of investor dollars that used to come to Sharjah from investors outside of our emirate is dwindling. We need those dollars to fund our industrial growth to diversify from our dwindling reserves of oil. My grandfather saw the pearl industry come to an end, and with it the source of his family's revenue. In a few years, we will see our oil revenues in Sharjah come to an end, and with it our current source of revenue." Omar paused for a moment, smiled, and asked, "So, Sarah, would you like to come to Sharjah for a real professional challenge?"

Sarah smiled in return. "Sounds intriguing, but I'm afraid I have my hands full here. But we must stay in touch."

"Absolutely," he said. "And I must tell you that the United Arab Emirates now has some fantastic new resorts. In fact, my family has one on the west coast of Sharjah in the planning stages. It is on a pristine stretch of the beach just north of Sharjah City. You will join us for the grand opening, right?"

"I'd be honored, and I'll hold you to that," she replied with a broad smile. It faded as she considered his invitation. "But as a businesswoman from the West, I could create quite a stir. I would not want to embarrass you by breaking any customs."

"Oh, on the contrary. The Koran teaches hospitality to strangers and kindness to travelers. You will find the citizens of the United Arab Emirates to be some of the friendliest people anywhere in the world. We have a gentle and exceptionally kind culture, one that will astonish you with its simple decency. There are a few basic rules. One is to remember to touch another only when a hand is extended to you first. And of course, there is no alcohol. It is considered rude even to ask an Arab to serve alcohol to you."

Sarah and Omar were so engrossed in their conversation that neither had noticed the waitress standing next to their table. She said politely, "I hate to interrupt such an interesting conversation."

Startled, Omar looked up to see the older woman standing at the table.

Smiling, she asked, "May I take your orders?"

Having been engrossed in their conversation, Sarah and Omar had forgotten they had yet to place their orders. They quickly glanced at the menus.

The waitress said, "Our specials today are veal parmesan and eggplant parmesan."

Sarah looked up and said, "I'll have the eggplant parmesan. It's always delicious here."

"It is. You have made a good choice." The waitress took her menu, turned to Omar and asked, "And for you, sir?"

Omar looked at the waitress and said, "I'll have the same," and handed his menu to her.

"Excellent," she responded, and headed for the kitchen.

They hadn't noticed before, but the restaurant was now bustling with the lunchtime crowd.

"Enough talk about me," said Omar. "Tell me about Uncle Jason. How is he? Is he still teaching? Does he get to your river cottage very often? What is the name you have for it?"

"Bella Vista. And yes, he gets there often. In fact, he and I had a wonderful time there over the Christmas and New Year's holidays. You should visit us there before you go."

"I would love to, Sarah, but I'm afraid I will not have the time before I leave, which brings me to ask. You mentioned on the phone that something was troubling you. What is it? Is that recurring dream still bugging you?"

Sarah paused a moment and shook her head. "No, I still have the dream, but that's not it. You know something of my company, Dutch Phosphate Corporation?"

"Yes. It is one of the world's largest producers of fertilizer. It also has a brilliant young woman named Sarah Carpenter as its chief operating officer."

Sarah smiled brightly. "Actually, we are *the* biggest producer of fertilizers in the world. Demand for our fertilizers has doubled in the past eight years, and we expect that to happen again in the next four."

"That's huge," said Omar. "Do you have the capacity to meet that demand?"

"Yes, we think so. Our revenues have been very strong over the past two years. In spite of those revenues, we've avoided paying large dividends. Instead, we've plowed much of our profits into expansion of our production capacity around the world."

"You obviously have huge demand for your products. Where is it coming from?"

"From multiple places. To start with, the worldwide population has doubled in the past fifty years. We now have six-point-five billion people on the planet who need food. Most of what we eat comes directly or indirectly from fertilized crops. We either eat the crops or we eat the animals that eat the crops. A recent UN report predicts that we will have nine billion people to feed by the year 2025."

"Yes," commented Omar. "And where are we going to find the farmland to feed us?"

"We can't. Our conservative estimate is that even today, without fertilizers to enhance crop growth, we would need fifty percent more farmland than we use now. As you and I know, cutting down more forests is not an option. Our forests are our best counter to the increasing problem of CO_2 emissions. Added to the demand for crops for food, we now have an explosion of biofuel plants. We already have a hundred up and running in the United States. We'll reach two hundred in the next two years. Those plants are currently consuming about thirty percent of our domestic corn crop. Even with our planned expansion, we can't come close to producing enough fertilizer to keep pace with demand."

Omar responded, "You have the problems most companies would love to have. So what concerns you?"

"Let's look at it this way. At what level of capacity are most oil wells operating today?"

"Well, we both know the answer to that, Sarah. Probably close to ninety percent. I think my family's wells are producing higher than that. Even if we wanted to produce more, we couldn't."

"Yes," said Sarah, "and what is happening to oil demand in the developing economies around the world?"

"We both know that answer as well. It's exploding, and there is no way all the oil wells in the world can keep pace."

"The price of oil is now at one hundred and ten dollars a barrel, and the projection is that we will see a hundred and fifty dollars per barrel within a year, assuming the world economies continue to expand as they have for the past five years." She paused. "Omar, what do you think is the biggest expense item for my company?"

"Probably to purchase those monster trucks and cranes I've read about," he said.

"That would probably be most people's guess, and they are expensive. Our biggest expense is the energy we purchase to run those monster trucks, cranes, and our fertilizer processing plants, plus we have the costs of transporting our products to virtually every corner of the world. Our energy costs have increased thirty percent a year for the past two years, while our net revenues increased ten percent for that same period. This is the main reason we've seen record sales yet lower profits. With the price of oil per barrel doubling in the past year alone, we find ourselves with a huge problem and no obvious options." Sarah paused for a moment.

Omar had been listening intently, nodding occasionally in agreement. "Sarah, there's another big unknown that you have not mentioned."

"What is that?"

"It is the political instability of the oil-producing countries themselves. Iran has a madman in charge of its military, religious sects, government, and oil industry. We have the power-hungry Mr. Chavez in control of the oil wealth of Venezuela. Both are openly hostile to the United States and the West in general. Nigeria, with its oil wealth, is in a constant state of turmoil. Then there is Russia, with its natural gas and huge oil reserves, which supplies many western European countries. It is returning to its dictatorial ways, and our relations with the Russians are deteriorating. Look at their recent invasion of Georgia, which has the pipelines of gas and oil that supply our NATO allies. Finally, there is Iraq. Even though the United States has poured close to a trillion dollars into the country, its political instability still threatens its ability to be a reliable source of oil production."

"It's not a pretty picture," observed Sarah, as the waitress appeared with their lunches.

Omar thanked the waitress and turned his attention back to Sarah. "So, where does the Dutch Phosphate Corporation go from here?"

"We're still trying to figure that out. I spent most of yesterday with a special committee that was set up at our last board meeting to explore our options."

"What are they?"

"There is simply only one: find an alternative to fossil fuels as a source of our energy supply."

"Good luck," he said cynically.

"I'm serious," said Sarah. "What choice do we have? You yourself know that even at full capacity, the oil-producing countries cannot keep pace. The world production of oil has peaked. We must find an alternative very soon."

Omar nodded, mindful of some of the USOCO projects recently mentioned to him by the Battses.

Sarah continued, "But when we get to the point where worldwide oil production cannot meet worldwide demand, the countries that have it will be in an enviable position. Oil-hungry countries will find themselves in bidding wars, or worse, for oil. The more ominous prospect is that countries with strong armies and no oil will forcefully take what they need from those who have it. Omar, my guess is that even if a major oil company like USOCO is fortunate enough to find an alternative energy source, it will have no financial incentive to share its findings with the rest of the world. At least not now, when there are still big profits to be made from a limited supply of oil and gas." Sarah saw Omar frown and wince slightly. "What is it, Omar?"

He sighed before responding. "I'm afraid that, from what I have seen firsthand for the past two months at USOCO, you may be right. But that's a discussion for another day, when I may have more proof of my suspicions. So, Sarah, how do you propose to develop an alternative source of energy at Dutch Phosphate Corporation? More importantly, how will you ever convince your board of directors to divert the enormous funds needed for such a project away from shareholder dividends to do it?"

"It is just as we have discussed. We simply have no choice. DPC has half a billion in cash right now. Also, we have an unusual board of directors. Many are from industries with large research and development budgets. They did not make their fortunes by sitting on their hands daydreaming. They know how to stay ahead of the curve. My intent is to keep our board members focused on the long-range outcomes rather than short-term profits, and I believe they will listen."

"Who will oversee such a project?"

"That is still unknown, but we're working on it. That is what my special committee spent most of last week doing. We interviewed a number of very capable people, but none of them overwhelmed us. We need someone who is not just very bright, but has vision and the ability to motivate and lead a team of equally bright people."

Omar stared across the room blankly and then looked Sarah directly in the eye. "I know just the man for this job."

Surprised, she asked, "You do? Who is he?"

"Kurt Benjamin."

"Hmm. From how you have described of him, he certainly sounds capable."

"Yes, and I suspect he could be lured away from USOCO for a project as exciting as this one. He has become disillusioned with the company. When Kurt starts looking around, he will have no problem finding a new opportunity. He expects a lot from his people, and they produce it. His team members have the utmost respect for him. I also sense something else is going on with him—and, for that matter, his whole team. It is as if they have a universal suspicion of USOCO because some of their more promising projects have been rejected by senior management. If he can't bring you results, no one can."

"Omar, I trust your judgment completely. How soon can you arrange for me to meet Mr. Benjamin?"

Omar replied, "Tell me when, and I'll call him right now."

"It needs to be soon. Our committee is under the gun. The board of directors is meeting in two weeks to vote this proposition up or down. I have every expectation that it will pass. When it does, I want this person on the ground running."

"Very well, then," said Omar. He flipped open his cell phone and dialed Kurt's cell number.

"Hello, Kurt. It's Omar. I am sitting here having lunch with someone you need to meet. She has a project that may interest you."

Although somewhat taken aback, Kurt chuckled and replied, "Well, sure, but what is it?"

"Why don't I let her tell you directly? Her name is Sarah Carpenter, and she is the chief operating officer of the Dutch Phosphate Corporation. Here she is."

Omar handed the phone to Sarah. After she gave Kurt a very general overview of the project, he had a few questions. Satisfied with her answers, he was intrigued. They agreed to meet in Houston the following Monday, March 24, and ended the call.

Returning the phone, Sarah said, "Thanks, Omar. He may well be our man."

"I don't think you will be disappointed."

After finishing their lunch, Omar and Sarah stepped out onto the noisy streets of Manhattan. After they exchanged a warm embrace, Omar hailed a cab for the trip to Kennedy Airport and Sarah strolled briskly back up Pine Street to her office.

MARCH 24, 2008 — HOUSTON, TEXAS

Kurt stepped out of the lobby of the USOCO building and walked across the parking lot to his Range Rover. It was a typical early spring day for Houston, with clear blue skies and the temperature already at sixty degrees. Moments later, Kurt was on Buffalo Speedway heading toward the River Oaks Grill for his eleven-thirty lunch appointment with Sarah Carpenter. Although both Kurt and Sarah had invited Omar to this luncheon, he had diplomatically declined. His excuse was simply that he had made the introduction, and the rest was up to them.

Kurt arrived early to secure a table that would offer some privacy. He found a suitable table in the corner by a window. He was sipping his unsweetened iced tea with lemon and enjoying the aromas drifting from the kitchen when he spotted the familiar short, plump figure of Tommy, a waiter, waddling toward him wearing his usual dark gray slacks and white jacket. Right behind him was a tall, slender, auburn-haired woman dressed in a dark blue St. John knit suit.

"Your guest, Mr. Benjamin," said Tommy.

Kurt rose and extended his hand. Sarah returned a brisk, firm handshake and spoke first.

"It's good to finally meet you, Mr. Benjamin. I've heard Omar say many nice things about you."

"Please, call me Kurt, and you can't believe everything Omar tells you."

Sarah shot back with a smile, "Oh, yes, I can. I have found Omar to be a very good judge of people."

Kurt smiled with a hint of embarrassment, thinking, *Omar didn't tell me I was having lunch with a model from* Vogue *magazine.* Regaining his composure, he responded, "And Omar speaks highly of you. I share your confidence in his judgment of people."

Tommy returned discreetly a few moments later with their menus, took Sarah's request for hot tea, and walked away.

"Omar told me about a recent sail he took on your boat in the Galveston Bay. What is your boat?"

"It's a Hylas 49."

"Those are beautiful boats, and by reputation very sea kindly, but I've never sailed one."

"So you are a sailor?"

"Oh, yes. I've been sailing as long as I can remember. My family has a place on the Pamlico River in eastern North Carolina. I started with a Sunfish. When I was a teenager, my uncle bought a Hobie 16. Since then, I have sailed a variety of boats."

After continuing their chitchat for a few more moments, Sarah directed the discussion to what was foremost on her mind. "Omar provided me with a copy of your résumé. You have a variety of very diverse interests and accomplishments. But none would seem to qualify you to manage a research project such as where you are now. Does working in such an environment feel stifling to you?"

Kurt's foot tapped the floor under the table. He thought, *She's not just drop-dead gorgeous. She also has the insightful ability to question like a trial lawyer.*

"Perhaps sometimes," he replied vaguely, "but they are an interesting group of very bright people." He immediately thought of his friends Jennifer and George Batts. He would certainly miss working with those two. Perhaps more importantly, he would miss their Thursday night dinners.

"Kurt, I only talked with you generally on the phone about what my company is about to do. It is my understanding that you have had some conversations with Omar about this project."

"Yes. I understand it in very general terms, and I have done a little research of your company's financials."

"Then you have seen the dramatic increase in our energy costs?" asked Sarah.

"Yes, and I'm surprised that some of the outside financial analysts have not noticed it as well."

"We have been fortunate to stay under their radar so far."

Kurt asked, "What else do I need to know?"

At this point, Tommy appeared to take their orders. Sarah studied the menu for a moment, handed it to the waiter, and asked him to bring her the shrimp linguine, served in a light cream sauce with broccolini and red potatoes on the side. He nodded and took the menu.

Turning to Kurt, Tommy said, "And you, sir, I suspect are going to have your usual, the red trout special."

"Yes," smiled Kurt. "You have a good memory." The waiter nodded as he scribbled the orders on his notepad, and then left them to their conversation.

Sarah spent the next fifteen minutes explaining the project, the financial necessity for it, the need to move expeditiously, and, finally and most importantly, the need for secrecy. Kurt asked a few questions, but mostly listened.

"There you have it, Kurt. We need an economically viable alternative to fossil fuels as my company's energy source within twelve months. Can you do it?"

Kurt moved his eyes from hers and stared across the room. The contents of the Enhanced Maize Project file he had broken into blazed through his mind, followed by images of some of the projects that Jennifer and George wanted to pursue. He brought his gaze back directly to Sarah for a few seconds before speaking. She shifted slightly in her seat as Kurt's penetrating blue eyes met hers.

"The magnitude of this project is beyond anything that your company, and probably any other company, has ever, and I do mean *ever*, undertaken. We're talking about the cost of resources in today's dollars that will go far beyond anything Nicola Tesla could have imagined when Morgan bankrolled his projects in the early 1900s. The cost of this will be enormous. I have no doubt that it will far exceed the fifty million you have budgeted." Kurt could see by Sarah's expression of disappointment that this was not what she wanted to hear.

"It would be a stretch to get that much committed from our board," she said. "We simply can't abandon our dividends and jeopardize our stock price. Otherwise, stockholders will take their money elsewhere."

As they were finishing their lunch, Kurt put down his fork and leaned forward. "Sarah, this is a very exciting project, and I will do it. But it appears that we need another source of capital. Could you find another company to participate with DPC as a joint venture?"

"I don't know, Kurt. I'll have to talk with our CEO, Jim Clark. Offhand, I wouldn't know where to start looking for such a partner."

Although Kurt attempted to pick up the tab for lunch, Sarah quickly snatched it from him. She did, however, accept his offer to drive her back to the airport. On the way, they returned to their earlier discussion of sailing. After dropping Sarah off for her return flight to New York, Kurt drove toward the USOCO building. The thought of getting out of the stifling USOCO environment and into such an exciting project had rejuvenated him. His mind was already racing with ideas for alternative energy being explored by his team of scientists, and he began thinking of which members of his team he wanted to take with him.

CHAPTER

7

The boardroom of the Dutch Phosphate Corporation was in full chatter when Jim Clark, CEO brought silence with three sharp raps of his gavel.

"Good morning, everyone," he announced in a booming baritone voice. "Thank you for coming. We have a full agenda, so let's get started. Mr. Secretary, would you read the minutes of our last meeting?"

"Yes, Mr. President." Julian Allan, with his proper British accent, proceeded to read the minutes. He had been with the company for over thirty years, and no one could imagine a board meeting without his stately presence, even at the age of seventy. With his thick, flowing silver hair and mustache, he was a double for Oliver Wendell Holmes.

After reading for about ten minutes, he paused, cleared his throat, and continued. "Finally, there was a discussion of the increasing cost of energy consumption by our plants worldwide. Ms. Carpenter presented the members with data on energy cost increases at our eleven mining and processing operations around the world. During the last two years, the increase has been at the pace of thirty percent while our net revenues have increased at ten percent. The board, after a lengthy discussion, approved a motion to authorize the president to appoint a committee including three board members, as well as Ms. Carpenter and Mr. Clark, to review options and bring us a specific proposal at the next meeting."

Julian removed his reading glasses and finished by saying, "And the meeting was adjourned at five twenty p.m."

"Thank you, Mr. Secretary," said Jim. Looking down the table, he asked, "Are there any corrections or additions to the minutes as read?"

The board members sat solemnly and said nothing.

"Very well," he continued, "they stand approved as read. Is there any other old business?"

The room remained quiet.

"There being none, we have several items of new business."

Jim then led a discussion of a variety of employee benefit and new capital expenditure issues. Once these were out of the way, he paused and looked around the room.

Sarah had been watching the board members closely, trying to discern who might be an obstacle to the proposal she and Kurt, who was not yet at the meeting, were to present. She thought the mundane business would never be over, and her mind was racing with thoughts of the resistance of the board and how to deal with it. She knew that she would have to convince them of the urgency of the need to dramatically reduce the company's huge energy costs. She firmly believed that if Dutch Phosphate succeeded, the company would achieve enormous energy cost savings and become a clear example of energy independence from fossil fuels. Their stock price would rise, and everyone involved would be handsomely rewarded. On the other hand, if the project failed, the company would face significant losses and a large drop in its stock value. Everyone involved in the decision, including the present board members would lose their jobs.

A half hour later, Sarah's stomach turned as she heard Jim Clark bringing the meeting's prior business to conclusion.

"We now come to the last and, I believe, the most important topic of this meeting, and perhaps any meeting this board may ever have," announced the CEO. "As we discussed at our last meeting, our energy costs have grown exponentially in the past two years. You as a board directed me to form a committee to study this problem and bring a proposal to you at this meeting. A committee has conducted extensive research on this issue. We also consulted with some of the leading experts on alternative energy sources. Many days and many late nights were spent reviewing our options. We are prepared today to report our findings and make a specific proposal. But first, let me begin by saying it is not a future problem, as we believed it to be at our last meeting. The problem is now. It is much more serious than we had feared. Today's meeting will be a defining moment for our company." Jim turned to Sarah. "Would you like to invite Mr. Benjamin to join us?"

While the board was sequestered in the DPC boardroom conducting its meeting, Kurt had arrived at the waiting room just across the hall. After settling into a chair next to the door, he had begun reviewing his notes for the presentation one last time. Although he had made many complex presentations during his career, he felt uneasy about this one. The information he was getting ready to deliver to the board would be shocking and would likely result in considerable dissent. He knew the cost of the project would be enormous, and its success was far from guaranteed. Still, he believed in the project and hoped this board would have the fortitude and foresight to take the required risks.

Suddenly, Sarah opened the door and stuck her head inside. "They're ready for us," she said in almost a whisper.

Kurt swallowed hard, nodded, and followed Sarah as she walked briskly across the hall into the boardroom. As he entered the room, Kurt saw five men and two women sitting at the long conference table. The only person he recognized was CEO Jim Clark, whom he had met a few days earlier.

Sarah directed Kurt to one of two empty seats adjacent to a lectern and a screen for their PowerPoint presentation. As he sat down, she walked to the podium to address the board.

"Before we start our discussion," she said with summoned confidence, "I would like to introduce a special guest we have with us today, Kurt Benjamin. Kurt is currently the director of Alternative Energy Operations at the United States Oil Company. Before that, he was involved in the search for and exploration of potential oil fields for USOCO all over the world. He also spent several years as a special attaché for the State Department, assigned to several projects in the Middle East oil regions. Finally, his academic credentials include a bachelor's from the University of Florida, with a double major in chemistry and geology, and a master's in geology from the University of Virginia. Kurt has been consulting with our committee extensively in recent days, and has agreed to lead the project that we are about to discuss, should the board decide to go forward with it."

As Sarah stepped to the computer and pulled up the PowerPoint presentation, Kurt studied the individuals before him. Most of them appeared solemn yet interested. One man with heavy brows sat back in his chair with his arms crossed. His scowl told Kurt to watch out for dissent from this guy. He would be the man to win over.

Turning her attention back to the board members, Sarah began by asking, "Has anyone heard of a man named Dr. Marion K. Hubbert?" The room was silent and a few of those present shook their heads. "Very few people have, much to the relief of OPEC and the world's large oil companies. Dr. Hubbert was a senior geoscientist with Shell Oil Company. In 1956, much to the dismay of his employer, he presented a paper at a meeting of the American Petroleum Institute. In this paper, he predicted that production of petroleum would peak in the United States in the early 1970s. At the time, he was dismissed as a quack. When 1970 came and the U.S. enjoyed the largest oil production year in history, oil industry experts recalled Hubbert's predictions and laughed about what a fool he was. However, just a few years later, oil production in the United States did begin to decline, and has continued to do so ever since. By the late 1990s, Hubbert's critics had become believers and the predictions he made in his 1956 paper are widely accepted by today's oil energy experts. In fact, his findings are often referred to as Peak Oil or Hubbert's Peak. From his research, he concluded that there were two peaks. One was the peak of discovery of oil reserves. The other was the peak of production of oil from these reserves. The latter obviously follows the former. As of 1970, the United States had been the world's largest producer of oil for over one hundred years. At that time, the United States produced twelve million barrels per day from domestic wells. Does anyone here want to venture a guess as to how much oil the United States produces today?"

Seeing only blank looks on the faces of the board members, she continued. "We now produce barely six million barrels per day despite new drilling. And that is not the most troubling of his predictions. It was also Hubbert's belief that the worldwide production of oil would peak around 1995. Fortunately, he was not right about that one. You are probably thinking, 'Then what's the problem?'" Turning to Kurt, she said, "At this point, I will turn the discussion over to Kurt. He is far more qualified to answer that question than I."

Kurt nodded and stepped to the lectern. Feeling he had the rapt attention of the room, he began slowly. "To answer Sarah's question, all we need to do is read this book." He held up a copy of a book in his left hand. "This is *Twilight in the Desert: The Coming Saudi Oil Shock and the World Economy*, which was published in 2005. It was written by an unlikely author named Matt Simmons. Simmons is a lifelong Republican and spent most of his working life in and around the oil industry as an investment banker. He has lived in Houston, the mecca for American oil companies, for the past several decades. According to Simmons, world oil production now stands at eighty-six million barrels per day. The United States consumes fully one-quarter of it. The Saudis are the largest exporter of oil, at twelve million barrels per day, but according to Simmons's extensive research, they are maxed out by even the most generous calculations. The Saudis have no more reserves to discover. He also reports that oil production from Prudhoe Bay and the North Sea is already in decline. Based upon extensive research, Simmons concludes that we are actually now at Hubbert's Peak of worldwide production, and that world production will decline in the years ahead at a rate of between four percent and five percent annually. What makes this really scary is that both the U.S. government's Energy Information Association and the International Energy Agency based in Paris predict that worldwide demand for oil will reach one hundred and fifteen million barrels a day by 2030."

After pausing for a moment to study his stone-faced audience, he continued, "These estimates are based in part on projections that developing third-world economies are coming forward demanding their share of this precious resource. In 1970, the African continent had little demand for it, and nor did most of South America. Even in the Middle East, where oil was being produced, there was little demand. But in China today, a recent poll showed that twenty percent of its population plans to own a car within the next five years, a significant increase from just five years ago. Adding China's increasing demand alone will strain the limits of oil now being produced. And we haven't mentioned the rapidly expanding economy in India. What happens when demand starts outpacing supply? What consequences will it have on the U.S., where we have grown accustomed to a limitless supply of oil? Will oil hogs such as airplanes be grounded because airports run out of jet fuel? Will countries such as China be willing to unleash their expanding military might to fight for this diminishing resource?"

Kurt studied his audience closely, trying to discern if what he and Sarah had presented thus far had registered with the board. Seeing only glum faces, he pulled his final graph up on the screen.

"As you can see, we have a bell curve that begins its upward slope gradually in 1870, when consumption of oil began, and peaks in the year 2008. From there, the line begins its descent, slowly at first, but then at an escalating pace until the year 2050, when worldwide production settles to 1950 levels. The rate of descent continues thereafter until it settles to early 1900s levels around the year 2080."

Kurt let the graph sit for a few seconds for its impact to sink in. Then he continued in an ominous tone, "This chart shows what some well-respected scientists believe will eventually be referred to as the age of the 'hydrocarbon man.' Enjoy it while it lasts."

The board members sat in shocked silence. Sarah, who had been standing to the side and studying the board members during Kurt's presentation, joined him at the podium. After a half dozen graphs showing past and projected revenue and expenses for Dutch Phosphate Corporation's worldwide operations, she came to her final graph. It showed the relationship of energy costs to net revenues in three years.

"Members of the board," Sarah continued, "as this graph illustrates, the company's cost of energy consumption is projected to surge ahead at a rate of thirty percent per year. Unfortunately, our net revenues are expected to increase by ten percent per year at best."

Even though Sarah knew this board was stacked with bright, insightful leaders from a variety of backgrounds, she could tell from their expressions of shock that they were not prepared for what was being presented. The silence was finally interrupted by Nathan Daniel, seated near the end of the giant conference table.

"Where is Thomas Edison when we need him?"

Nathan, a brilliant and very successful stock analyst from Morgan Stanley, single and by reputation a serious party boy, was the youngest member of the board. He could always be counted on for a quip to lighten the air of a stuffy boardroom. However, this time there were no smiles or chuckles.

Kurt responded, "You're not far from one of the areas of alternative energy that should be explored. However, Edison is not exactly who we need. Instead, it is actually one of his contemporaries and his nemesis, Nicola Tesla. While Edison opened the door for Tesla's career in America and became his mentor, the two came to differences and parted ways over Tesla's work with alternating current. Edison's fortune was based upon direct current, which was the world's primary source of electricity at the time. Edison may have had an inquisitive mind, but he could not, or would not, accept Tesla's competing alternating current. Edison simply felt threatened financially by Tesla's new technology.

"Tesla's belief in a radical new concept called alternating current changed our world a hundred years ago. As we all know, alternating current is what now powers our toasters and microwaves, and heats our homes. It is also the energy that powers Dutch Phosphate Corporation's giant cranes and processing plants all over the world. That discovery was over a hundred years ago. Tesla was awarded hundreds of patents and is credited with many inventions, such as X-rays, the radio, fluorescent lights, air-conditioning, remote control, robotics, beam weapons, and an electric car. It is said that he had many more he never took the time to patent or record. At his famous Wardenclyffe Tower on Long Island, Tesla was close to other discoveries about energy sources from what he called 'the vacuum,' or zero-point energy, when his financial support suddenly ended. J. P. Morgan, the oil magnate and his financial benefactor, came to realize that what Tesla was working on would end demand for oil, the commodity that drove Morgan's financial empire. Seeing no way to make a profit on Tesla's free energy from 'the vacuum,' Morgan not only abandoned the inventor but also blackballed him. That resulted in Tesla, arguably the greatest inventor ever known, being written out of the history books.

"Tesla was so far ahead of his time that his ideas seemed like science fiction to the people of his day. Strangely, when he died penniless on January 7, 1943, J. Edgar Hoover, the director of the FBI, was one of the first people notified of his death. And a curious thing then happened to this now discredited inventor. The FBI went to his New York hotel apartment and removed all his papers. What was the FBI trying to find? Or hide? Many of his papers have since disappeared. Years later, the FBI finally released some of Tesla's papers to his heirs. What happened to the ones the FBI failed to return? But I digress," Kurt said apologetically. "Are there any questions?"

A long period of silence was finally interrupted by a question from Jim Clark. "So what are our best short-term options for an alternative to oil?"

"There are a number of options," Kurt replied. "As we all know, there are efforts already under way to develop biofuels from things such as corn, sugarcane, and sawgrass. I have some very bright scientists at the USOCO Laboratory for Alternative Energy Research who are involved in some very promising research in those areas. We should leave out nothing at this point."

Kurt paused and nodded to Sarah, and she stepped forward to join him at the podium. Smiling comfortably at the audience, she picked up the presentation. "So you look at us and ask, 'Why have we been talking about what took place a hundred years ago with people like Tesla?' The answer is that we believe a clear parallel can be drawn to the competing interests of OPEC and the major oil companies with emerging alternative sources of energy being developed today. The only difference is that the stakes are much higher for the oil industry and OPEC than they were for J. P. Morgan or Thomas Edison a hundred years ago. If a viable alternative to oil is discovered, it could mean the loss of billions of dollars in revenue to all oil-producing countries and the major oil companies in our own. While Edison did cruel things to discredit his competitor, such as public displays of animals being electrocuted by what he claimed was Tesla's alternating current, we should expect far worse from those who need to protect their oil wealth today. The stakes are simply too high for them not to resort to virtually anything to prevent their precious oil from being replaced as the world's primary energy source."

After Kurt answered several more questions from board members, Jim Clark thanked him for his comments, and Sarah escorted him into the hall.

"Well done, Kurt," Sarah said with a wink and a smile. "Can you meet me back at my office around three o'clock?"

"Sure, I'll see you then."

Returning to a hushed boardroom, Sarah resumed her place at the podium. "So, what incentive do the major oil companies, and oil producing countries, have to find an alternative?" she asked. "They have a vested interest in protecting their investments and keeping prices and profits as high as possible. We are in this energy mess today thanks to people who continue to hold on to their vested interests, just as J. P. Morgan did a hundred years ago. The difference now, however, is that there are sources of revenue, such as the Dutch Phosphate Corporation, that are able to fund the research needed to discover the alternative sources of energy which Tesla, and others like him, believed are there to be found."

At this point, the CEO looked around at the board members and sensed it was time to bring the matter to a head. "Is there a motion concerning this project?"

John Taylor, the former president of MIT, quickly stood. "I move we accept the proposed alternative energy project as presented."

Sarah knew John Taylor was the perfect person to be on the study committee and to make the motion. As the former president of a university highly respected for its cutting-edge research, he had served on a number of special energy projects for the White House during both Democratic and Republican administrations.

"Is there any discussion?" asked Clark.

With the words barely out of Clark's mouth, Joe Edwards, whose career had been spent in banking, stood to speak. His frown and bushy eyebrows gave away his obvious disdain for the proposal.

"Our shareholders expect to see dividends remain at two dollars per share. Otherwise, they will vote all of us out at their very next meeting. How can we possibly spend a hundred million dollars a year for the next two years and still pay that dividend? I'll support no more than twenty-five million on this long-shot idea."

Clark turned to the chief financial officer, Paul Fetzer, who was also a member of the committee. "Can you address that question, Mr. Fetzer?"

With his own PowerPoint presentation, Fetzer proceeded through a series of graphs to illustrate their projected revenues and expenses for the next three years. His presentation was slow and deliberate. He concluded his analysis by saying, "The bottom line is that our current three dollars per share dividend will not be sustainable. With our projected future energy costs, we will be paying only fifty cents per share in dividend in three years. Something dramatic has to happen to reduce our energy costs."

The message was clear: unless there was a dramatic reduction in the ratio of energy costs to revenues in the next three years, their dividend would be of no interest to stock investors.

Sarah suffered through two more hours of debate before the board finally voted by a narrow four-to-three majority to approve a compromise expenditure of fifty million dollars. The board members who approved the project shook their heads in stunned resignation as they voted; to their minds, the amount was staggering.

After the vote, Sarah returned to her office with a sense of uncertainty as to what she had orchestrated the board to do. Stepping over to her desk, she dialed Kurt's cell phone number.

"Hello, Sarah. I'm dying to know how it went."

With a deep sigh, Sarah replied, "They approved only fifty million, and that was close."

"Judging the response of your board members during our presentation, that is probably the best we could have expected."

"Maybe," Sarah replied, with a sense of both relief and apprehension. "But I have a feeling the most difficult challenges lie ahead."

"Are we still on for three o'clock this afternoon?" asked Kurt.

"Yes, we'll see you then."

As Kurt hung up the phone, he wondered who Sarah meant by "we."

CHAPTER

8

APRIL 16, 2008 — DUTCH PHOSPHATE CORPORATION HEADQUARTERS, NEW YORK CITY

As Omar stepped off the elevator into the luxurious lobby of the Dutch Phosphate Corporation headquarters, he wondered why Sarah had urgently requested to see him. It occurred to him that she would have met with Kurt by now. Also, her board of directors was to meet this morning. *Is any of this tied together?* he wondered.

Moments later, Sarah strolled confidently into the lobby and warmly embraced her friend. "Good afternoon, Omar. Thank you for coming on such short notice. I hope this wasn't an inconvenience."

"Not at all, Sarah, I had some things to take care of here for my family before I leave. Your timing was excellent. I would have come anyway, of course, since you are like family to me."

"Let's talk in my office."

Omar followed Sarah into her corner office, a spacious, glass-walled room overlooking the Manhattan skyline from its tenth-floor vantage point. Omar was not surprised to see pictures of Sarah as a young teenager with her Uncle Jason digging for fossils at various dig sites. There were also pictures of the two of them sailing the family Hobie Cat on the Pamlico River. Sarah directed Omar to join her at a round table in the corner overlooking Pine Street.

"So, how is Uncle Jason?" asked Omar, as he picked up a picture of Sarah and Jason standing on the pier in front of their Pamlico River home, Bella Vista. "How does he spend his time now that he's retired?"

Sarah laughed, remembering the river cottage when she last visited.

"The last time I saw him, there were books, articles, and papers spread out all over the cottage—research for his new book."

"Oh, and what is he writing about?"

"Life in eastern North Carolina in the eighteenth century."

"Hmm, wasn't there a pirate named Blackbeard who operated out of that area?"

"Yes, there was. In fact, his home base was in Bath, not far from our cottage on the Pamlico River. But Blackbeard's days ended in the early part of the eighteenth century, when he was beheaded during a battle with a ship deployed out of the Virginia colony by its Governor Spotswood. Jason's book talks about how Blackbeard was in cahoots with North Carolina's Governor Eden and the council secretary of the colony, Tobias Knight. It seems Virginia's governor found out about the connection between Knight, Eden, and Blackbeard, and took it upon himself to get rid of him."

"That sounds interesting. What brought Jason to write about this?"

Sarah laughed. "This may sound a bit strange, but Jason has the diary, or what still remains of it, of Tobias Knight. I'm actually a descendant of Mr. Knight. When Jason started researching to try to figure out what was in the missing pages of Knight's diary, he was in the midst of eighteenth-century life in eastern North Carolina. At that point he said, 'What the heck? I can turn this into a book.' But enough about Uncle Jason. I'll bet your family is really excited about your homecoming."

"My father is anxious for my return," he said tentatively. "But I sense my brother, Naji, may be a bit concerned that I will usurp some of his current power. I guess that is to be expected, given how long I've been away." Omar paused and studied Sarah closely. "You didn't ask me to meet you at your office today to talk about our families. What is on your mind?"

"You know me too well. Omar, I have a very serious matter to discuss with you. Please hear me out, because I have a specific proposal to make to you and your family."

He gazed at her curiously, wondering what was coming next.

"Omar, I've done some research on your family's company, Sharjah Oil. Back in 1982, it claimed oil reserves of half what it does today. Since then, no additional oil fields have been discovered in Sharjah. Of course, during the 1980s, OPEC started basing the permitted output of its members on their oil reserves. Then, miraculously, the reserves of the OPEC member countries started going up dramatically. My research shows that Sharjah Oil claimed to have eight hundred million barrels of oil reserves in 1982. Even though no new oil fields have been discovered there since then, it now claims to have reserves of sixteen hundred million barrels. Sharjah Oil's Annual Report for fiscal year 2007 states that it is producing about twenty-two million barrels per day. At that rate, and based on 1982 reserves, your family's company will run out of oil in 2018. This is 2008. What happens in 2018?"

Omar, wondering where she was going with this, nodded and said, "Please continue."

"I've also studied the investments made by Sharjah Oil to improve health care, education, and infrastructure. With its oil wealth, your family has transformed Sharjah from a nomadic wasteland with mostly poverty-stricken and uneducated citizens to a country with schools, hospitals, and infrastructure that are the envy of any developing country on this planet. You have excellent free health care and schools available to all of your people. You also have experienced dramatic growth in industrial and technological innovation. But my question remains: what happens in 2018? Will you have diversified enough by then to sustain this modern miracle?"

Omar studied his friend and let out a deep sigh. "As always, you have done your research. Those are my concerns as well. Sharjah must make the most of the oil revenue we now have. We must invest wisely and diversify widely. That being a given, why are we discussing this?"

"What if Sharjah could be a part of a project that could develop an alternative source of energy?" asked Sarah. "What if this project could replace Sharjah Oil's lost oil revenue by the time it ends in 2018?"

Omar felt Sarah's penetrating blue eyes studying him closely. Responding stiffly, he replied, "We are fortunate that Abu Dhabi, our sister emirate to the south, has oil and gas reserves that could sustain the United Arab Emirates for another hundred years."

"Yes," Sarah retorted, "so they may claim. But at what price?"

There was an uncomfortable pause in their conversation.

"They are a part of our country," Omar responded. "We are both brothers of the United Arab Emirates."

"Yes, Omar, but as we both know, it is a loosely connected federation of autonomous emirates. Each emirate, and especially Abu Dhabi, has an emir who controls his own underground wealth. It has ninety-four percent of the proven oil reserves of the United Arab Emirates. Sharjah has one-point-five percent. Sharjah may not be much better off than the rest of the oil-dependent countries by 2018. So, how generous do you expect the emir of Abu Dhabi to be when there are huge demands for his underground treasure from all around this oil-thirsty world? Will he share his oil with his other loosely connected confederate states, or will it go to the highest bidder?"

Omar sat silent for several moments contemplating Sarah's pointed questions.

Sarah continued, "What will become of all the dramatic gains Sharjah has achieved because of your family's generosity? Will your family just walk away with your wealth, or will you continue to support and create opportunity for the people of Sharjah? Do you want to control your own destiny and find an alternative to being at Abu Dhabi's mercy?"

"So, where are you going with this, Sarah?"

"You have spent the last few months surrounded by people like Kurt, who believe passionately that all of us on this planet must find an alternative source of energy. We must find a way to wean ourselves from our worldwide addiction to oil. Kurt thinks his lab personnel may have stumbled upon some very feasible alternatives to fossil fuel energy." Sarah paused briefly to choose her next words carefully. "Kurt seems concerned that USOCO has been less than sincere about its proclaimed goal of finding alternative energy sources. While he did not come right out and say it, he seems to suspect that USOCO has been less than transparent about what it has learned about sources of alternative energy. Kurt wants to take the brightest scientists on his USOCO team with him to Dutch Phosphate Corporation's energy project. I think he is concerned that if he doesn't, the progress his team has made will disappear forever."

"Sarah, I still don't understand where you are going with this. My family's companies have made huge strides in developing new industries besides oil. We now have production facilities for food, furniture, jewelry, plastics, and building materials. Our share alone of total non-oil industrial production of the United Arab Emirates is forty-five percent and climbing."

Sarah listened patiently and nodded. "But again, what will your revenues be in 2018? Sharjah will be out of oil. Some projections from people like Matt Simmons have oil prices at five hundred dollars per barrel by then. Will you manufacture enough plastics, building materials, and jewelry to produce enough revenue to purchase your oil needs at that price? If not, that will likely lead to work cutbacks, unemployment, and hungry, angry citizens demonstrating and rioting to have their basic needs met. Fuses will be short now that they've tasted the good life."

After another long pause, Sarah decided to make her proposal. "Omar, I'm very serious about this. I have an idea that I want you to take home and offer to your family and your country. The Dutch Phosphate Corporation authorized me to secure a compatible partner in our alternative energy project. We need a partner that we can trust to share our vision. I believe you and your family should be that partner." Sarah watched Omar's reaction closely.

He sat back in his chair and looked at her inquisitively. "So, Sarah, how would you propose that we go about this joint venture?"

"I have the utmost confidence in your friend Kurt Benjamin. With the proper resources and support, I believe he can make things happen. Although he is certainly not the eccentric genius Nicola Tesla was, he knows how to motivate and direct people who are. He also seems confident that his team at USOCO would leave with him for such an exciting opportunity."

After a long pause, Omar asked, "So, has Kurt made any specific proposals to you about how he would undertake this project and the direction it would take?"

"It's interesting that you should ask. He's in the lobby waiting to talk with us. I asked him to join us at three o'clock. What time is it?"

After glancing at his watch, Omar chuckled and shook his head. "It's five after three. Let's bring him in."

Picking up her desk phone, Sarah asked her administrative assistant to bring Kurt to her office. Moments later, Kurt strode into the room. Seeing the surprised look on his face, Sarah quickly apologized.

"I should have given you a heads-up that Omar would be here. But things were falling into place quickly. I thought the three of us should talk."

After Kurt and Omar exchange brief pleasantries, Sarah directed them back to the round table in her office.

"Kurt, I think we've found the perfect partner for our project," she pronounced confidently. "But we need to convince him that he should come on board."

"And who is it?"

"Look across the table from you."

Kurt looked inquisitively at Omar, who looked back with an affable smile.

"Well, I'll be damned," said Kurt. After a short pause, he smiled. "And I thought I was getting away from working for this guy."

The three shared a good laugh before Omar sat back and looked directly at Kurt. "I do not know if my family will agree to join this project. But assuming they will, how do you see this thing unfolding?"

Kurt stood, walked to the windows, and contemplated the New York streets below. "How much energy does it take to run this city on any given day? How much oil or gas is being burned to do it? And what amount of CO_2 is being released to eat away at our ozone layer? At what point is the ozone protection so depleted that we melt the North and South Poles and flood the streets of New York City? 'Never,' say some scientists. 'In five hundred years,' say others. Some say much sooner than that. Who really knows?"

Kurt paused for a moment, looking at the cars, buses, and trucks. "Did you know that Henry Ford's first car ran on ethanol? Soon after, he and the other auto manufacturers discovered a thing called rock oil that, after being slightly refined, held more bang for the buck than ethanol. It wasn't until 2000, almost a century later, that fuel ethanol regained any serious interest. Of course, it's now only at the level of a ten-percent additive, at most. Most of the ethanol in the United States is brewed from yellow feed corn, which requires an enormous amount of oil to produce.

"And we have Brazil. Its cane alcohol production is a huge success story. Sugarcane yields six hundred to eight hundred gallons of ethanol per acre, which is twice what corn can produce. The waste cane is burned to power the distillery that refines the ethanol, which has the benefit of lowering fossil fuel use. Brazil is now virtually an energy-independent country."

With his hands behind his back, Kurt turned to face Omar and Sarah, who had been listening intently.

Sarah nodded and said, "I agree, Kurt, but let's talk about the specific direction of our funds. A lot of money is going to be invested in this project. Where will it go?"

"To answer your question, I think our focus should be on a number of areas. Let's start with biofuel because we can use it in current combustion engines. We should experiment with sugarcane-type plants that have the short-term potential to produce significant quantities of biofuel. I don't think we should totally ignore what we might be able to accomplish with genetically altered corn products grown in very controlled environments. And there is also cellulosic ethanol. This involves using perennial prairie grasses such as switchgrass grown on land that is typically unfit for crops. Research in our lab has suggested that this has potential as well.

"The most intriguing source of ethanol is algae. Jennifer Batts believes it's possible that algae, grown in the right conditions, could perhaps double in mass within hours. Corn can produce around three hundred gallons of ethanol per acre a year, and soybeans around sixty gallons of biodiesel per acre a year. But some of Jennifer's studies suggest that algae could turn out more than five thousand gallons of biofuel per acre. This may be where we hit our home run. But, I must tell both of you that I can make no promises at this point, and we should close no doors.

"Another alternative is the wind. American multibillionaire tycoon T. Boone Pickens is attracting a lot of attention with his sixteen-billion-dollar investment in land from Canada down to Texas for installation of a system of wind generators. The Chinese are heavily involved with wind energy as well. There are many windy places on our planet where turbines could produce electricity. And, of course, there is solar energy. We will certainly work toward solar panel perfection. Last, but not least, is hydrogen. Omar, you know about the project Stan Moore in our lab is working on."

"Only very generally. What is it?" responded Omar.

"It's an intriguing continuation of work done with H_2O by a number of scientists and inventors over the years. You may have read about the water car that literally runs on water. Electrical current from the generator releases electrons that produce electric power to run the car."

As Kurt sat down at the table, Omar asked, "How about the work that George Batts was doing? He seemed very excited about it when we last talked with him."

Kurt nodded. "We should not leave George out of this. Although perhaps our brightest scientist, he is rather secretive about his work. As best I can understand it, he is focusing on the work of Nicola Tesla. As Tesla's theory goes, there is an unlimited supply of energy available to us from what he called 'the vacuum.' Modern scientists are calling it 'the zero-point field.' The problem is that we haven't figured out how to tap into it."

The three of them had been in Sarah's office for over four hours. Glancing at her watch, Sarah said, "Hey, guys. It's now seven thirty. Shall I have some dinner brought in?"

Kurt and Omar readily agreed. Sarah knew that Omar's time in the United States was short, and their time together at this stage was critical to the future success of the project. Sarah stepped over to her desk, opened the bottom left drawer, and pulled out an assortment of menus.

"What'll it be?" she asked. "Italian, Chinese, or Mexican?"

The three settled on Italian, and Sarah called in their orders to Antonio's. After hanging up, she announced," We'll have food in about thirty minutes. At this hour, security won't let the delivery guy come to the office, so they'll call us to go down and pick it up. Let me give the guard station a heads-up that it's coming." After talking with the guard, Sarah returned to the table and the conversation continued.

"Kurt, what can I say to my family about the specific short- and long-term goals of the project?" asked Omar.

"I think you can talk with them about all the areas of alternative energy we've been discussing. During the first year of the project, we hope to make breakthroughs with biofuel. If we perfect a way to produce it for forty dollars per barrel, we can make a profit. Long term, our focus should be on things like hydrogen/water-driven energy production. That type of technology is more challenging, but I think that with the right people and resources, we can make the breakthroughs we need."

"By 'right people,' I assume you're considering some of our own people at the lab."

"Exactly," Kurt replied. "For starters, I feel certain I can get Jennifer and George on board."

"But they are in their fifties," observed Omar. "Their USOCO retirements have not yet vested. Why would they leave USOCO at this point?"

"After I remind them of what USOCO has done with some of their research, they will jump at this opportunity, especially Jennifer."

"Are you talking about our recent discussion with them at lunch?" asked Omar.

"Yes. You saw their attitude about how they thought top-echelon management would react to their latest idea. They suspect that no matter how promising their proposals may be, USOCO will shelve them. I also think they are idealists and would quickly join us to work on something this exciting."

At this point, Kurt thought about telling Sarah and Omar about breaking the code on the Enhanced Maize Project file. He decided they had enough on the table for now, and that information could be discussed later.

"As to who else might join us from the lab," Kurt continued, "I daresay most of them would jump at the chance to join us on this project. I have completed a random audit of some of our lab's past projects. Some of these looked very promising. But inexplicably, they were scrapped by upper management. I can see why many of our scientists are disgruntled. One of our scientists is working on a hydrogen fueled car and believes he is close to a breakthrough. It needs significant funding from USOCO to reach the next level, but as you know, upper management has refused to fund it."

"Okay," pressed Omar, "assuming that you will have no problem recruiting these capable people, let's talk about where to conduct this project. What are your thoughts about where it should be located?"

"We'll need a place with seclusion, lots of fresh water, and at least seven months of warm weather per year. It should also be fairly close to a place where our personnel would want to live."

The three sat in silence, pondering the question. Sarah felt her eyes drifting to a picture of a sailboat on the wall behind her desk. With her voice barely above a whisper, she said, "I know just the place." With both Kurt and Omar now staring at her, she continued, "It's near one of the Dutch Phosphate Corporation's mining facilities in a remote area of eastern North Carolina. While some of our management personnel choose to live in the nearby town of Aurora, most live in Greenville, which is about a forty-five-minute commute. Greenville is where I grew up. It used to be a sleepy college town, but that is changing. The students number around twenty-five thousand, still a third of the total population. But the local schools are excellent, and a variety of cultural attractions are available in the college community. As to the need for water, the mine sits on the banks of the Pamlico River. Kurt, I might add that Pamlico Sound offers some of the best sailing waters anywhere in the world."

Omar studied Sarah and Kurt cautiously, wondering what he might have started.

"When can we take a look at this place?" asked Kurt.

"DPC has a plane that flies there from New York on Thursdays. Can you break away from USOCO again that quickly?"

"I'll find a way," Kurt responded.

CHAPTER
9

APRIL 24, 2008 — LONG ISLAND MACARTHUR AIRPORT, NEW YORK

As Sarah and Kurt walked up the gangway to the Dutch Phosphate Corporation's Piaggio P180, they were greeted by its pilot at the top of the stairs.

"Kurt, I want you to meet our pilot and my good friend, Kate Burns," Sarah said.

Kate greeted Kurt with a broad, toothy smile and a firm, friendly handshake. After a few minutes of pleasantries, she returned to the cockpit and was all business.

"Kate is one of my favorite people. She's full of energy, funny, and is a damn good pilot. Like me, she's single and grew up in coastal North Carolina. She's also a sailing buddy of mine. But I have to warn you. She's a free spirit and will say anything."

Kurt thought, *Yes, and she also looks pretty strong in those tight black slacks.*

Sarah was in the seat next to Kurt as they taxied down the tarmac. They were studying an aerial photo of the remote five-thousand-acre tract of land where the DPC mine was located when Kate announced, "We're next in line for takeoff."

The plane was one of three Piaggio P180 Avanti II turboprops owned by the Dutch Phosphate Corporation. Its two rear-thrust engines provided a cruising speed of 385 miles per hour, comparable to most jets of its size, but with far better fuel efficiency. More importantly, it could land on the short runways of DPC's usually remote mining operations.

Within minutes, they were just off the Atlantic coast flying south. Two hours later, while Sarah and Kurt were still engrossed with plans for selection of a site for their project, Kurt felt the plane beginning its descent. Moments later, Kate announced, "Kitty Hawk is below us on the right side of the plane. That's where we first started flying these fake birds. Thank you, Wilbur and Orville Wright. Did you guys have any idea what you were starting?"

Kurt smiled and looked down through his window at mile after mile of long, slender barrier islands known as the Outer Banks.

"When the Wright brothers were here, those islands were barren strips of sand with almost no vegetation and very few people," commented Sarah. "Look at them now. Row after row of fragile wooden structures perched on sand dunes just a few storm waves away from an often-unfriendly ocean. We spend millions of dollars each year to restore the sand on the beach that Mother Nature insists on moving around with each winter nor'easter."

A few minutes later, the pilot put the Piaggio into a steep bank to the right and announced, "That's Ocracoke Island below us. Except for the small village of Ocracoke, it's an uninhabited national park and has, in my opinion, some of the most beautiful and unspoiled beaches in the world. There are also some very secluded areas that are great for skinny-dipping. Kurt, if Sarah won't take you there, I will."

Kurt and Sarah broke into a good laugh. "I see what you mean," said Kurt. "She will say anything."

Through the window, Kurt could see Pamlico Sound and its miles of open, sun-sparkled water below. "This looks like a great place to sail. How much depth do you have here?"

"Generally about twenty feet," replied Sarah, "although there are a few well-marked shoals down there. You will find plenty of open water in Pamlico Sound. This is a sailor's dream place. The really good news is that it's a still-undiscovered secret. How much water does your Hylas draw?"

"Six feet."

"Then you could easily sail her here. We could find you a berth at the River Rat Yacht Club. You could sail with us on our frequent weekend jaunts around the sound. Belhaven, Bath, Washington, Ocracoke, Oriental, and Cape Lookout are some of our favorite destinations. We have a potluck dinner every second Saturday night of the month.

I think you would enjoy the River Rats. They're a fun-loving group of sailors. And if you need crew, I'll be the first to volunteer."

"Sounds great, but getting my boat here would be a challenge."

"I understand, but you're welcome to join us anyway. And I'll give you a first option anytime as crew on my boat."

"Thanks, Sarah. Don't be surprised if I take you up on that."

Kurt felt the plane suddenly descend. Looking out the window, he saw the tree line of the north shore of the Pamlico River less than two hundred feet away, at what he guessed was an altitude of only a hundred feet. Seconds later, Kate's voice came over the intercom.

"Sarah, I think I see your Uncle Jason on the pier up ahead. Let's let him know we're here."

Sarah leaned over Kurt to look out the window. Kurt couldn't help but notice her right breast pushing gently into his left shoulder.

"Yes, that's my Uncle Jason down there," she said happily. "I can't wait to see him again." Sitting back in her seat, she continued, "When we land, I'll give him a call to let him know we're here. Jason loves to cook and will insist that you stay with us tonight. And he doesn't take no for an answer."

"Sounds great, but I would hate to just barge in uninvited."

"Not a problem. He will welcome the chance to have another guy around."

Just before the Piaggio reached the pier, Kurt felt the plane tilt to the right, followed by a tilt to the left. On the pier below, Kurt could see a man waving his hand as the plane flew over him. Kate accelerated the engines and brought the plane into a steep bank to the south out over the Pamlico River. Seconds later, they had almost crossed the three-mile width of the river when Kate banked hard to the right. After the Piaggio leveled, Kurt looked out the left windows and saw the tree line on the south side of the river. A thump came from the bottom of the plane as the landing gear descended. After touching down on the runway, Kurt noticed a two-story, glass-walled office building pass by on the left side of the plane, with the Pamlico only a hundred feet to the right.

Hearing the cockpit door open, Kurt looked up to see Kate with a mischievous smile on her face. "I guess I should have asked if you get airsick," she said. Seeing that Kurt was smiling, she and Sarah both had a good laugh.

Looking at Kate, Sarah asked, "We'll see you in a few hours at the Lee Creek terminal?"

"Sounds great. That will give me time to go through my maintenance checklist, get this bird refueled, and catch up on some paperwork." Kate, still giggling, returned to the cockpit.

As Kurt and Sarah descended the stairway, a tall, slender, redheaded man stood on the tarmac to greet them. Kurt guessed he was in his late thirties.

"Kurt, this is Mike Mahoney, the DPC plant manager."

"Pleased to meet you," said Kurt, and the two men briskly shook hands.

"The pleasure is mine," replied Mahoney stiffly.

After placing their bags in the back of a Jeep, Mahoney drove the short distance to the DPC office building that Kurt had noticed as they were landing.

Once inside, Mahoney led them to a large second-floor conference room with a scenic view of the expanse of the Pamlico River below. Kurt immediately noticed several aerial photos on the long conference room table. In his previous phone conversations and e-mail exchanges with Mahoney, Kurt had explained in general terms the type of site that was needed for the project. Kurt surmised that Mahoney already had some ideas for them to consider.

As the three studied the maps on the table, Mahoney began going through some of their options.

"One site to consider is located right here within the perimeter of the production facility itself. It has fences, a guard gate, and twenty-four-hour security. The area consists of about twenty acres of open land that was mined last year and could easily be converted to what I think you want to do. Another option is several miles to the east on what is called Alligator Island. It consists of eighty-plus acres of high ground in the middle of a very forbidding swamp. Indians once somehow lived there a couple hundred years ago. Who knows how they survived in that godforsaken place. Over the years, Mother Nature has taken it over with dense, low vegetation. If you really want a remote location, that would be it."

Kurt interjected, "That sounds interesting. It has the seventy acres we need. It could also provide us with the absolute privacy we need."

Mahoney thought for a moment before responding. "I have an even better idea. The old lab here inside the premises is secure. We have twenty-four-hour guards, and no one gets into or out of this area without proper identification. How would that do?"

Kurt and Sarah exchanged glances. Neither was comfortable with what they were hearing. Kurt spoke first. "I'm afraid that won't be enough room and won't offer enough seclusion. A lot of people come through the plant gates twenty-four hours a day, seven days a week. Maybe I need to explain better the scope of this project. For starters, we will need to erect five large, insulated aluminum buildings and three glass greenhouses, all with power, climate control, and Internet access. I think Alligator Island sounds like a better option."

Mahoney laughed. "Mr. Benjamin, you don't understand. The place you are thinking about locating this project would make construction very difficult. There is no road for access. The only way in and out now is by boat or in a four-wheel-drive vehicle in very dry conditions. People are afraid of the place. We would have trouble getting local construction workers to go there. The last people who ventured onto that island were Indians who lived there until they suddenly vanished about two hundred years ago. No one knows what really became of them, but some believe they lost their battle with the swamp's alligators for control of the island. This strange breed of alligator still infests that place today. As you may know, most alligators reach a size of about twelve feet in length and shy away from humans. The alligators in this hellhole are often over twenty-five feet long, four feet thick, weigh as much as an F250 pickup truck, and are very aggressive. They will eat whatever is on the menu. That includes you."

"All the more reason to use that place," Kurt persisted. "We could use the lab here within the perimeter for the first few weeks while we start our experiments and build what we need at the island."

Mahoney rolled his eyes. "Mr. Benjamin, you are talking about an enormous construction project that under the best of circumstances could take six months. Why not put it closer to the plant here, where we already have electricity, water, and an established infrastructure? You could save millions of the company's dollars by doing so."

Annoyed with Mahoney's inflexibility, Kurt looked at Sarah for assistance.

"Mr. Mahoney," Sarah interjected, "money is not an issue. Time is. The board of directors of our company has authorized me to deliver a clear message to you and whoever else is on the payroll. We will provide Mr. Benjamin with whatever he needs for this project on a priority basis. Your projection for the outlying lab was six months? We'll need it done in two. Do you understand?"

Mahoney stared at her in disbelief for a few seconds before responding. "Very well, but I think you need to see with your own eyes what it is we're dealing with."

"Why don't we go look at it now?" Kurt suggested.

Mahoney glanced at his watch and said, "It's four p.m. We should be okay unless there's a late afternoon thunderstorm. The only pathway in and out is low and wet. We'll need to get out of there fast if a storm comes up."

As they passed through the rear gate of the mine in Mahoney's Jeep, it was four thirty. In two hours it would be sunset; in three it would be dark.

"It's been several years since I've been out here to the island," Mahoney commented. "But that was with plenty of daylight."

The pathway through the swamp was every bit as challenging as Mahoney had described. Although there were still traces of the old roadbed used thirty years before, most of it was now washed away or covered with underbrush.

"How the hell do you know where you're going?" asked Kurt.

"I don't, really, but I do have a general idea of where the high ground is. The vegetation provides clues of where to go. So far, so good."

Large, ancient cypress and live oaks towered above them. The few areas of high ground were covered in thickets of ferns and wax myrtle. Thick Spanish moss dangled like spiderwebs from dead branches of cedar overhead. At one point along the way, Mahoney stopped and pointed to an open area in the swamp about one hundred feet to their left.

"See that gator over there on the bank in the shadows of the swamp? That's the type of alligator that infests this place."

"Look at the size of that guy!" exclaimed Kurt. "He has to be twenty feet long. Where the hell did he come from?"

"It's probably a she," said Mahoney. "The female is bigger than the male, and they rule this place. Local legends have these guys dominating this godforsaken swamp for eons of time."

Those guys would deter anyone from coming in here, Kurt thought, as he studied the giant creature.

"You guys want to keep going?" Mahoney asked sarcastically.

"Absolutely," Kurt shot back.

"Very well," Mahoney replied. He put the Jeep back in gear and moved slowly forward. After another half hour of bouncing over the narrow spit of high ground and slogging through the swamp, the Jeep finally ascended onto higher ground. "Here we are," said Mahoney. "If you want seclusion, privacy, and security from unwanted human guests, you certainly have it here."

Sarah and Kurt said nothing as they studied their surroundings. Exiting the Jeep, they walked to the edge of the island and then around its circumference, pausing occasionally to study an aerial map. When they had almost completed their inspection of the island, Kurt heard a low rumble from the west. Looking across the island at Mahoney, Kurt saw him pointing nervously at the sky to the west.

Returning to the Jeep, Kurt pulled out the aerial photograph of the island. "According to my calculations from the scale on this map, we have about ninety acres here. My guess is that some of it will not be usable, but we easily have enough land to make this location work." Turning to Mahoney, he asked, "When can we get a usable roadbed in here?"

"I can mobilize the necessary crews and equipment tomorrow, if that's what you need."

"It is," replied Kurt firmly.

"We'll need three weeks, assuming no rain. If it rains, all bets are off."

Another rumble from the west caught their attention. Within seconds there was another, but louder. Then there was a third, and this one shook the ground.

"Not good," barked Mahoney. "Let's get out of here."

In moments, flashes of lightning seemed to appear from every-where. The swamp appeared to erupt from an attack of artillery.

Suddenly, there was a blinding flash of light followed by a violent explosion. Kurt watched in amazement as a giant oak fifty feet to his left split open from its top to its roots. It was as if an axe had been driven down from the sky to slice the old tree in half. The rain was now cascading across the swamp in sheets.

"Hang on!" yelled Mahoney over the deafening drumbeat of rain pelting the roof and windows. "We have to get out of here fast."

At times, the four-wheel-drive Jeep seemed to mire down. At other times it seemed to be sliding sideways off the pathway and into the swamp. Mahoney drove like a possessed NASCAR driver in the final laps.

After what seemed like an hour to Kurt, but was only fifteen minutes, the Jeep bounded up onto a firm gravel road and left the swamp behind. Moments later, the rain let up and the storm departed as quickly as it had arrived. As Mahoney approached the plant gate, he slowed and dimmed his headlights. The decal ID, along with most of the vehicle, was covered in mud, making them unidentifiable potential intruders.

The guard stepped forward and waved for them to stop. With the driver's side window down, he immediately recognized Mahoney. "Mr. Mahoney, what happened to your Jeep? Where have you been?"

"You don't need to know," Mahoney replied bluntly. "Have a good evening."

There was no conversation in the Jeep as Mahoney drove through the plant to the Lee Creek tugboat terminal. When they arrived, Kate, who was seated on the dock, turned to wave. After Kurt removed their bags from the vehicle, Mahoney bid them a gruff good evening and drove away.

Moments later, the running lights of Jason's twenty-five-foot Grady White appeared in the terminal's channel and approached the dock. Jason tossed a bow and then a stern line, which Kate and Sarah caught easily and tied with clove hitches to the oversized pier pilings. Only one tug with its barge sat quietly in the harbor behind them.

Although he was sixty-five years old, Jason's six-foot frame was still trim and muscular. Hopping up easily onto the dock, he warmly embraced his niece, Sarah, and then turned to Kate, giving her a warm hug as well.

"Nice flying up there, hot rod," Jason laughed. "As soon as I heard those turboprops, I knew it had to be you. But Sarah, you didn't tell me you were coming. This is a very pleasant surprise."

Sarah replied, "Jason, this is Kurt Benjamin, the friend I was telling you about. He will be working on a project at the mine for a while."

Jason turned to Kurt with a warm, friendly smile and offered a firm handshake. "Welcome, Kurt."

Once everyone was aboard, Kurt and Sarah removed the dock lines and coiled and stowed them in a compartment on the starboard side of the boat. Moments later, they were skimming across a light northeasterly chop, crossing the Pamlico River. The orange glow of a giant rising moon was slowly emerging above the shoreline to the east. Jason crossed the three-mile expanse of river and then turned east, following the northern shoreline past the mouth of North Creek for another mile. Jason then pulled the throttles back, and the twin two-hundred-horsepower Johnsons settled down to an idle as he headed into a brightly lit dock. Once Kurt and Sarah had the boat tied off, they unloaded their few bags and headed up the pier toward shore.

The cottage sat on a bluff twenty feet above a sandy beach in front of the pier where Jason docked his Grady. On the beach, Kurt noticed a Hobie 18 and two sea kayaks.

A large screened-in porch covered the entire front of the cottage. Just inside the glass double doors, there was a large living area with a fireplace to the right. Behind the living area was an open dining area, and beyond that was a counter and a well-appointed kitchen, with a vaulted ceiling above.

"Would anyone like a libation?" asked Sarah.

There was a unanimous response: "Yes!"

"What'll it be?" she asked.

Kate responded, "I'll have a Heineken. What'll you have, Kurt?"

"A Heineken sounds good to me."

"That's easy," said Jason. "Four Heinekens it is. Why don't you guys enjoy the view from the porch while I finish dinner?" he suggested. "I'll just need a few minutes to warm things up."

On their way out to the porch, Kurt paused to ask Sarah about some of the pictures of her, her parents, and numerous others of her growing up on the river. One photo of her hiked out on the windward hull of a Hobie in a rough, frothy white sea caught his eye. *Skittish women don't do that*, he thought.

The three of them settled into comfortable rockers facing south and the river. Speckles of silver bounced off the moonlit ripples on the water below. The call of a whip-poor-will floated from the forest behind them. Jason soon stepped onto the porch to announce that dinner was ready.

The dinner conversation was spirited and lively, although there was no discussion of the DPC Alternative Energy Project. After dinner, they all pitched in to clean up the kitchen and put things away. After a round of B&B in large brandy snifters on the porch, they were all yawning and ready for a good night's sleep. With a warm southerly breeze carrying the sounds of the waves from the beach below, Bella Vista soothed her guests into a sound, peaceful sleep, except for Sarah.

After sleeping for several hours, she was awakened by a recurring dream where she saw a young Indian woman standing next to a distant fire. After lying awake awhile wondering again what this dream meant, she finally drifted off to sleep.

CHAPTER
10

Kurt was at his desk at the USOCO Laboratory for Alternative Energy Research, contemplating a graph on his computer screen, when he received a call from Jeffrey Morton, USOCO's chief of operations. At Morton's request, Kurt agreed to meet with him in his office in an hour. On his way to Morton's office, Kurt considered what he might say if Morton offered him the position of vice president of Alternative Energy Research.

Morton greeted him warmly, and after exchanging a few pleasantries, he offered Kurt the job. Kurt felt a fleeting sense of guilt, knowing his own resignation was only a few weeks away. But he reminded himself of what he had discovered in the locked computer file, and those guilty feelings were quickly overwhelmed by indignation. He accepted the position.

It was ten thirty a.m. when Kurt returned to his office. Seated once again behind his desk, he stared out the window at the Houston skyline, mentally retracing the rapid pace of recent developments.

"Good morning, stranger."

Kurt turned to see his friend Jennifer Batts standing in the doorway, smiling.

"We missed seeing you last Thursday. You took a hasty long weekend. Who is she?" Until Jennifer learned of Kurt's loss of his fiancée during his days with the CIA, she had wondered why such a handsome, intelligent, and successful man wasn't married.

Kurt smiled. "No, Jennifer, it's nothing like that, but it was quite a weekend."

Jennifer nodded and said, "Sounds interesting. We want to hear all about it this Thursday evening. Are you going to stand us up again?"

"I'll be there," Kurt replied, motioning for Jennifer to step into his office and close the door. In barely above a whisper, he continued, "Morton just offered me Omar's position, and I accepted."

"That's fantastic!" she said, giving him a warm hug. "We'll have something to celebrate this Thursday. But wait, you don't seem very enthusiastic about it."

"To be quite honest, I'm not. I need to talk to you and George about leaving USOCO and joining me in a very interesting project. Tell George to be prepared to have his socks knocked off Thursday night."

Jennifer stared at him wide-eyed, with her mouth open. "I'm speechless," she replied. "What is it?"

"I can't tell you. It's too involved and too big to discuss here. Just be ready, because something very exciting is ahead for you."

⊕ ⊕ ⊕

At dinner that evening, Jennifer told George the news of Kurt's promotion and also his veiled reference to wanting them to join him in an exciting new venture. Although George acted inquisitive, old feelings of resentment resurfaced that, as outsiders, Omar and Kurt had been given the top two jobs at the USOCO Department of Alternative Energy. In George's mind, Kurt's job should have been his. Now, USOCO had once again passed him over.

Carefully concealing his bruised ego, George asked, "What the hell is this project?"

"I don't know, George. I guess we'll know Thursday night."

"Why would he give up a fantastic promotion like that?" George asked thoughtfully. "Until now, I thought the young man was very levelheaded. I hope he hasn't done something rash. This should make Thursday a very interesting evening."

When Thursday evening came, Jennifer greeted Kurt at the door of their residence with her usual warm welcome. The aroma of George's lasagna filled the den. George had his own secret special recipe that Kurt had so far been unable to pry out of him. "If I told you, it would no longer be a secret," George kept telling him.

On this occasion, George had a reason for it to be on the menu. With it and the Caesar salad pre-prepared, he would be able to give his full attention to whatever it was that Kurt would present to them. He also planned to do something unusual; he was going to sip his wine judiciously that night.

Over dinner, they enjoyed small talk about the weather, the Houston Astros' loss the previous night, Omar's sudden departure, and then the status of their current projects at the lab. With the dishes done hastily and put away, the three of them returned to the den with their wine.

"Okay, Kurt," said George, "you've kept us in suspense long enough. You get promoted this week to Omar's position as the vice president of Alternative Energy Research. Then you tell Jennifer that you're leaving USOCO for some strange project and want us to leave as well and join you. What in the world could be so important to cause you or us to leave USOCO now?"

Kurt nodded his understanding. "Yes, the timing does seem a bit strange. But after you hear me out, I think you will understand. Even if they promoted me to CEO, I would still do this. It's that big. Before I begin, you must promise to keep this conversation to yourselves. Even if you choose not to join me, what we discuss here must be kept confidential."

In unison, Jennifer and George nodded and said, "Absolutely."

Kurt began with his introduction to Sarah and a synopsis of his discussions with her about Dutch Phosphate Corporation's proposed Alternative Energy Project. "And as the three of us have discussed many times, the production of energy from fossil fuels cannot keep up with the exponential growth of the world's demand. There must be another source."

Jennifer and George nodded in agreement. Kurt was cautious in what he revealed as he explained the offer from Dutch Phosphate Corporation in general terms and the huge monetary investment being made. He chose not to mention the fact that this venture might have a silent partner, the Sharjah Oil Company. The potential involvement of Omar and his family was not something they needed to know.

"How does this involve us?" asked George.

"I want you to join me and be a part of this exciting project. This is an opportunity for you to finally have your talents and discoveries appreciated. More importantly, you will participate in the actual trials of your work and see the results. It will be well funded, fully and honestly tested, and implemented if proven economically viable. I have seen your work. You and Jennifer have some ideas that have enormous potential."

Both looked at him questioningly.

"What's that supposed to mean?" sneered George. "According to USOCO, our discoveries have proven to be failures when subjected to economic viability testing."

The file Kurt brought with him lay on the coffee table in front of them. Kurt slowly reached forward and handed the file to Jennifer. "I suggest you guys take this to the dining room where you can spread it out to study. In the meantime, I need to make a phone call."

Jennifer and George dutifully returned to the dining room, turned up the light that had been dimmed during their dinner, and spread the file's contents out on the table. They took turns reviewing the various portions of the file.

Kurt stepped onto the back patio and dialed Mahoney from his cell phone. Kurt hoped he would still be in his office at this late hour.

After three rings, Mahoney's answered, "Hello, Kurt. How goes it?"

"All is well here. How's our project coming?"

"Kurt, those bureaucratic bastards at the Department of Environment and Natural Resources issued a stop work order on our road construction to the swamp. At first, there was a flat refusal to reconsider. However, after our company's attorneys got involved, DENR was made to realize that the roadway was actually a repair to the grandfathered roadbed that had been constructed thirty years ago. The obstructionists at DENR have now promised that they will issue our permit tomorrow morning. All the necessary materials, equipment, and crews are ready to restart work as soon as we have the permits."

Mahoney continued with a brief description of the progress in awarding the contracts for construction of the buildings and greenhouses, and the lab equipment, power, and phone lines that the two of them had spent all day last Monday planning. When Kurt hung up the phone, he smiled in pleasant disbelief and thought, *Mahoney has gone from a skeptical naysayer to an energetic and efficient managerial machine. This guy knows how to get things done.*

Kurt stepped into the dining room to find George staring across the room as if in a trance. Jennifer slammed the document she had been reading on the table.

"Those slimy bastards!" she sputtered angrily. "They lied to us, and we believed them. We were onto something big, and this proves it. Instead of pursuing it, they locked it in a cellar, thinking no one would ever find out. To hell with those bastards! I'll resign from USOCO tomorrow. Kurt, when do we start?"

"Whoa, Jennifer, let's think about this," said George. "We have eighteen years at USOCO. Our retirements will vest in two more years. If we go now, we leave not just our jobs, but our retirements and our health insurance as well. This new project could last two years, and it could be a bust. Besides, when Kurt leaves, one of us may be promoted to his position.

"George, I don't give a damn. You can stay. To hell with USOCO, and to hell with my retirement. What they've done is criminal. I'll have to puke every morning before showing up for work at that damned place again."

George was silent and thoughtful. Kurt realized he had created a huge rift in what he thought was a rock-solid relationship. Pangs of guilt went through him, but at the same time he felt the same indignation toward USOCO as Jennifer did. It also was clear that George had more pent-up anger than he'd realized—until tonight.

Kurt proceeded cautiously with his words. "George, there is no need to make a decision tonight. How about if you guys just think about this for a few days? If I'm welcome to return next Thursday, can we discuss it further then?" Kurt paused before adding, "But I am certain of one thing. The two of you are onto some ideas that need to see the light of day. Your work deserves to be fully and fairly tested and developed. George, I truly believe you and Jennifer are close to some very big accomplishments. This is the chance of a lifetime for both of you."

After changing planes at London's Heathrow Airport, Omar boarded an Egypt Air Boeing 747 bound for the Sharjah International Airport. As the plane reached its cruising altitude of thirty-six thousand feet, Omar's thoughts turned to his upcoming reunion with his family. There were many unanswered questions on his mind. *Will they really accept me after all this time in America? Will they be receptive to joining the Dutch Phosphate Corporation project? Will Naji view me as a threat?*

The call two days earlier informing him that his grandfather had died in his sleep saddened him, yet he was relieved to learn that the old man had gone peacefully. The memory of the meeting he'd had with his father and grandfather shortly before he left Sharjah came back to him. Although the details had faded over the years, they had recently returned to haunt him with images as vivid as ever. It was on his sixteenth birthday. Omar remembered his grandfather's story of the American oilmen coming to his home with their contract. The attempt by these men to cheat the family out of its oil wealth was a lesson his grandfather wanted him never to forget.

The story his grandfather had told of his life crept through Omar's thoughts. He remembered his words clearly.

"Omar, your great-grandfather was a very fortunate man. He was one of the few pearl divers to break out of the system of debt that destined most of them to a lifetime of economic slavery. He fortunately escaped the clutches of his *Nahkota*, the captain of the dhow and his master.

"At the beginning of each pearling season, every pearler was given an advance to tide him and his family over until the end of the season. As often as not, by the season's end, the pearler's share of profits from the dhow's pearl sales would not cover the advance. This meant he was indebted to return to dive for his *Nahkota* the next season. Some of the pearlers unfortunately began their slavery because they had inherited their father's debt to the *Nahkota*.

"In turn, the *Nahkota* was indebted to his merchant who financed the pearling season. The merchant often would pay his *Nahkota* a fraction of what the pearls were worth at the season's end, and then sell them for several times that amount in the market. If, in the judgment of the merchant, the dhow's profits were not sufficient to cover the amount advanced to the *Nahkota* for the pearling season, the difference remained as a debt. Until the debt was paid, the *Nahkota* was required to serve his merchant for another season."

Over the years since hearing this story, Omar had often tried to rationalize this system with the Islamic law that forbade the charging of interest on lent money. This whole system was just another form of debt, but with very harsh consequences for failure to pay. Nevertheless, he understood that this was the culture in which his family had somehow prospered.

His grandfather had continued, "My father had an unusual season. Allah was surely with him every day. As they began opening the oysters by the firelight on the deck, amazing things fell in front of them. It was a rare night that they did not see a large pearl of very high quality in the day's catch. At the end of the season, even after the *Nahkota* and the merchant had raked off the cream of the profits, the pearlers were handsomely rewarded. While most pearlers lived recklessly and blew their year's pay within weeks, my father took his share and invested it in a small dhow of his own. The next year, with a crew of six, he had a very good season. The following year, he purchased a second and larger dhow. It was another very good season. Eight years later, he had a fleet of twenty. He never borrowed from a merchant, and was soon in the role of a merchant himself.

"He was one of the very few lucky pearlers not to die pearling. Each day as a pearler, he made at least thirty dives to depths often over one hundred feet. With each dive, he was under water for a minute and a half or more, descending to the ocean's bottom with his feet on a large stone, to gather as many oysters as he could. Once out of breath, he would pull the line to signal his handler to haul him up. At the surface, he would gasp for air and repeat his dives until he had completed ten. He would then have a rest on deck in front of a fire to try to stop shivering after his exposure to the cold waters below. The cycle was repeated until the day's dives were completed. The daily cuts from barnacles and the sharp edges of the clams inflicted wounds that were painful and slow to heal. For some pearlers, the wounds did not heal, resulting in infections that led to a slow death at the back of the dhow. From the years in which my father endured the hardships of pearling, he left our family something far more valuable than pearls. He had the insight and guidance from Allah to take the money he had made and purchase what most people thought was worthless land in the desert. Its value today is far more than anything he could ever have dreamed at the time. Unfortunately, the value of what we have was not lost on greedy men from the West. They would have taken everything we have if we had not been careful and fortunate. They have a foothold in our lands and are here to stay. We must learn to deal with them. We must learn how they think. We must learn their ways. We must learn everything about them. The world as we know it is forever changing."

"Why are you telling me this, Grandfather?"

"Omar, I want you to honor this by completing a task. I want you to do what we are going to ask of you."

"What is that?"

"We believe you need to be educated in the United States. Your teachers tell us that you are more than capable of competing with students anywhere. After you have completed your education, and have worked in and learned the Western business world, you will return to us. We will call you when it is time to return."

Omar's reflections were suddenly interrupted by the pilot's voice on the intercom. "We are on our final approach to Sharjah International. We will be on the ground in twenty minutes."

CHAPTER

11

Omar's father and his younger brother, Naji, greeted him when he arrived at the Sharjah airport. Although he and his father exchanged the traditional greeting of hugs and the touching of noses enthusiastically, Omar noticed that Naji's embrace was mechanical and without any real enthusiasm. Omar wondered if this might be an indication that Naji felt slighted or jealous about his return to take over the family's businesses.

With Naji at the wheel of the big family Mercedes, they drove through Sharjah City. High-rise buildings with offices, apartments, and upscale restaurants had replaced the dilapidated buildings along the desert waterfront that Omar remembered as a teenager. As Naji maneuvered the Mercedes through the busy traffic of Sharjah, Omar watched men dressed in traditional tunics with kaffiyeh headwear, and women wearing burkhas, walking briskly along concrete sidewalks. An eerie sense of unease about what lay ahead suddenly crept over him.

Leaving the city, Naji drove along a coastal highway that ran parallel to the turquoise blue waters of the Persian Gulf. Arriving at a gated entrance, Naji turned onto a long driveway bordered on either side by rows of tall palm trees. A large stucco mansion soon appeared ahead of them, surrounded by lush, neatly groomed gardens. Behind the massive structure lay the wide expanse of the Persian Gulf.

Their dinner that night was a feast. Omar's mother and sister had supervised two kitchen servants for the entire afternoon to prepare it. Omar, dressed in a tunic and kaffiyeh, joined his mother, father, Naji, and his sister, Shallah, for the meal. Being a more liberal Arabic family, they did not follow the custom of women and men eating separately.

As dinner progressed, the servants brought generous portions of traditional Arabic dishes. The three children listened patiently as their parents reminisced about their childhood days and told stories passed down by the family's ancestors. At one point, Omar sensed Naji glaring at him, but feigned not to notice.

After dinner, as Omar's mother and sister supervised the kitchen servants, Naji, Omar, and their father retreated to a large living area. Plush Persian carpets covered the room's floor. In one corner, there was a small, low, round table with cushions for seating. Omar's father and Naji proceeded to light their favorite Arabian cigarette, an unfiltered Shisha.

Once they were settled around the table, Omar's father turned to him and said, "You have something that you want to talk to us about. On the phone, you told me this was a very important opportunity for our family, and our country. What is it?"

"Yes, Father," answered Omar. "I have had the good fortune to come to know some very remarkable people while in the United States. The first one I want to talk about is my friend Sarah. We became good friends during my studies at Wharton. After graduation, we went our separate ways, but stayed in touch."

Omar continued by telling of Sarah's progression at the Dutch Phosphate Corporation and his own at USOCO and how he came to know Kurt Benjamin. He then turned to the huge power needs of DPC and its concerns over its escalating energy costs.

Naji interrupted him. "Omar, corporations all over the world are experiencing the same thing. Thanks to Allah, the United Arab Emirates has the oil they crave. As industrial growth around the world increases, so will the demand for oil. The more the demand, the more they have to pay for it. The more they pay for it, the wealthier our country becomes. So why do you tell us about something we already know?"

Omar studied his brother patiently and said, "Yes, I agree, Naji. We also have our own industrial growth here in Sharjah. We now have access to the most expensive clothes and jewelry money can buy. There are over forty-five museums in the city of Sharjah alone. Our hospitals are as well equipped and our doctors as well trained as any in the world."

Omar paused for a moment, studying his father closely, and then continued. "But we have a problem. Some of our own estimates indicate our oil reserves running out in as little as four years and eight at best. While we are making investments that will provide some revenue in the future, will it be enough to replace our current revenues from oil? And at the point that our oil reserves are gone, we will find ourselves dependent upon the emir of Abu Dhabi to supply us with oil to run our industrial projects. By that time, oil may well be selling for as much as three hundred dollars a barrel. Is Abu Dhabi going to give us a break on the price? If so, what will be expected in return? Regardless of what happens, we will be at the mercy of our oil-rich neighbor."

"So, Omar, what is this opportunity?" asked his father. "How does it affect us here in Sharjah?"

"I will tell you," said Omar. "While we have been blessed, we need to find another source of cash flow for our family and our emirate. When the flow of oil stops, the influx of money that we have used to invest in industrial growth will end. The project I am going to propose to you could give us a large interest in a company developing other sources of energy that could replace oil. To explain what this opportunity is, I need to backtrack to what I have witnessed at the USOCO Laboratory for Alternative Energy Research over the past year."

Omar proceeded to explain several of the projects and why they had potential. He concluded by stating, "The bottom line is that we must find an alternative energy source to oil, and find it soon. I firmly believe that with our investment, Kurt Benjamin and his team at DPC will find a viable alternative to oil."

His father interjected, "What do these American friends of yours have to offer us for our investment?"

"While I do not have a complete proposal yet, I believe we could get Sarah's company to sell us a very large number of shares of preferred stock. As Naji knows, with preferred stock, we receive interest during the time we own it. More importantly, we would have the option to convert these shares to common stock at a set price, probably around the thirty dollars a share that Dutch Phosphate Corporation trades at today. If this project succeeds, the stock could be worth tenfold what we pay for it."

"And what if it doesn't succeed?" interjected Naji. "Do we want to put millions of dollars into the hands of the officers and board of directors of an American company over which we have no control?"

"Naji, you raise a good point. But I think your concerns will be lessened when you hear more. If we make this investment, we will be in a position to own twenty percent of the shares of Dutch Phosphate Corporation, should we ever choose to convert our preferred shares into common stock. This is enough to guarantee three seats on the board of directors. We will also own stock in one of the largest producers of fertilizer in the world. The food required to sustain the world is produced almost entirely with the assistance of processed fertilizer. Oil produces luxuries; food is a fundamental necessity."

Naji scowled. "But you have to admit, this project is a long shot."

"Yes," responded Omar, "but so is drilling for oil. Besides, even if we don't find the energy source, we will own a large amount of stock in a very sound company of a secure industry. The world population is growing rapidly, and so is the demand for food. Consequently, the demand for fertilizer is going to increase. I believe we win whether we find the energy source or not."

The three sat quietly for a moment before their father asked, "Do we have enough cash on hand to invest the hundred million dollars?"

"We do," Naji replied reluctantly, "but the money would be better invested here to create industrial projects that we know and can control."

"Yes," said Omar, "but up to now, almost all of our money has been invested only in projects here in Sharjah. Would we not be wise to diversify elsewhere?"

There was another long period of silence, until Omar turned to face his father, followed by Naji. Finally their father spoke.

"Many years ago, the people of our young emirate thought the pearl industry would last forever. As we know, it did not. We must also remember our own family's history. We were not always so blessed with good fortune as we are today. Your great-grandfather was a poor young pearl diver when he received his good fortune from Allah. He could have remained a simple pearl diver. Instead, he had a vision, and he followed it. He constantly reinvested his earnings until he had a fleet of dhows that made him a rich man. When your great-grandfather bought the oil-rich land, the presence of oil was only a dim possibility. The important thing for us to remember is that he had a vision and seized an opportunity to pursue it. I believe we must continue on his path. He taught us never to be debtors, which we will be in a few short years if we stay on our current course. Even if our brother emirs are generous with their oil, they do not extend favors for nothing. We cannot allow ourselves to be in their debt. If your great-grandfather were here tonight, I believe he would tell us to seize this opportunity and invest in this project. That is what we will do."

Omar studied Naji closely. He sat with his arms crossed and a look of disgust on his face. Omar easily surmised that he was not happy with their father's decision.

Days after the dinner with Kurt, George was still reeling from the contents of the USOCO internal file that Kurt had presented to them. His analytical mind pondered the recent developments and his options. He and Jennifer had engaged in several heated discussions about where they would go from here. George was not at all convinced Kurt knew what he was getting into. George had been working in alternative energy research for years and knew the realities. Kurt Benjamin was new to the company. What did he know? In contrast, he and Jennifer had spent their whole careers in the nuts-and-bolts end of scientific experiments. It was about time the upper echelons of USOCO recognized him for his valuable contributions. And now that the VP position would be open after Kurt's resignation, why not step forward to take it? But Jennifer was dead set on leaving to work on Kurt's project. He would have to go along, but inside he seethed with anger about this lost opportunity. He finally came up with a plan.

Sitting at his computer, George typed a carefully worded e-mail to Jim Hayes, the chief executive officer of USOCO. *I know what happened to the Enhanced Maize Project. I also know something about that project that USOCO does not. Would you like to know what that is?* Finishing the e-mail, George sat back in his chair, smirked, and clicked the *Send* button.

When George's e-mail appeared on the computer screen in front of him, the CEO of USOCO searched his memory, trying to recall the Enhanced Maize Project. Then it hit him. Picking up the phone, Hayes pressed the speed dial for his general counsel, Bert Thornton.

"Got a minute? We need to talk ASAP."

"Jeez, Jim, I have a lunch meeting in thirty minutes."

"Can you reschedule it?"

"Damn, this must be big. I'll be right over."

Moments later, Bert walked into Jim's outer office. Like most CEOs, Jim Hayes wanted his legal counsel close by. To accomplish that, Bert's office was on the same floor as the CEO's, only a few steps away. Being summoned at the last minute was nothing unusual. Like most general counsel, there was an unwritten part of his job description that he was on call 24/7 for the CEO.

Julie, Jim's administrative assistant, was usually at her desk in the outer office, guarding his doorway. Today, she had taken an early lunch and was not present to greet their frequent visitor. Jim was standing with his back to the door, looking over the Houston skyline through the glass walls of his enormous corner office, when Bert approached the doorway. Hearing footsteps, Jim turned just as Bert stepped into the plush office.

"Bert, close the door and come look at this," Jim said, pointing to his computer screen.

The heavy door of Jim's office closed with a thud. Bert leaned over Jim's screen and read Batts's e-mail. The attorney then read it again, out loud. "'Would you like to know what that is?'" Bert stood back and looked at Jim incredulously. "Who the hell is this guy?"

The CEO finally turned away from the window. "I looked him up in the firm directory. He's one of the weirdoes down at the Laboratory for Alternative Energy Research. Bert, I thought Jeffrey Morton buried the Enhanced Maize Project where it could never see the light of day. What happened?"

"He did," replied Bert. "Or at least he said he did. There's no *way*, unless a very clever hacker got through a very secure firewall and got in. I'll talk to Morton and our IT guy, who actually built the firewall, and find out if or how the code was broken."

"Bert, if it was, we have a big problem."

"No doubt about that," replied Bert. He opened the large door to the CEO's office and headed down the hall.

Two hours later, following his investigation on the lower floors of the tower, Bert reappeared. Julie had returned to her guard station outside Jim's office. As Bert strolled into the outer office, she looked up with no expression and said flatly, "Go in. He's expecting you."

After Bert crossed the threshold of the inner door, he closed it behind him. "We do have a problem. Morton has determined the file was breached by someone using Kurt Benjamin's computer. Whoever did it was not your run-of-the-mill hacker. He or she is very clever."

"Maybe Batts is our hacker?" said Jim.

"We don't know. But I'm afraid we have to assume he has the information that the hacker got from the file."

Jim frowned and stared at his trusted lawyer. "And assuming that, Counselor, where do we go from here? What are our options?"

"I'm afraid not to meet with him. We have to find out how much he knows and who else knows it."

Jim looked directly at Bert and, in a voice as cold as steel, he asked "Can you take care of this?"

"Yes. And as CEO, you know nothing of this matter. You will not be involved." Moments later, Bert was back in his office in front of his computer.

The e-mail that arrived on George's screen was simple. *George, can you meet with me in my office in an hour? Best regards, Bert.* George smirked at the friendly tone of the e-mail and glanced at his watch. It was three thirty p.m. He had driven separately from Jennifer that day, having told her he had errands to run after work.

The smirk stayed on George's face as he typed his response to the general counsel. *I'll be there in an hour.* George shut down his computer and left the lab.

⊕ ⊕ ⊕

With a smug sense of confidence, George arrived at the office of the general counsel of United States Oil Company. Bert Thornton's office was as George had imagined it. Law books lined the wall behind the enormous desk, which was cluttered with stacks of files and paper.

On one front corner of the desk was a mahogany box labeled "In Box" and on the other corner was another labeled "Out Box."

Bert greeted George with a warm smile and a firm, friendly handshake. "Thank you for coming to see me on such short notice. Please have a seat," he said, and gestured to a corner sitting area with large brown leather chairs, next to a small conference table and adjacent to a wet bar. "Can I get you something to drink?"

"Some water would be nice," answered George.

"Certainly, and in this Houston heat, we can't drink too much of the stuff."

Bert pulled two bottles of water from the bar's small refrigerator and handed one to George. Bert took the chair directly in front of George where he could make direct eye contact.

"So, Jim Hayes showed me your e-mail. He's in the middle of something right now and asked me to follow up with you about it. What was this Enhanced Maize Project that you mentioned in your message?"

George thought, *He's going to pretend that he knows nothing about it.* Raising his eyebrows, George responded, "You don't know about it?"

"No," Bert responded coolly. "Please tell me about it."

George explained the research he and Jennifer had done and the promising results from it, up to where the results were submitted to upper management at USOCO for review. He then said that, six months later, they were informed it was not economically feasible to pursue their proposed project, based on trials that had been run by other independent experiments.

"Your e-mail said you know what happened to the Maize project. What does that mean?"

George thought for a minute and then replied, "Let's just say I know the trials of our theories proved very promising. I now firmly believe we were close to creating an alternative energy source that, with some further adjustments to our formulas and protocols, would have been commercially feasible. For whatever reason, we were told that the trials revealed that our work was not economically viable. But as you and I know, the trials actually revealed that our findings were correct and could have provided an economically viable source of alternative energy."

Finishing his description of the project, George watched Bert for any reaction. Bert sat motionless, gazing directly into George's eyes as if studying a poker hand.

The attorney finally spoke. "Tell me, George, how did you come by this information?"

George smiled and delivered his well-thought-out response. "You don't need to know. And this is not what the e-mail was about. The real question is what happens to the information I have. In the wrong hands, it could prove very damaging to USOCO. I have a good friend at the *Houston Chronicle* who would love to get his hands on this story. It would be a career-maker for him. As for USOCO, the headlines would be just the beginning of its problems. After the story breaks, there will surely be some ugly congressional hearings. Some high-level people at the company will be subpoenaed to Capitol Hill to testify under oath. If they do not testify truthfully, they could be indicted for perjury. If they do tell the truth, USOCO will have to give them the axe to save face with a public outraged by the current cost of a gallon of gasoline."

George finished his response and studied Bert intently, knowing he was dealing with a seasoned lawyer who had survived countless courtroom and boardroom brawls. But he sensed his words had struck a nerve, as if a lightning bolt had struck the top of the USOCO office tower.

"Why are you telling me this?" Bert finally asked. "Do you want me to do something with this information?"

"Yes. Jennifer and I plan to resign our positions tomorrow at noon. We've been asked to join a well-funded team to further our work from the Enhanced Maize Project, along with some other intriguing ideas that may have much more potential than that one. The question for you to deliver to Mr. Hayes is simple. Would he like to keep the contents of the USOCO Enhanced Maize Project file away from my friend at the *Houston Chronicle*?"

George took a sip of water with a slightly tremulous right hand. Although he thought he had just delivered a hammer blow to Bert's gut, and his stomach should be churning like a concrete mixer, he watched the cool and collected lawyer studying him like a seasoned poker player. With no outward show of emotion, Bert leaned forward slowly and looked George in the eye.

"And how can that be made to happen?"

George's eyes darted over the man's head to look out the window before returning to Bert's piercing stare.

"Jennifer and I will have vested retirements in two years. To keep the file to ourselves, we need to have sabbatical status with full pay and benefits for the next two years. Our retirements must be guaranteed after this two-year period. We will also require a severance package of one hundred thousand dollars, in cash, to be paid within five days."

Bert stared intently at George for several seconds before finally responding. "I see." He then shifted his gaze from George to the Houston skyline. After several calculated seconds had passed, he returned his steely gaze to George and continued. "You will have to give me some time to review the matter with senior management."

George responded quickly, "It can't wait. This new project is moving fast. Millions of dollars are being spent on it as we speak. I need an answer before we tender our resignations at noon tomorrow. If not, the file goes to my friend at the *Houston Chronicle*. Also, if I don't place a certain phone call by noon tomorrow, a copy gets mailed to my friend regardless. So, Bert, don't send your stooge Jeffrey Morton off to do anything funny."

After sitting motionless for several long seconds, studying George like a lion calculating his kill, Bert finally responded. "I can't promise anything."

George stood and handed Bert a slip of paper. "This is my cell phone number. Call me on it. Do not call me at my home or at the office. This is the only safe contact number for me."

Bert's mechanical warm smile was gone as he escorted George to the door of his office and wished him a good evening.

Stepping into the empty elevator, a wicked smile crossed George's face as he considered the message he had just delivered. As the elevator began its descent, he muttered confidently, "It's now check, Mr. Thornton, in our little game of chess."

CHAPTER

12

George Batts stepped through the glass-paneled front door to the Buffalo Grill and looked around the large, open expanse of the restaurant. The night before, Bert Thornton had called to request that George meet him there at seven thirty a.m. and bring the file. He soon spotted Thornton seated in a back corner booth, studying him. George stepped quickly yet nervously across the restaurant toward Thornton.

After George was seated, Thornton began immediately. "Here's what we can do. We're putting you and Jennifer on sabbatical status for two years. USOCO will then accept your notice of retirement. You will receive all of your vested retirement benefits at that time. In the meantime, you will be entitled to full medical and other related benefits of a USOCO employee on sabbatical. Jeffrey Morton will deliver a check for a hundred thousand dollars to you by noon tomorrow." He paused. "Of course, this is on the condition that you and Jennifer return whatever files on the Enhanced Maize Project that you have and never speak of it to anyone again."

George stared at Thornton for a moment before responding. "We can deliver on the latter, but unfortunately we do not have the file to give you."

"Who does?"

There was another long pause.

"I'm not at liberty to say."

"George, we know the file was hacked from Kurt Benjamin's computer. So I gather he is the one who has the file."

"I cannot tell you that."

Thornton's thoughtful stare at George was soon transformed into an evil smirk. "Okay. Enough said."

The two men then shook hands and walked across the crowded restaurant to the door. Once outside, Thornton stopped and turned to face George directly. With George's face less than two feet from his, Thornton's steely eyes glared menacingly into the startled eyes in front of him. In a voice that was barely above a whisper, he issued his warning.

"If word of the Enhanced Maize Project ever sees the light of day, you, your lovely bride, and Mr. Benjamin will pay the consequences. Do not underestimate USOCO's ability to reach you, no matter where you are."

With his message delivered, Thornton turned abruptly and walked away.

⊕ ⊕ ⊕

At USOCO headquarters, Kurt had just finished his exit interview with Jeffrey Morton. The meeting had brought back memories of his resignation from the CIA. Once again, he was leaving an organization whose objectives he had come to question. But at least this time, his departure did not involve the loss of a loved one. Nevertheless, memories of the death of his fiancée in the embassy bombing flooded over him. Then, as now, he somehow felt responsible for her death. He should have discouraged her from taking such a dangerous assignment.

Kurt fought back the urge to get up and walk out when Morton began lecturing him about what USOCO could do for his career and the importance of being a member of its team. When that did not work, Morton stood and said angrily, "Give me your key to the building."

Kurt was prepared for this and quickly tossed his key onto Morton's desk.

"You have one hour to remove yourself and your belongings from the building," Morton snarled.

After departing Morton's office, Kurt went back to his office to pick up the last box of his personal articles. As he walked down the hall to the elevator, he stopped at the lab where Jennifer and George Batts conducted their experiments. Stepping into the semidarkness of the lab, he saw empty worktables, bookshelves, and clean desktops.

The eerie silence of the room sent a tingling sensation up the back of his neck. Yet a smug smile came across Kurt's face as he contemplated that Jennifer, George, and the best of the USOCO Laboratory for Alternative Energy Research personnel were now at or on their way to the DPC facility in North Carolina.

⊕ ⊕ ⊕

The phone rang as Kurt was entering his home in West U. The caller ID indicated it was Sarah Carpenter at the Dutch Phosphate Corporation.

"Hello, Sarah. I just walked in the door."

"How are things going there?"

"Well, I officially resigned and was immediately ordered to get off the USOCO premises."

"That should have come as no surprise."

Kurt chuckled. "It didn't."

"Kurt, I have one of DPC's P180s coming tomorrow morning. It should be there by seven thirty, to pick you up and fly you to Greenville."

"Okay, I'll be there."

"Jason has an apartment in his home in Greenville and you can stay there. That way, you won't have to take a chance on some unknown apartment situation or waste time looking. Besides, Jason enjoys your company."

"That's very generous, Sarah. How should I contact Jason?"

"I will e-mail his contact information to you. He told me he would be around for most of tomorrow. What will you do for transportation?"

"I'll rent a car at first. A neighbor of mine will drive my Range Rover to Greenville next week. He's also going to keep an eye on my house for a while. I'll probably sell it. I think I'm done with Houston anyway."

"How about your boat?" asked Sarah.

"I'll probably leave it at the Houston Yacht Club and have a diver clean the bottom once a month so it will be ready to sail, should I get the opportunity. And if the sailing is as good as you say it is, I may eventually hire a captain and sail it to North Carolina."

"As I've said before, you can always sail with us. We have a Tartan 37 and would be happy to have you join us."

"Thanks. You're certainly making this transition easier for me. I really appreciate everything you're doing."

"You're welcome, Kurt. I'm glad to help. Just let me know if I can do anything else."

⊕ ⊕ ⊕

The next day, Kurt entered the private plane terminal at George Bush Intercontinental Airport and strolled to the windows. Dropping his satchel and glancing around, he spotted the P180 with its conspicuous aft-wing turboprops. On the tarmac underneath its starboard wing was a fuel truck, its hose extending up into the wing. As time was of the essence, the Dutch Phosphate Corporation was flying Kurt directly from Houston. Otherwise, he would have to deal with the congested commercial terminals and the inevitable two connecting flights from Houston to Greenville. Upon his arrival in Greenville, he planned to rent a car and make living arrangements for what he expected to be at least the next year, possibly two. He was mentally going back through the planned facility construction timeline when he felt a light tap on his shoulder. He turned to see Kate Burns.

"You look like you need a ride. Can I give you a lift somewhere?" she asked with a come-hither grin.

Without shifting his eyes, Kurt saw that she was wearing her Dutch Phosphate uniform's standard white shirt with pilot's bars on each shoulder. Most importantly, she was wearing her close-fitting black knit slacks.

Kurt grinned and replied, "You bet, Captain. When do we take off?"

"Let's go," said Kate.

Just at that moment, Kurt's eyes picked up a familiar face across the room. It was USOCO's chief of operations, Jeffrey Morton, who had conducted his exit interview and had been persistent in questioning why Kurt would leave now. Morton was standing sideways and talking with two other men Kurt recognized: Jim Hayes, the CEO, and Bert Thornton, the company's general counsel. Kurt's smile faded to a frown.

Right away, Kate noticed the change in his expression. "What is it, Kurt?"

"There are some people behind you who do not need to see me with a Dutch Phosphate Corporation pilot, much less see me boarding one of its airplanes. How can I get out of here unnoticed?"

Without turning, Kate thought for a moment. "There's a hallway straight behind you. I will go there and wait for you. Wait a few seconds and then follow me. This is where the restrooms are located, so if these people see you, they may well assume that's where you are going."

After Kate walked away, Kurt turned to face away from the three individuals and look out the terminal windows. After about ten seconds, he turned to his left and walked idly across the room, with his satchel on his left shoulder shielding his face, and down the hallway as Kate had directed. She grabbed his hand, pulled him into one of the pilot's rooms, and slid the *Occupied* sign into place.

"That was close," said Kurt. "Hopefully those guys out there didn't notice me."

Kate replied, "Wait here. I'll be right back." A few minutes later, she returned with a pair of maintenance coveralls, a baseball cap, and earmuffs. "Put these on. What is your cell number?" Kate quickly added the number Kurt gave her to the list of contacts in her cell phone. "Okay. I'll call you when I'm ready. I'm going out to start the engines and get clearance to taxi to the runway. Once that's done, I'll call and give you instructions about how to get to the airplane." Kate quickly turned, opened the door to the small room, and departed.

As Kurt waited, he noticed the Spartan furnishings available to transient pilots who needed to get the obligatory sleep required by the FAA. There was one single bed, a table, and a chair. Twenty minutes later, Kurt's phone rang.

"We're gassed up and have clearance to go," Kate said. "Take a right out the door and go to the emergency exit at the end of the hall. Once outside, you will see a luggage trolley. That's your chariot to get here. Park it a hundred feet from the plane and get up the stairs as quickly as possible. The ground crew will then push the stairs away and remove the chocks. Got it, Mr. Benjamin?"

"Got it."

Kurt snapped his cell phone shut, grabbed his bag, and headed down the hall wearing his newly acquired coveralls, cap, and earmuffs. As he approached the door, he saw the *Emergency Use Only* warning sign.

As soon as he opened the door, the alarm began. Without hesitation, he sprinted across the tarmac to the luggage trolley, tossed his bag in the back, jumped into the driver's seat, and turned the ignition key. Careening around the corner of the building, he made a beeline for the P180. As Kate promised, two men were standing on each side of the stairway. After parking the trolley, Kurt grabbed his bag, bounded up the steps two at a time and stepped inside the fuselage. Kate quickly closed the door behind him and latched it.

"Come up here and strap yourself in," barked Kate.

The ground crew, as instructed, immediately pushed the stairs away from the plane and removed the chocks from the wheels. One of them then gave the "all clear" signal. Kate pushed the throttles forward and the plane picked up speed as it taxied down the tarmac. Moments later, Kate received the clearance to take off and pushed the throttles forward. Once aloft, she put the plane in a forty-five-degree bank to the east and climbed to cruising altitude of twenty thousand feet.

"Okay, cowboy, who were those bad guys back there?"

"My former employers," responded Kurt.

"So, what's with all the secrecy? They have to expect you will work somewhere. What's the big deal about working for Dutch Phosphate?"

"The project I'm running in North Carolina needs to be kept under wraps for a while. Only a few people at Dutch Phosphate know why I am on this plane. Let's leave it at that."

"No problem, cowboy," she snickered coyly. "Sounds as if we'll need to keep you under cover for a while."

⊕ ⊕ ⊕

The three USOCO executives, like everyone else in the terminal, were startled by the alarm that sounded when Kurt went through the emergency exit. Ten minutes after airport security had shut off the alarm, it was announced over the public address system that it had been accidentally set off by someone opening an emergency door.

As the executives continued their conversation, Jeffrey Morton interjected, "Changing the subject for a moment, on my way in from the parking lot I saw a young guy driving off in a Range Rover that looked like the one owned by our recently departed Kurt Benjamin. But I haven't seen him in the terminal."

"Didn't you conduct his exit interview?" asked Bert Thornton.

"Yes, I did."

"What did he tell you about why he was abandoning his promotion to vice president of Alternative Energy just a couple of weeks after he got it?"

"He was very guarded about what he was planning to do," said Morton. "I really got nothing out of him. But if that was his car, then he's probably gotten on a plane departing from this terminal."

"Is there a way to find out what flight he took?" asked CEO Hayes.

Looking across the terminal with his steely gray eyes, Morton pondered the question. He had been hired by Bert Thornton five years ago as USOCO's chief of operations. Before that, he had served as a lieutenant colonel in the U.S. Army Special Forces. Although on the organization chart he appeared to be under the direction of the company's CEO, most of his assignments came directly from Thornton. He was exactly what Thornton wanted, a yes-man who never questioned why. He simply got the job done, whether by force or finesse.

What had really earned Thornton's trust and confidence was the manner in which Morton had recently dealt with an inventor who had developed a way to route gasoline through the exhaust system of a typical gasoline-fired engine to quadruple its gas mileage. The patent now belonged to USOCO, and the whole concept was buried deep in the bowels of warehoused files. The inventor went from rock-star notoriety to the status of a wealthy recluse overnight. It was an expensive undertaking, but Morton got the job done.

Morton smiled wryly and replied, "I have some connections with airport security personnel who have access to that information. Do you also want me to keep up with our former employee, Mr. Benjamin?"

"Yes," replied Thornton, "keep an eye on him for a while. I suppose he gave his forwarding address in the exit interview."

"Unfortunately, all he would give me was a post office box in Houston, and that's no help. He claimed he didn't yet know exactly where he was going. It's interesting that the other lab employees who resigned recently also left only Houston P.O. boxes as their forwarding addresses. These folks really don't want us to know where they're going."

Thornton thought for a moment, and then reached into his pocket, pulled out a slip of paper, and handed it to Morton. "This is the cell number for that weirdo, George Batts, that I just dealt with. He worked closely with Mr. Benjamin at the lab."

"Ah," said Morton, "with this, I can have my phone company connections track where his calls are originating."

With a smirk, Thornton said, "Yes, and I have a hunch that when you find him, you'll find Benjamin and all the rest of his lab gang who recently disappeared on us. We believe they will all be working on a project similar to ones you have neutralized for us in the past."

Morton nodded. "If they are, how should I proceed?"

"Let's first find out what the project is," replied Thornton. "When you do, we'll have a discussion concerning what to do about it."

"I understand," said Morton.

CHAPTER

13

MAY 27, 2008 — GREENVILLE, NORTH CAROLINA

After picking up his rental car at the Greenville airport, Kurt followed Jason's directions to an old subdivision known as Brook Valley. Winding his way through its narrow streets, he soon arrived at Jason's home. It was a Tudor-style brick, stucco, and wood structure that reminded Kurt of an old English country villa. The property was heavily wooded, with natural areas of low-maintenance pine straw and English ivy. True to the subdivision's name, a brook actually ran along the back side of Jason's property.

After a brief discussion about the trip from Houston, Jason showed Kurt the apartment. Situated on the back left corner of the house, it overlooked a large, well-manicured yard with the brook behind it. There was a bedroom with a queen-sized bed, a living area, and a kitchenette. In a corner beside the window was a small desk.

"This is perfect," Kurt said.

"It's all yours," responded Jason. "There's a back entrance if you want to use it. However, I suggest that you park your vehicle in the extra space in the garage and just come through the house. I'll give you a key, and you can come and go as you please. I may or may not be here. I'm spending a lot of time at our river cottage, Bella Vista, working on my book. Just make yourself at home."

"Thanks," said Kurt. They wandered back through the house to a large room filled wall-to-wall with shelves of books. In one corner by a bay window was a large antique mahogany desk with a computer surrounded by stacks of papers and books.

"It's seven fifteen," Jason said. "Are you hungry?"

"Yes, I am. Because of my flight schedule, I missed lunch. What do you have in mind?"

"Let me call the Beef Barn. It's close by, and it has a great selection of steaks and seafood. I'll call to see if we need a reservation tonight."

While Jason was calling, Kurt began browsing the library. There were books on every imaginable subject, and his attention was caught by a grouping sitting on a table in the corner. Several had torn pieces of legal pad paper sticking out from the tops as bookmarks. What really caught his eye was a book titled *The Works of Nicola Tesla*. He thumbed through it and noted various paragraphs highlighted in yellow. The torn strips of paper that were inserted among the pages had a variety of numbers and some page references to other books.

"Do you have an interest in Tesla?"

Kurt had been so absorbed that he had not heard Jason return to the library. "Sorry, Jason, I didn't mean to be snooping. But yes, I've actually had an occasion recently to do some research on him."

Jason studied Kurt closely. "Why were you interested in Tesla?"

Kurt considered the question thoughtfully. "How much has Sarah told you about our project?"

"Only that it is a high-priority item for the Dutch Phosphate Corporation and involves alternative energy sources. She also told me that it is highly confidential and she could not give me any specifics right now."

"What I learned is that Tesla is the reason we have alternating electrical current, which is used to power almost all of our electrical equipment and appliances today. He was also apparently a peculiar bachelor whose only marriage was to his work. Most of his research remained buried in his notes and papers until recently."

"You are correct, Kurt. And you seem to know a great deal about him. While we don't know what he might have ultimately accomplished, we do know that Tesla's financial backer, J. P. Morgan, suddenly pulled his funding out from under him. It seems to have happened when Tesla began experimenting with what scientists refer to as energy from 'the vacuum.' In theory, it is a virtually unlimited source of energy. Of course, oil was what was emerging as the world's primary energy source at the time and had made J. P. Morgan a very rich man. Unfortunately, Tesla was a man ahead of his time."

During dinner, the two men enjoyed a bottle of wine and a lively discussion on a wide range of topics. Kurt was amazed by the professor's knowledge of geology, the history of the local area, and some of the very same potential energy sources the Dutch Phosphate Alternative Energy Project was about to explore. On the drive back to the house, Kurt was eager to learn all he could from Jason.

"If we're so advanced now," Jason said, "why can't we figure out how stones weighing many tons got to the top of the pyramids? And an even bigger question is what happened to the knowledge of how it was done? It's as if we have to start all over because someone threw the instruction manual away. And here we are in 2008, facing an oil shortage in the United States, when over thirty years ago we went through the same thing with the Arab oil embargo. You would think we would have learned our lesson then and developed alternative fuel sources. Instead, we continue to go all over the world to buy oil at exorbitant prices from countries that are openly hostile to us. We're literally bankrolling our enemies." Jason paused. "Sorry, I didn't mean to rant."

"You are not ranting. Your points are well taken. This is the reason why we must speed up our search for ways to free our country of its dependency on foreign oil."

"Absolutely," Jason responded enthusiastically, "and there are probably countless times throughout history that knowledge—such as that needed to build the pyramids, or of brilliant people such as Tesla—somehow got lost or misplaced. In fact, there may even have been an old energy source near where your project is to take place. It too has been lost over time."

As they were pulling into the driveway, Kurt looked at Jason curiously and asked, "Really? And what was that?"

"Why don't we continue our discussion in the library with a glass of B&B?"

Kurt nodded and replied, "Sounds like a great idea."

After pouring an ounce of the brown liqueur into two large snifters, Jason handed one to Kurt and took a seat across from him at the cluttered library table. "You may have guessed that the names for rivers such as Pamlico and Pungo have Indian origins. Some of our history books would lead us to believe that the Native Americans in this area were uncivilized savages. In truth, their culture and way of life were quite advanced for the time period when the English colony of Bath was established. Instead of being nomads living in wigwams, they often lived in villages and had public buildings, governmental officials, and shamans, who were like priests and medicine men. Across the Pamlico River from Dutch Phosphate, at the mouth of North Creek, there was an Indian village that was known in the early eighteenth century as Secotan. Sarah and I are actually descendants of the tribe's medicine man and shaman who lived there at the time. According to legends, and some concrete evidence passed down in our family through the generations, Secotan had a broad main street with connecting paths leading to houses that had multiple rooms and yards with garden plots of squash, corn, and tobacco. More importantly, they also had a mysterious green liquid they burned in clay lamps and heaters. This shaman, it seems, knew how to extract this liquid from something called pocosin. He also mixed it with other plants and herbs to create a very effective salve that could heal infections."

"Interesting. But why don't we know what this pocosin was?" asked Kurt.

"Kurt, it's just another example of knowledge disappearing. Unfortunately, all we have from the Secotan of that time is a strange, sealed clay urn that has been passed down in our family over generations, and parts of a diary kept by one of our ancestors, Tobias Knight. He was secretary to the council that governed the Bath colony during the time that the inhabitants of Secotan suddenly disappeared. From reading his diary, it appears to me that he knew where the villagers went, but told no one. His diary also refers to a list of sacred ingredients that are inside the urn, but does not reveal what they are or what they make. According to the diary, a descendant daughter who possesses the urn will someday know when to open it. Interestingly, the urn has always been passed to the only or oldest daughter of each generation."

"Who has it now?" asked Kurt.

"It is Sarah's. Her mother was my sister. She and her husband were killed in an automobile accident when Sarah was a child. I kept the urn in a safe-deposit box until giving it to her on her eighteenth birthday."

Jason pointed to a safe in the corner of the library. "It's stored there." He walked to the safe and spun the combination. With a low click, the door opened. Stepping back across the room, he gently set an old cedar box down on the only open spot on the library table. Both men studied it for a moment in silence.

"From reading the diary of Tobias Knight," Jason continued, "I learned that he and Selu, the daughter of the tribe's shaman, had a daughter together, Wahnenauhi. Tobias was an interesting fellow living a double life. He would spend time with Selu and his daughter in Secotan, and then return to Bath where he was a prominent citizen. His diary states that the urn in this old box will someday be opened by a descendant daughter of Selu."

"Does the diary say which descendant daughter that will be?" asked Kurt.

"It does not. It only says that she will come to know it is time. Who knows when that will be?"

At the Aurora Fossil Museum near Dutch Phosphate Corporation's mine, Jason was preparing to give another lecture on marine geology. He had taught a class in the subject at East Carolina University for more than twenty years. Even now, as professor emeritus, he continued to teach it. Although marine geology was the only class he still taught, it remained one of the most popular on campus. It consisted of six lectures, each conducted at the Aurora Fossil Museum about thirty miles east of Greenville. Each of the six three-hour sessions included a lecture and a guided discussion of a wide variety of the fossil remains that were on display, as well as an actual dig in the mine by the students.

Visitors started their tour of the museum in the media room where Jason conducted his lectures. In a twenty-minute video, visitors would see the rich history of the previous fifteen million years. It was with this video that Jason liked to start the first lecture. On the walls of the theater were murals depicting various strata of soils, from the surface down to about 150 feet. Each had a reference to when the strata of deposits were left.

Once the video was over, Jason began his lecture. "Where you sit was one hundred and fifty feet below sea level fifteen million years ago. The coastline of North Carolina was near Raleigh. New York and Philadelphia were also probably a hundred feet under water. Then our climate changed. Temperatures dropped, the ice formations at the poles increased, and the oceans retreated.

"Many scientists think that the opposite of this process is in progress today. They believe our climate is warming and causing the melting of our polar ice. If so, we can expect our sea levels to rise again. Where we sit may be under water as soon as twenty-five hundred years from now. This same cycle has occurred, we believe, four times since this planet came into existence four and a half billion years ago.

"With each cycle, there was another layer of eroded sediment from upstream runoffs deposited on the remains of sea creatures on the ocean floors. A variety of sea life was covered, including whales, porpoises, seals, and sea cows, to mention only a few. As the upland streams deposited more sediment, the layers of eroded materials thickened and compressed the organic materials underneath. Over time, as much as a hundred and fifty feet of sediment was deposited on top of this rich material we now know as phosphoric rock. This is the stuff that the Dutch Phosphate Corporation uses to make fertilizer.

"The world's crop-growing regions were depleted of their naturally occurring phosphorus years ago. In your reading materials, there is a reference to a president who first called our attention to phosphate. Does anyone know who that was?"

Several hands went up. "Okay, Jane, you're on the front row. What did you find?"

"It was Franklin Delano Roosevelt."

"That is correct. And what did he tell us about phosphate?"

Jane thumbed through sheets of paper on her desk for a few seconds. Finding what she was looking for, she responded, "It was in a speech he gave in 1938, and I have an excerpt of it here. He said, 'The phosphorus content of our land, following generations of cultivation, has greatly diminished. It needs replenishing. I cannot over-emphasize the importance of phosphorus not only to agriculture and soil conservation, but also to the physical health and economic security of the people of the nation.'"

"Excellent, Jane, thank you. In another fifteen minutes or so, the bus will arrive to take us to the fertilizer processing plant at the mine. There, we will be able to see firsthand how these phosphates that were created over millions of years are processed to make fertilizers. This

144

process hasn't changed dramatically since Franklin Delano Roosevelt gave his speech. However, there are some people working very hard to find ways to improve the process so that we can achieve much more powerful fertilizers for more efficient crop production. We are long overdue for a major breakthrough."

⊕ ⊕ ⊕

It was just past six a.m. when Kurt turned his Ford Fiesta rental car onto Highway 33, heading east out of Greenville. He figured it would take him about forty minutes to reach the Dutch Phosphate facility near Aurora. With his mind focused on the enormous task ahead for the research project, he wondered how many of the construction requirements he had delegated to Mahoney had been accomplished. Knowing he would be responsible for delivering results for DPC's massive investment gave him an adrenaline rush for the first time in months.

The Fiesta was a far cry from his Range Rover, but it would do for another week. Jason had warned him that by eight thirty, traffic in Greenville would be a mess, even with only half the usual twenty-five thousand students on the road. From his own research, he had learned that Greenville was exploding from a Southern college town into a mecca for high-tech and pharmaceutical companies in search of an inexpensive, skilled labor force. The medical school, with its new heart center, was attracting many well-paid doctors and nurses, and a variety of technical staff. There was also a large influx of retiring Northern baby boomers in search of the perfect setting for the golden years of their lives. The AARP had recently touted the Greenville area for its health care, wide variety of entertainment, moderate temperatures, and close proximity to the Atlantic coast. As a result, Greenville had become a magnet for cold-weary retirees. The once sleepy college town was no more.

Twenty minutes after leaving Greenville, Kurt passed through the little town of Chocowinity. From Jason's short history presentation the evening before, Kurt had learned that this old community derived its name from the Indian term for "fish from many waters." Five miles farther east, Kurt was in the flat lowlands of coastal North Carolina. For miles, he saw thick pine forests interspersed with enormous fields of soybeans, corn, and cotton. Jason had explained that twenty years earlier, these fields would have had few crops other than tobacco. The local farmers no longer had government subsidies to support the tobacco crops that had been their mainstay for many years. With their crutch taken away, they were forced to make the transition from their dependence on tobacco to other forms of agriculture in order to survive. His thoughts drifted to a comparison that could be made to the dependence of the United States on foreign oil. It soon would also be forced to give up its dependency crutch, find alternative energy sources, and stand on its own.

When Kurt arrived at the Aurora facility, Mahoney greeted him like a long-lost brother.

"You have to see what we've done," Mahoney said proudly. "Let's go for a ride." Kurt and Mahoney jumped in Mahoney's old Jeep and headed out the back gate of the mine.

Mahoney turned onto the previously potholed dirt road Kurt had experienced less than a month earlier. It was now paved, with three lanes for travel. A mile down the road, Mahoney turned onto a graveled causeway.

"Kurt, this is the route we took last month into the swamp to Alligator Island. Do you recognize it?" he asked proudly.

"No, this is a far cry from what I remember. Good work."

What had been a sloppy pathway through the swamp was now a well-grounded gravel road thirty feet wide, sitting five feet above the swamp. Moments later, they arrived at the entrance gate to the island. As they were waved though by the gate's security guard, Kurt was astounded to see several large metal buildings under construction. The buildings were in front of sixty acres of cleared land, with furrowed rows sprouting seedlings of corn and sugarcane. In the northwest corner, two long greenhouses were nearing completion in front of one of the large metal prefabricated buildings. Mahoney drove around behind the greenhouses to the entrance of one building. Stepping around construction workers and equipment, Kurt saw five people in the far corner of the building, wearing white lab coats and staring at computer screens. In the opposite corner, he saw four more lab-coated personnel peering into microscopes. Spotting Jennifer Batts looking at one of the microscopes, Kurt left Mahoney and walked across the open, concrete-floored space in her direction.

As Kurt approached, Jennifer looked up at the sound of his footsteps on the unfinished concrete echoing across the room. A broad smile appeared on her face, and she jumped up to give Kurt a warm hug, chiding, "It's about time you got here."

Kurt smiled. "Good to be back, Jennifer. What's cooking?"

"We've come a long way in a short time," she said, beaming. "And I can't tell you how nice it is to be gone from those dishonest jerks at USOCO. It finally feels like I'm part of a serious research program."

"That's great to hear. How is George faring with his projects?"

With a bit of a frown, Jennifer replied, "Funny you should ask. While I think he's relieved to be away from the USOCO environment, he has been rather aloof and quiet about his work."

For Kurt, it was great to see his old friend and lab employee smiling. From the gleam in Jennifer's eyes, he could tell she was truly excited about the project. This was a far cry from the dejected Jennifer he had known toward the end of their tenure at USOCO.

CHAPTER

14

With a sense of pride and confidence, the emir of Abu Dhabi, Sheik Fayyad Fadil, sat at the head of the large conference room table and studied his personally selected board of directors. He knew these men well as a group of bright, talented, and well-trained professionals. Although the emir had made each of them rich, he worried at times that, even so, he might not have their total loyalty.

In his confident, casual tenor voice, the emir called to order the meeting of the board of directors of the Abu Dhabi Sovereign Wealth Fund. The board consisted of Hussein Mubarek, the president of Abu Dhabi Oil Company; Hasad Domani, the minister of finance of the Abu Dhabi Sovereign Wealth Fund; the sheik's personal director of operations, Abdul Ahad; the director of special security operations for the emirate of Abu Dhabi, Haydar Ghazi; and the emir's eldest son, Massud Quasim bin Fayyad.

"Let's start with our finances. Hasad, what is the state of the investments of the Sovereign Wealth Fund of Abu Dhabi?"

"Yes," replied Hasad. "Last month, we were fortunate to receive another record contribution from the Abu Dhabi Oil Company of slightly over three billion dollars. As you know, over the last ten years, we have funded the construction of many schools, hospitals, parks, and universities for the benefit of our citizens. We have also invested heavily in the development of the emirate's industries. We will soon have desalinization capacity to irrigate enough land to be totally food self-sufficient. However, to make that happen, we still need a reliable source of large amounts of fertilizer. To do that, over the next few months, we hope to invest most of the contributions to the fund into the purchase of a controlling interest in a major worldwide fertilizer producer. We are already funneling our revenues into discreet offshore investment companies for this purpose. We must be very careful. All of us remember the uproar in the United States Congress over the contract our brothers in Dubai had to manage the New York Harbor. You would have thought Osama Bin Laden himself was going to take control of the port.

"The brightest spot for us is the large investment we secretly have already made in Western financial institutions. The recent meltdown of some of the West's most powerful and prestigious banks made some of them desperate for huge amounts of cash to keep them afloat. We had it to invest, and we did. We now have become a major shareholder in two of the largest financial institutions in the United States."

When Hasad was finished, the emir turned to Hussein. "What is the status of our oil production?"

"Your Eminence, we continue to produce at last year's levels, but Washington is putting a lot of pressure on us to increase production. While we are in the process of constructing more pumping facilities and adding two more supertanker terminals, they probably will not be operational for another year. The good news is that even though the price of oil has dropped to one hundred and fifteen dollars per barrel, down twenty-eight dollars per barrel from its high this summer of one hundred and forty-three dollars per barrel, we are still doing very well. With our net production costs at twenty-seven dollars a barrel, our net profit each month is just shy of five billion dollars. As you know, we send two billion per month to the minister of finance for the operation of the country and the continued investment in our growth and infrastructure, and the remaining three billion goes to the Abu Dhabi Sovereign Wealth Fund. We anticipate that at current oil price levels, our net profits will continue to be strong for many years to come."

"Thank you, Hussein. Let's turn to an investment that we have discussed at previous meetings of this board. How do we expand our investments into the production of fertilizer? To do this, I believe we must purchase a controlling interest in a major fertilizer-producing company. We have a stranglehold on the rest of the world with its desperate need for our oil. But when you look at basic survival, one thing that every living being on this planet must have is food. Whether it's the corn people eat or the corn that is fed to the cows that are used to make hamburgers, the world has to have fertilizer to grow the corn, or whatever the crop may be."

"I am afraid someone has already beaten us to it," interjected Massud, the emir's son. "But I also have information that may be even more troubling."

"And what information is that?" asked the emir, as he and his board members stared at Massud.

"Father, you remember my friend Naji al Rashid from Sharjah."

"Yes, I do," replied the sheik. "He was your roommate at the University of Sharjah, and you are still good friends."

"That is correct. We are friends, and I spent this past weekend with him in Dubai. As you know, the consumption of alcohol is prohibited in Sharjah. This is unfortunate for Naji because of his taste for good cabernet sauvignon. Dubai does not have that prohibition, so, on this weekend, Naji was making up for lost time. At dinner Saturday night, the wine loosened his tongue considerably."

Massud cleared his throat and continued. "It is also helpful to know that Naji is the older of Kareem's two sons. He would never admit this, but he feels overshadowed by his younger brother, Omar. And he is feeling quite threatened by the return of this prodigal son, who will likely take control of the family's businesses. Omar was educated in the United States and earned an MBA with honors from the Wharton School. He then rose quickly through the ranks of junior executives at USOCO before being summoned home earlier this year.

"In any event, I was teasing Naji at dinner about what all the members of OPEC know about Sharjah's oil production. Specifically, that it has consistently pumped far in excess of its permitted oil quota for years. I said to him, 'Naji, Sharjah has only two-point-four percent of the known oil reserves of the United Arab Emirates. However, rumor has it that you pumped twice your OPEC allotment last year. At that pace, your true oil reserves will be exhausted in four years.'

"To this, he replied defensively, 'So what's your point? All the members of OPEC, including Abu Dhabi, started drastically inflating their stated oil reserves in the late 1980s to get higher quotas from the organization. To protect our own quotas, Sharjah had to inflate its known reserves as well. So there may be other oil-producing countries besides Sharjah that may soon have a problem.'

"I continued to needle him, saying, 'You also appear to be spending every *dirham* you make on luxurious parks and museums. So when your wells run dry in four years, what will you do for revenue to fund such projects?'

"Naji took another sip of wine before he answered. 'Yes, that is true, but we have also built many large high-rise office buildings. Those skyscrapers now have some of the world's biggest and most powerful banks occupying them. We're also spending huge amounts of money on our own industries, the products of which are now being exported to all points of the globe.'

"I replied, 'Sure, but by then you will have competition from other exporting industrial nations for a finite amount of demand. Right now, you and all the rest of the world's oil exporters have the luxury of virtually no competition and an ever-increasing demand for oil.'

"After another long sip of wine, Naji placed his glass on the table and, fiddling with it, said, 'We do have an alternate plan to replace these revenues. As a trusted good friend, I will tell you, but you must promise to tell no one else. We have invested heavily in a project that Omar believes has great promise for the production of an economically viable alternative to oil.'

"I said, 'Let me guess. It's an ethanol product.'

"He said, 'That is part of it. But other ideas that appear more interesting than that are being considered. From experiments so far, the people running this project hope to develop the capability of producing a barrel of ethanol at a cost of forty dollars. While the price of a barrel of oil has slid back to one hundred and fifteen dollars, from its previous high this year of over one hundred and forty-one dollars per barrel, we could still make a tidy profit. A few years ago, with the oil price at forty dollars a barrel or less, there was no incentive to invest in this technology, but now there clearly is and we are investing heavily in it.'

"I replied, 'Abu Dhabi can produce oil for thirty dollars per barrel. Why should we be concerned?'

"My friend continued, 'It is simple. The world's demand for oil now exceeds its ability to supply it. And as you should know, oil production in the United States is down to six million barrels per day, from its peak in 1970 of twelve million barrels per day. Saudi Arabia may not admit it, but it is maxed out at twelve million barrels per day. The North Sea oil will dry up by 2020. And with the rapid industrial development going on in China, India, Vietnam, and the rest of the developing world, demand for oil will grow exponentially in the next ten years.'

"I asked, 'Where do you get this information?'

"He said, 'Go read Matt Simmons's book *Twilight in the Desert: The Coming Saudi Oil Shock and the World Economy.*'

"I asked, 'Who is Matt Simmons, and what is this book?'

"Naji replied, 'I asked my brother Omar the same question. At his urging, I read this book, and it opened my eyes to what lies ahead for us. Simmons is an American who has spent his career in the oil industry and knows it backward and forward. His book sets forth a compelling argument that Saudi Arabia and all the other oil-producing countries combined are producing the most oil now that they ever will. You need to read his book, Massud.'

"'Maybe I will, Naji. But tell me, where is this project taking place? I haven't heard of any cornfields sprouting in the deserts of Sharjah yet.'

"'The project is situated in a very remote location which is far different from a desert environment. It's actually an island in the middle of a swamp.'

"I said, 'You're kidding me,' and filled his wineglass again. I did not want his loose tongue to stop. 'Where is that?'

"'Have you ever heard of a company called the Dutch Phosphate Corporation?'

"Of course, I know it is the largest producer of fertilizer in the world, but I did not want him to know that I knew, so I answered, 'No.'

"I clearly had him on the defensive, because his jealousy of his brother had now been replaced by an apparent need to defend his family. He proceeded to explain how Omar had connections at a very high level at the Dutch Phosphate Corporation and was able to purchase for his family a large number of shares of the company's preferred stock. He also bragged that with this stock came the right to convert it to shares of common stock. This would guarantee them three seats on the board of directors and would put them in striking distance of purchasing enough additional common stock to have a majority of the outstanding voting shares of the company. He even boasted that if they could not take control with a friendly takeover, they would make it a hostile one.

"Seeing that he appeared very proud about all this, I refilled his wineglass yet again and asked, 'But, Naji, all this depends on a giant breakthrough being made with this project. Sounds like a pipe dream to me.'

"Getting defensive, he shot back, 'Maybe you think so now, but we think there is a way to make a biofuel that could be mixed at a fifty-fifty ratio with gasoline or diesel. And what if we perfect a biofuel that will require no gasoline or diesel at all?'"

After a pause, Massud looked directly at the emir and continued. "Father, I have read Mr. Simmons's book. I am afraid Naji may be correct. Sharjah may well be ahead of us in its quest for control of not only a major fertilizer-producing company, but in a source of alternative energy as well."

The emir had been watching his chosen board members during Massud's account of his weekend with Naji. "Any comments?" he asked, looking first to Hussein Mubarek, the president of Abu Dhabi Oil, and then to Haydar Ghazi, the director of special security operations for the emirate.

Hussein nodded thoughtfully and responded, "Dare I speak the obvious when I say this could become a big problem for us? We now control the United Arab Emirates through our oil wealth. We are also making large investments in the world's banking institutions and industries of all kinds. If oil demand grows as is forecasted over the next ten years, we could become one of the most powerful countries on earth, and we will have attained this power without spending billions on a military to control or conquer anyone. We will simply garner control with our cash investments."

Hasad Domani, the minister of finance of the Abu Dhabi Sovereign Wealth Fund, broke in, "We cannot allow anyone to derail our current path. We must remember that we are Allah's chosen people. That is why he has given us our oil and the opportunities that it provides for us."

Hussein interjected, "But we must be very careful. If the demise of this project were ever traced back to us, the world's condemnation would be devastating. Wars have been precipitated by far less."

The emir frowned, nodded thoughtfully, and turned to look at Haydar Ghazi. In a low but commanding voice, the emir said, "You will not fail us, will you, Haydar?"

Haydar nodded and replied, "I will not fail. Allah will be with me."

Two hours later, Haydar was airborne in one of the Abu Dhabi Oil Company's Gulfstream Citations. As he mentally went through his options, the emir's final words—"You will not fail us, will you, Haydar?"—kept echoing in his mind.

As Kurt turned his Range Rover into the entrance to the Bayview Ferry Terminal, the ferry *Governor Hyde* was idling slowly toward the dock. The night before, he had dinner with Jason at Bella Vista. To avoid having to drive back to Greenville and then to Alligator Island the next day, Jason had offered Kurt Bella Vista's guest room for the night. At five the next morning, Kurt's internal alarm went off, and his mind immediately began organizing the day's agenda.

The ferry terminal was only a fifteen-minute drive from Jason's cottage. After a short wait, Kurt followed a line of cars and trucks on board and parked as directed by a ferry crewman on the starboard side of the vessel. As scheduled, the *Governor Hyde* pulled away from the terminal at six a.m. Glancing at his watch, Kurt estimated it would take forty minutes to reach the Aurora Ferry Terminal located on the south side of the river. The only passengers on board at this time of day were the regulars headed for the first shift at the Dutch Phosphate Corporation's mine and processing facility. Most of the plant personnel had parked their vehicles in the terminal parking lot and walked onto the ferry. Braced against a strong northerly wind, they climbed the stairs to the ferry cabin. Although not fancy, the cabin was warm, had two TV sets, and a choice of seating—either booths along the walls or one of the rows of seats in the middle of the room. Settling in for the trip across the river, they quietly fell into their usual routines. Some sat in the booths playing cards, some on benches read or engaged in small talk of the day, and some reclined and slept for the duration of the three-mile trip.

Kurt followed the passengers up the steps to the cabin and found a seat on one of the benches. Opening his laptop computer, he began outlining his agenda for the day. A few minutes later, Walter Brinn, whom Kurt recognized as one of the mine's security personnel, settled into a spot on the bench in front of Kurt. After exchanging pleasantries, Kurt returned his gaze to his laptop. Seconds later, Kurt heard the rustle of a paper being opened, and looked up to see Walter reading the local newspaper, the *Down East*. Shortly after, another mine employee took a seat beside Walter, and Kurt heard him say, "Morning, Walter. How's it going?"

"I don't know, Josh. Would you look at this?"

Curious, Kurt looked up to see Walter pointing to the headline, "USOCO Announces Record $20 Billion in Fourth Quarter Profits."

"Those greedy bastards!" growled Walter. "I paid three twenty-five a gallon for gasoline for my truck today. Something ain't right."

Josh looked at the article for a moment and replied, "Yep, the price of gas is eating up our paychecks. After putting gas in my car, there's not much left over to buy a beer or go fishing with, not to mention trying to support a family. Something ain't right. Those towel-headed Arab sheiks and fat-cat oil company bosses are gettin' rich, we're gettin' poor, and our congressmen ain't doin' nothin' about it."

"Hell, Josh, they're gettin' rich, too. Otherwise, this wouldn't be happenin'." Walter studied the article and said, "This reminds me of something I was reading just the other day, about a guy in California who came up with a modification to his car's engine that gave him six times his usual gas mileage. He routed the gas through the exhaust system to vaporize it. Burning the vapor instead of gasoline increased the efficiency of the engine so that there were almost no pollutants produced. The only problem was that it required removal of the car's catalytic converter, which is against the law. When his congressman introduced a bill to make an exception for this type of product, the oil industry mounted a huge lobbying effort to defeat it."

"What happened?" asked Josh.

"Good question. Same question the guy writing the article asked. It seems this inventor suddenly went quiet. He just disappeared. Eventually, the bill his congressman introduced died a slow death in a legislative committee. The guy writing the article tried for a year to find this inventor. He finally got lucky and tracked him down. This guy now lives on a fancy ranch outside of Dallas, with iron-tight security. Seems mystery man has an unlisted phone number and refuses to talk anymore about his invention."

"Well, it doesn't take a rocket scientist to figure that one out," replied Josh. "That man got bought, and it was by somebody with a lot of money, like USOCO, who had a reason to bury that invention."

Pondering this conversation, Kurt sat with his eyes focused on his computer screen. His thoughts returned to the Enhanced Maize Project file he had broken into while at USOCO. The words Jennifer Batts had used the evening he shared the file with her in Houston suddenly jumped into his head. "Those slimy bastards" was still resonating in his mind thirty minutes later as he drove his Range Rover off the ferry and headed for Alligator Island.

By eight thirty, Kurt was standing over a large table in the conference room of the administration building, reviewing a spreadsheet and a large map prepared by Mahoney setting out the progress of construction. Thanks to Mahoney's aggressive work, Kurt could see that Alligator Island had been transformed from an overgrown thicket of wax myrtle and scrub oaks only a few months before into a beehive of productive activity. The construction of eight greenhouses covering four acres on the north end of the island was complete. Multiple mutated varieties of corn and sugarcane were growing at the island's south end. Most of the crops were the direct result of experiments formerly conducted by the Battses and other USOCO lab employees who were now working on the project. Being applied to the variety of plants was a rotating sequence of experimental nutrients from fertilizer products provided by the nearby mine.

On the western portion of the island, the map depicted a greenhouse that, by itself, covered an acre. It was devoted totally to algae experiments. In the greenhouse, several varieties of algae were also being nourished with DPC fertilizer products. On a ten-acre expanse behind the greenhouse were rows of plastic tubes growing algae. The idea was to take advantage of every bit of ground on which Mother Nature could provide heat and sun this time of year. When winter arrived, all the projects would have to be moved into the greenhouses.

Still under construction was a small refinery situated near the east entrance to the island. It was specially designed so that it could refine the variety of potential biofuels being produced on Alligator Island.

Just to the east of the main entrance to the island, a blue metal building had been erected that housed George Batts's experiments. A large water tower stood fifty yards behind it, near the west end of the island.

It was nine a.m. when Kurt heard footsteps in the hallway outside the conference room. Looking up, he saw Mahoney standing in the doorway.

"Ready to take a look around the island?" Mahoney asked.

"Let's go," replied Kurt. He stood and followed Mahoney out to his Jeep. As they rode through the island, Kurt surveyed the progress of construction that was now almost complete. When they reached the building where George was conducting his experiments, Mahoney pulled the vehicle to a stop facing its front. Kurt and Mahoney studied an elaborate system of pipes running from the building to the water tower behind it, and Kurt said, "Mahoney, I have to tell you that I am truly impressed. You sure know how to get things done."

"Thanks, Kurt. But this Batts guy is about to drive me crazy. He seems absolutely possessed."

"Why do you say that?"

"Well, just look at all that pipe work connecting from his lab to the water tower. Looks like somebody's intestines. And he wants his part of this project completed yesterday and ahead of the others. My welders and pipe fitters think the man is mad."

Kurt considered Mahoney's comment and wondered why George was beginning to give him a sense of unease.

"We shall see," Kurt finally replied in a tone of feigned indifference.

An hour later, Mahoney dropped Kurt off at the administration building, and Kurt returned to his office. Sitting at his desk, his mind began assessing what he and Mahoney had seen during their tour of the island. His concern now more than ever was security. When construction began, Kurt had allowed Mahoney to provide security on Alligator Island with Dutch Phosphate Corporation plant security people looking for extra hours. While their level of security was adequate for the phosphate plant, Kurt knew he would need a security team far better trained and equipped than the one that guarded the plant. With an investment of this magnitude in such a short time, he knew rumors would flourish. He also knew firsthand from his experience at the CIA, and most recently at USOCO, that certain entities with a vested interest could be motivated to sabotage such a project.

Through Nighthawk, a discreet paramilitary agency with which he had worked at the CIA, he had assembled the team needed for the task. They all had prior combat training with the Army Special Forces, Navy SEALs, or Green Berets. A former Navy SEAL named Tom Gabriel was hired as chief of security. He was a six-foot-six-inch, 210-pound African American and former star fullback at the Naval Academy. His active-duty years had been spent on a variety of classified missions in hot spots around the world. Kurt had actually worked with him indirectly during his Saudi Arabian assignment with the CIA.

Kurt had no doubt that Tom Gabriel—or Gabe, as he preferred to be called—was the man for the job. He was all business and understood the potential that this project could be a target. At their first planning session, Gabe set the tone exactly where Kurt thought it needed to be.

"Kurt, we're going to attract some potential intruders, probably locals who are just curious. We're also going to attract some weirdoes whose intentions could be hard to predict. We can handle these types of folks with firm diplomacy, or intimidation if necessary. But if this project accomplishes what you expect it to, some very dangerous people will probably try to get on this island and destroy everything here and those who are running it. There may well come a time when precautions need to be taken to protect you and your inner circle of people who are in charge of this project. I need to know who they are."

"Primarily George and Jennifer Batts," replied Kurt. "They report directly to me. Although they have their own research teams, they also help supervise teams of other areas of research on the island. Each team focuses on a different potential source of alternative energy."

"As long as you have complete trust in the Battses, my security team can work with that arrangement. My next concern is who has access to the island. I suggest that no one have access until they have passed my clearance standards and are approved by one of the three of you." He paused. "Again, that assumes you have complete trust in the Battses."

"Absolutely," Kurt responded. "They're like family. I trust them completely."

"Very well."

"What else do we need to ensure the security of the projects?" asked Kurt.

"We should probably install electronic sensors to detect any efforts to penetrate through the swamp."

Kurt laughed. "We have the biggest damned alligators on the planet hungrily waiting in the swamps surrounding this place. If anyone dared try to penetrate that hellhole out there, God help them. But if you think we need sensors, get them."

CHAPTER
15

Kurt stood alone in the watchtower overlooking Alligator Island. Although he was pleased by the progress of the project, he had a nagging sense of concern. For some strange reason, his gut kept telling him the project was vulnerable. It was this concern that had led him to hire Gabe and to insist on the rigorous security measures that were now in place. Viewing the island from the tower, Kurt could see the ten-foot electrically charged fence with a top layer of coiled concertina wire that encircled the island. The watchtower with tinted windows hovered a hundred feet above ground, providing a panoramic view of the swamp and causeway, the only possible approaches to the island. Motion sensors were mounted around the perimeter of the island, along with hidden video cameras focused on the swamp. Speed bumps began on the causeway three hundred feet from the front entrance gate. The workforce had grown to forty-six people, who all arrived by bus. The only vehicles permitted on the island were Kurt's Range Rover, the Battses' Volvo, Gabriel's Suburban, and the bus that brought in the projects' research personnel. Otherwise, no vehicles, including material delivery vehicles, were permitted through the front gate until they were thoroughly searched by Gabriel's security force. In keeping with their mission to guard the island, Kurt and Gabriel selected uniforms of light-gray fatigues for daytime and black body suits for night. Each guard carried a Walther .38 on his hip and an M4 automatic rifle over his shoulder.

Kurt's thoughts were interrupted when he remembered that Sarah was scheduled to land at the DPC airstrip at ten o'clock. Glancing at his watch, he saw that it was 9:40. Knowing the drive to the airstrip took fifteen minutes, he quickly descended the tower's staircase and walked to his Range Rover.

Arriving at the airstrip, Kurt crossed the runway with the three-mile-wide expanse of the Pamlico River in front of him. He felt the warm, brisk southwesterly breeze on the back of his neck. With consistent whitecaps sweeping across the river, Kurt estimated the wind speed at twelve to fifteen knots, perfect conditions to be on the river sailing. It had been months since he had been sailing, and he was hungry to be back on the water.

The sound of turboprops approaching brought him back to reality. Turning to the east, he saw the P180 approaching with flaps down and landing gear descending. Moments later, two brief puffs of smoke appeared as the plane's wheels touched down on the short runway. With the props in reverse, the plane soon slowed, made an about-face, and returned to within one hundred feet of where Kurt was standing.

Soon after the cabin door opened, Sarah bounded down the stairs and gave Kurt an unexpected big hug. "It's so good to see you, Kurt. I certainly didn't expect the head of this project to find time to pick me up."

Kurt smiled. "I wanted to bring you up-to-date on progress before you got to the project. I think you're in for a pleasant surprise."

In truth, Kurt had actually felt a twinge of excitement at the prospect of being around Sarah again. He picked up her two bags energetically and placed them in the back of his Range Rover. On the way through DPC's phosphate production facility, Kurt outlined the construction activity of the past two months.

"Mahoney has been a huge help. Thanks to him, we were able to find labor and materials on short notice. He really does know how to get things done. Of course, knowing the chief operating officer was watching was probably a great motivator."

"I don't think so, Kurt," replied Sarah. "I never applied pressure after our initial meeting with him. I suspect you are the one who did something to motivate him."

"Maybe. Anyway, we now have twenty acres of sugarcane and thirty acres of corn under cultivation. Jennifer Batts's team is working with various strains of algae. All of these are being grown as mutations under a rotating system of nutrient formulas. Getting the fertilizer materials from right here at the plant has saved us enormous amounts of time and money."

"What is this algae project? Who would ever think that slimy stuff would be good for anything? Most people think of it as a nuisance."

"Good question. The algae project is a continuation of work Jennifer started at USOCO. Most of it is being grown outside to take advantage of the intensity of the summer sun while we have it. We will have to move it and all the other growth experiments inside in a couple of months. The large greenhouses you'll see under construction should be ready by then. When Jennifer was at USOCO, she conducted some very successful experiments with algae that she's trying to reconstruct here."

"Why are we putting so much emphasis on algae?" Sarah asked. "I thought the focus of most biofuel work was on things like corn and sugarcane."

Thinking he had adequately answered her original question, Kurt found it odd that Sarah was persisting.

Sensing that Kurt might be annoyed by her question, Sarah quickly added, "I'm not second-guessing, just curious."

"I understand," he said. "I guess I should tell you something, and I would ask that you not share it with anyone else."

"Agreed," she said, curious.

"When I was at USOCO, I happened to stumble upon a locked computer file. Some of Jennifer and George's algae work had been given the misleading name of the Enhanced Maize Project and locked away by USOCO. What I found in that file is what caused me to leave the company, and is probably why I'm here today."

"Really! What on earth did you find in that file?"

"I learned that a research department of USOCO independent of our Laboratory for Alternative Energy Research had conducted very successful trials using their work."

"What happened to it?"

"Nothing. The project and its trials were buried in the bowels of computer files USOCO thought were securely locked. But fortunately, I was able to get in."

Sarah stared at Kurt, smiled, and shook her head. "I don't recall seeing 'expert computer hacker' on your résumé."

Kurt raised his eyebrows and responded with a smile of his own. "But I wouldn't be here if I hadn't broken the code and gotten access to what was done with their work. Until I did, Jennifer and George believed USOCO when they were told that field trials of their work had proven to be economically unfeasible."

"So is the project economically feasible?"

"The USOCO trials suggested that it could be, but Jennifer is very frustrated right now. While she remains convinced that algae holds promise, she hasn't found the right algae, the right fertilizer to grow it, or an efficient way to convert it through the refinery to biofuel. But I want her to tell you about this project personally. George is distracted now with a project of his own. You'll have an opportunity to hear all about her project when we meet with Jennifer later today."

As Kurt drove the Range Rover onto the Alligator Island causeway, he said, "Last but not least, we need to visit George's special project. His experiments may be years away from producing anything, but they could truly be blockbusters. He's working on some ideas first envisioned by the inventor Nicola Tesla."

"You spoke of Tesla at the board of directors meeting and suggested that he may have been close to some other very important discoveries. But I wonder if he wasn't way ahead of his time."

"That may be so. Unfortunately, he lost a lot of his work and notes in a curious fire. After that, he struggled to continue until finally his financial support dried up, and much of his later work had to be abandoned. Your Uncle Jason knows a lot about his work. I must tell you, Jason is an amazing guy and I enjoy his company. Thanks for arranging for me to have a place to stay at his house in Greenville."

Sarah smiled. "I am so glad you like Jason. He has been like a father to me."

Kurt slowed the Range Rover as it reached the exaggerated speed bumps at the approach to the island's front gate. He lowered his window and brought the car to a stop at the gate, and a guard stepped forward.

"Good morning, Mr. Benjamin," the guard said cheerfully. "How goes it?"

"Very well, Jeff. My passenger is Sarah Carpenter. She has clearance, but you should check the file of permitted personnel and follow the protocol as you would for everyone entering, of course."

Several minutes later, the guard returned. "Wow, Mr. Benjamin, you didn't tell me she was the chief operating officer of Dutch Phosphate. Welcome to Alligator Island, Ms. Carpenter."

Leaning toward Kurt, she looked directly at the guard and responded, "Thanks, Jeff. It's good to be here. You're going to see a lot of me from now on."

"I hope so, ma'am," he replied. "Have a nice day." As the car drove onto the island, Jeff muttered to himself, "No problem recognizing a drop-dead gorgeous woman like that."

Kurt parked in a small lot beside a plain prefabricated metal building in the center of the island. "This is our administrative building. It's not fancy, but it will suffice."

Once inside, Kurt led Sarah down a long, narrow hall to his office, located at the end and across from a conference room. Next to Kurt's office was a guest office. Stepping into it, Kurt flipped on the light. "I hope this will meet your needs while you're here. The computer is secure and should take care of your requirements. However, if you need anything else, just let me know. I'm right next door."

A few minutes later, Jennifer and George Batts arrived at the conference room, and Kurt made the introductions. "Sarah, these are my very good friends Jennifer and George Batts."

"I'm pleased to finally meet both of you," Sarah said effusively, and the three shook hands. "Kurt has said many nice things about you. And George, I'm looking forward to one of your famous pot roasts. We are fortunate to have you involved in this project."

"We are delighted to be a part of it," replied Jennifer warmly. "We also think a lot of our boss, and jumped at the chance to join him in something as challenging and exciting as this."

Kurt could not help but notice that George's only response to Sarah's obvious compliment was a distant look and a casual nod.

For the next half hour, Jennifer and Kurt gave Sarah an overview of the projects being conducted by the various research teams on the island. George said little. Afterward, the team leaders for corn, sugarcane, and sawgrass arrived at one-hour intervals and gave detailed presentations as to what was happening in their phase of the project. When the other project presentations were completed, Kurt asked George to talk about his.

"My work may take the longest to produce results," George said softly, looking directly at Sarah and removing his wire-rimmed glasses with his left hand. "But when it does, the potential will be mind-boggling. I am convinced that Tesla was really onto something with his energy from 'the vacuum,' or zero-point energy, as it is often called today. My project will turn our world's production of energy on its head."

After George had spent fifteen minutes giving mind-numbing explanations of his theories, Kurt saw Jennifer place her right hand on George's left, as if to signal to him "enough." Kurt had been studying George closely throughout his presentation, and noticed him frown with a hint of anger at Jennifer's admonition.

Kurt cleared his throat uncomfortably and said, "Okay, Jennifer, let's hear about what you're doing with algae."

Jennifer began with a description of her work at USOCO on the Enhanced Maize Project. Kurt was pleased to see her passionate enthusiasm as she presented her previous work, her theories, her work on the island to date, and her frustration over not yet achieving a clear breakthrough.

"There is a key to unlocking algae's potential, but we haven't found it," she sighed. "We have tried every process known to modern science, with no clear progress."

Kurt listened intently as Sarah dove into Jennifer's project protocols and procedures; she was showing far more interest than she had with any of the other projects presented. Like a relentless detective examining a suspect, Sarah took Jennifer back through her work on the Enhanced Maize Project at USOCO. She had Jennifer reexamine in excruciating detail what she had done with algae there. Sarah finally came to the end of her questioning, sat back in her chair, and pronounced, "If the upper management at USOCO found Jennifer's work such a threat to have buried it in their locked computer files, something big has to be there."

As soon as the presentations were done, George quickly excused himself, saying he had an experiment in progress at his lab that he had to get back to. Kurt and Jennifer asked Sarah if she would like a tour of the island's projects, which she immediately accepted. Along the way, she couldn't help but notice the rigid security in place. When

Sarah and Kurt were back in his office, she closed the door. Seated in front of him, she looked at him sternly.

"Kurt, I am absolutely impressed with what has been accomplished here in three short months. My board of directors and our friends in Sharjah will be impressed when I report back to them. But I have a question. Why is there so much security? This place looks like Fort Knox."

"I understand, but what we may discover here could prove to be far more valuable than all the gold stored there. We suspect that certain people might go to great lengths to make this project fail. My job is to make it succeed. Please trust me on this for now."

"Kurt, I trust your judgment completely." After a brief pause, Sarah said, "Enough talk about business. I spoke with Jason earlier. He should be on his way over in the boat to pick us up."

Kurt looked at her inquisitively.

Sarah returned the look with a smile. "It's Friday. You've obviously been working very hard. Jason and I want you to spend the weekend with us at Bella Vista. You look like you need to go sailing."

Kurt studied Sarah for a few seconds as he considered her proposal. The prospect of getting away from the tension of the past few weeks for some sailing and good company seemed very enticing. "I'd love to Sarah, but I don't have any extra clothes with me."

Sarah glanced at his slim, muscular physique. "You're what, six foot two and about a hundred and eighty pounds?"

"That's close."

"Well, that's a little bigger than Jason, but I'm sure we can find something that will fit you. Besides, all you'll need is a pair of shorts and a T-shirt. We have guests who sometimes forget things like razors and toothbrushes, so we keep a supply of stuff like that."

A big smile broke out on Kurt's face. "I accept."

"Great," said Sarah. "Jason will be arriving at the DPC dock at four thirty to pick us up. What time is it?"

Kurt glanced at his watch. "It's four o'clock."

"Well then, let's not keep him waiting."

Twenty minutes later, Kurt and Sarah entered the parking lot of the DPC tugboat terminal to find Jason standing on the dock waiting for them.

As they walked across the lot toward him, he smiled and called out, "Well, well, Sarah. You did tear him away from that place. I didn't think you could do it." He gave Kurt a hearty handshake and said, "Glad you can join us."

"Thanks, Jason. I'm looking forward to this."

The three of them stepped down into Jason's Grady White. Moments later, they cleared the red and green entrance buoys of Lee Creek, and Jason pushed the throttles forward, bringing the boat onto a plane heading northeasterly on top of the Pamlico River chop.

Turning to Sarah and Kurt, Jason asked, "What do you say we dock the Grady at the cottage and drive over to Jordan Creek for a sail up to Belhaven for dinner?"

Kurt had spent the last month immersed in twelve-hour days of supervising the construction on the island, hiring personnel, and dealing with a multitude of start-up issues. He was ready for a break. "I'm game. Sarah, is that where the River Rat Yacht Club you told me about is?"

"It is. Maybe you'll have a chance to meet some of them this evening. They really are a fun-loving bunch of people."

Jason added, "It's an easy one-hour sail up the Pungo from there. We'll have dinner at the Back Bay Café, a restaurant owned by some friends of ours. Then we'll have a night sail back down the river."

Kurt took a deep breath and sighed quietly. He could feel his muscles relax as he soaked up the warm afternoon sun. "I've heard about that restaurant. Does it have a wine shop and bookstore as part of it?"

"Yes, it does," Jason replied.

"My good friends and co-workers at the project, Jennifer and George Batts, rave about the place. They actually invited me to meet them there for dinner tonight, but I declined. Maybe we'll see them."

⊕ ⊕ ⊕

Haydar Ghazi watched the entrance to Dutch Phosphate Corporation's Lee Creek tugboat terminal with binoculars as Captain Jeremy Beacham navigated his Fountain 30 to a discreet half-mile distance off the terminal's entrance. With twin 250-horsepower Mercurys on back, Haydar was confident they could outrun or run down any boat on the river. As Jason's Grady White cleared the entrance to the Lee Creek terminal and headed northeasterly across the river, the Fountain took a heading due east down the middle river at a safe distance. From there, Haydar watched the progress of the Grady White closely. He doubted that at this distance the occupants of the Grady White took any notice of them, but if they did, they would just assume the Fountain was out for a late afternoon spin on the Pamlico.

Haydar had been annoyed that none of the other local charter captains would rent to him. It was as if they thought he was some sort of terrorist. However, Haydar overheard a conversation on the docks that Jeremy Beacham, a commercial fisherman and part-time marine contractor, was a month behind on payments for his Fountain cigarette boat and his Toyota Tundra. When Haydar offered him two thousand dollars up front and another thousand when the two days were over, he readily agreed.

⊕ ⊕ ⊕

As Jason throttled down and headed into the dock in front of Bella Vista, the Fountain slowed to an idle in the middle of the river. From a mile away, Haydar focused his binoculars on the three occupants of the Grady White as they stepped onto the dock and headed toward the shore. There was no question in his mind that the young male was the one he was seeking.

Lowering the binoculars, Haydar turned to Jeremy and asked, "Who owns that property?"

Jeremy fidgeted slightly and cleared his throat before answering. "I'm not sure. I think he might be a retired professor of some sort."

Sensing Jeremy's hesitancy, Haydar spoke sternly. "You know who owns that property and who is on that dock. I am paying you well. If you want the rest of the fee we agreed on, I would suggest your memory improve."

After another long pause, Jeremy cleared his throat again and responded, "I think his name is Jason. His niece is supposedly a big executive-type with the Dutch Phosphate Corporation. I think that's her on the dock with him now. They also own a fancy sailboat over in Jordan Creek."

"Where is Jordan Creek?" Haydar asked.

"You go down the Pamlico, round Wade's Point, and then up the Pungo River for a few miles."

"Show me Jordan Creek on this nautical chart," demanded Haydar, as he spread it open.

"We're here," Jeremy said, pointing toward Pamlico River Buoy Number 3. "Indian Island is to the south behind us. We round Wade's Point to our east and turn north up to Pungo River. At Pungo River Buoy Number Three, you take a course of three hundred and twenty degrees that will take you directly into the channel at the mouth of Jordan Creek. Once in, you take a dogleg left into the middle of the creek. Their boat is docked at the first marina to the east. There are a lot of hardy sailors in there. The two marinas are part of a group known as the River Rat Yacht Club. Some of them are very good seamen. In fact, last winter during a bad nor'easter, a few of them saved some local commercial fishermen who got in trouble out in Pamlico Sound. Rumor has it that they also know how to party."

"Let's go over and take a look."

The Fountain was soon up on a plane heading down the Pamlico at fifty-five miles per hour. Rounding Wade's Point and Buoy Number 2, Jeremy headed the Fountain north up the Pungo River. Reaching Pungo Buoy Number 3, he proceeded on a heading of 320 degrees toward Jordan Creek. At that moment, a sail appeared at the mouth of the creek a half mile in front of them.

"Throttle down and head back out toward the middle of the river," commanded Haydar.

Once in the middle of the Pungo, the Fountain progressed at a steady ten knots a mile off the mouth of the creek, unnoticed by the occupants of the sailboat.

Haydar handed his binoculars to Jeremy and asked, "Who is that?"

After studying the sailboat for a few minutes, Jeremy lowered the binoculars and said, "Well, I'll be damned."

"You know that boat?" asked Haydar.

"Sure do. That's Jason, the fella you were so interested in over there in the Pamlico."

"Where are they going?"

"Who knows? My guess is probably up to Belhaven for dinner. The wind is just right from the southwest, and they should have a full moon rising around nine o'clock tonight for their trip back down the river."

"Okay. Let's pull back and keep a good distance behind them."

Haydar picked up his binoculars to focus on the sailboat as it cleared the entrance to Jordan Creek and headed into the deeper waters of the Pungo River. The woman Jeremy had identified as Jason's niece was at the helm.

⊕ ⊕ ⊕

On board the sailboat, Sarah barked the sailor's course change warning, "Prepare to jibe."

Kurt and Jason scrambled to deck positions for the change of course command that would soon follow. Once in position with the port sheets in hand, they responded, "Ready jibe."

Hearing that her crew was ready, Sarah gave the course change command, "Helms over," and began turning the wheel to port. At the same time, Kurt released the port jib sheet while Jason eased the main over toward the starboard side of the boat. A few seconds later, the southerly breeze picked up the boom and pushed it to starboard with a solid thud. Kurt and Jason quickly adjusted the starboard sheets for their new heading to the north. With its sails now full, the *Phoenix* began slicing its way through the waves of the Pungo River toward Belhaven. Kurt settled back contentedly against the starboard stern railing. This was his favorite spot on a sailboat, because it was where he could fully appreciate the craft's performance rhythm.

A few minutes later, he was jolted to reality by a sensation he always dreaded. It was a feeling he had first learned to detect during his time with the CIA—he was being watched. Looking out over the Pungo in all directions, the only boat he saw was a small motorboat a hundred yards behind them. He tried to rationalize that it was just someone out for a late afternoon spin on the Pungo.

An hour later, they slid past the opening in the breakwater that protected Belhaven's harbor. After Kurt and Jason had the main and jib sails furled, Sarah steered along the town's waterfront of upscale condos and marinas. The low throb of the sailboat's thirty-horsepower

Yanmar diesel could barely be heard as it pushed them quietly through the harbor at three knots. With Sarah at the helm, Jason and Kurt were standing on the deck at the bow watching the waterfront go by.

"Looks like some serious development money has been spent here," Kurt commented.

"Yes, it has," replied Jason. "Twenty years ago, this waterfront was full of commercial fishing vessels and seafood processing plants."

"What happened?" asked Kurt.

"Everyone has a different theory. The commercial fishermen blame cheap imports, nitrogen releases from upstream farming and development, and even the fresh water dumped into the Pamlico by the Dutch Phosphate Corporation. The developers and farmers claim the fishing industry itself caused the problems by years of over-fishing. And then there are the environmentalists who blame all the above for contributing to the problem. Regardless, this once sleepy fishing village has lost its old mystique and character. It will never be the same."

Kurt, Jason, and Sarah were too preoccupied with the waterfront's scenery to notice the Fountain powerboat that had crept into the Belhaven harbor behind them. All the while, Haydar's steely eyes followed their every movement through his binoculars.

As the sailboat reached the town's public docks, Sarah slowed the engine and turned the bow away from the dock and out into the harbor. Pushing the gearshift into reverse, she slowly backed the *Phoenix* into a berth at the Belhaven Municipal Dock. Once Kurt and Jason had the dock lines secure, she choked off the diesel engine.

"Nicely done, Sarah. You know how to handle a boat," remarked Kurt, as they walked up the dock toward the shore.

"Thanks. I had a good teacher," she responded with a bright smile, punching Jason's left arm.

After they crossed Water Street, Jason led the way along an old sidewalk on the west side of Pamlico Street before stopping abruptly in front of a large sign that read RIDDICK AND WINDLEY HARDWARE.

"When I was a child," said Jason, "this store was run by two old fellows that, as you might expect, had the names of Riddick and Windley. Back then they really had an old-time hardware store. It was about a tenth of the size of the current store. While they still sell nuts and bolts, nowadays you can purchase anything from a chainsaw to a cell phone, or even a bottle of expensive wine."

As they reached the intersection of Pamlico and Main Streets, the location of the town's only stoplight, Jason stopped and pointed to a patched hole in the concrete. "You won't believe this, Kurt, but there used to be a pipe right here where artesian water flowed naturally from a depth of about twenty feet below. It flowed every day, all day, without the need for electric pumps. It was the town's public water fountain."

"What happened to it?" asked Kurt.

"Well, there were a lot of those wells in this part of the county in the 1960s, before the Dutch Phosphate Corporation began mining. For them to get their cranes down to the level of the phosphoric rock, the mine had to pump millions of gallons of fresh water a day from the subsurface soils. That lowered the water table for miles around. As a result, all the free-flowing artesian wells around here dried up." Jason paused before making the sarcastic comment, "The things we do for progress."

"Yes, there often seems to be a downside to much of what we do in the name of progress," mused Kurt.

In the next block, on the left Kurt saw a sign for Wine and Words hung from a post in front of an old single-story home. Sarah explained that it had been renovated to accommodate the current owner's wine shop and bookstore and the Back Bay Café. Kurt followed Jason and Sarah through the front door into a room crammed with racks holding a wide assortment of wines from all over the world.

Sarah turned to Kurt. "While I really like the food here, what I like most is that we can taste and select our dinner wine and then buy it at close to retail price for the table with only a modest cork fee, unlike most restaurants that routinely double the retail price of their wines."

"I like that," Kurt mused, as he studied a South African pinot noir.

Jason had wandered back to an area where there was a tasting table with several bottles of wine and a few wineglasses on top. Behind it was a middle-aged man with brown hair graying at the temples, studying the small print on the back of a wine bottle through half-moon reading glasses perched on the end of his nose.

Jason cleared his throat before asking a question of the man seated behind the table. "Is the food any good here?"

The man paused in his reading for a moment, instantly recognizing the voice of one of his frequent and favorite patrons. Without looking up, he answered casually, "No. Still stinks, just like it does every time you come in here, Jason."

Both men laughed heartily and exchanged a good handshake.

"Good to see you, and welcome back," said James, from behind the table.

At that moment, Sarah and Kurt appeared from around one of the wine racks.

"And there is Sarah," said James. "What a pleasant surprise to see both of you!"

"Hello, James," said Sarah. "And this is our friend Kurt Benjamin."

James said, "Hello, Kurt," as he reached over to shake Kurt's hand.

"Nice to meet you," replied Kurt.

Seeing Sarah holding a bottle of wine, James asked, "What do you have there?"

"It's a Joseph Phelps Insignia."

"Oh, do you ever know how to pick them! That's one of our best labels. It's a full-bodied, hearty wine with an aftertaste of dark chocolate. It will go great with the flank steak Yvonne is preparing tonight."

Jason said, "Sure, let's try it."

The threesome made their way into the restaurant's small dining area. As soon as Kurt stepped into the room, he spotted Jennifer and George Batts seated at a small table in the corner next to an open area filled with racks of books.

Seeing Kurt, Jennifer smiled and said loudly, "Well, look who just walked in."

Kurt and Sarah chuckled and walked over to their table, with Jason right behind. Jennifer and George stood to greet the new arrivals.

Looking at Sarah, Jennifer grinned and said, "Kurt, I see why you turned us down for tonight. You obviously had a much better offer."

Kurt laughed and turned to Jason. "These are my good friends I mentioned a while ago, Jennifer and George Batts."

Shaking hands with both, Jason immediately suggested that they join them for dinner.

"We just arrived ourselves," said Jennifer. "That would be great."

"So you guys know each other," said James, as he cradled the Joseph Phelps in his right arm.

"Yes," said Jason. "Any chance we could all dine together at that round table over there?"

"Not a problem. Let's go."

When they were seated, Jason looked up at James. "How about two more glasses so George and Jennifer can share the Insignia with us?"

"Absolutely. I'll be right back."

A few minutes later, James returned with two more glasses and poured a splash into a full-bodied wineglass on the table in front of Sarah. After rolling the velvety red wine around to let it aerate, she tilted the glass under her nose and drew in its fragrance. "Wow, this is superb. I think you guys will like this one."

After they all enjoyed their first sips of the Phelps Insignia, Jennifer said, "So, let me guess. You guys sailed up here tonight?"

"We did, and it was great," responded Kurt. "Jason and Sarah are good sailors and have a fantastic old boat."

"Hmm, there's usually an interesting history behind a boat like that," ventured George.

"You are right, and there is," said Jason. "She's an old Tartan 37. Her former owner signed her over to his insurance company for salvage after she was beaten up by Hurricane Ophelia a few years ago. I paid the insurance company salvage value and had her towed to a boatyard in Washington. Our friend Bob Stephens did the work. The guy is a genius when it comes to restoring a fine yacht. He is the epitome of what you might expect of a master craftsman: shoulder-length hair, mustache, and a fierce intolerance for workmanship that doesn't meet his standards of quality. As such, some of the guys in the boatyard thought he was a grouchy asshole. But everyone who knows him respects the quality of his work. Bob's workmen replaced all the chain plates and standing rigging. When Bob finished his repairs, Sarah thought it only fitting that we rename the boat *Phoenix*, after the legendary Greek bird that rose from its own ashes."

Sherry Anne, the restaurant's only waitress, stepped through the door from the kitchen into the dining area and immediately caught Jason's eye. With a broad grin, she strode briskly over to their table.

"Good evening, Jason. And do looka here," she said, smiling effusively at Sarah. "Sarah Selu, where have you been? I haven't seen you in over, what, two years?"

"She's left us for the bright lights of New York City," Jason quipped.

Sherry Anne looked at Sarah sternly. "Girl, my cousin went up there when she was your age thinking she would find a great job and a rich husband. After three years and a divorce, she was happy to hightail it back down here. I hope you have better luck than she did."

Sarah smiled warmly at her. "So far so good on the job part, Sherry Anne, but I haven't had time to do much in the dating scene yet."

Somehow, Kurt felt pleased to hear this piece of information.

"Well, while you've been away, we have kept your Uncle Jason and his sailing buddies very well fed." Without missing a beat, Sherry Anne looked at Kurt. "Who is this handsome fellow you have here? Something Sarah Selu should tell me about?"

Sarah laughed. "Sherry Anne, this is my colleague Kurt Benjamin. He's working with me at DPC. He'll be at our Aurora facility for a while. You'll have to look after him now, too."

"I will," Sherry Anne replied enthusiastically. "All he has to do is show up here. Jason is in here all the time. Kurt can just come along with him."

"I will," said Kurt, smiling comfortably.

Pulling her notepad from her pocket, Sherry Anne asked the question all servers ask. "So, have you folks decided on what you would like?"

"I know what I want," said Sarah. "How about you guys?" She glanced at the others.

Everyone nodded or said, "I'm ready."

Sarah proceeded to order the flank steak, and Kurt and Jason both ordered the pork tenderloin. Jennifer selected the salmon, and George chose the filet mignon.

"Those are great choices. They'll go well with that Joseph Phelps Insignia. Let me go get them started." Sherry Anne turned, walked briskly across the small dining room, and disappeared through the kitchen door.

Kurt looked curiously at Sarah and thought, *Sherry Anne called her Sarah Selu. Isn't Selu the name of her Indian ancestor Jason mentioned that night in Greenville?*

Jennifer, who had been enjoying her wine, proposed a toast. "Here's to unlocking our secret source of energy."

Their wineglasses clinked in unison with the words, "Hear, hear!"

As the evening progressed, Jason had an idea.

"Sarah, why don't we have everyone over tomorrow?" he suggested. "I could cook some ribs for lunch, and you guys could chill for a nice day at Bella Vista. You all need to get away from your work for awhile."

"We'll be there," replied Jennifer instantly.

"Excellent. We'll expect you guys at Bella Vista tomorrow for lunch and an afternoon of fun."

⊕ ⊕ ⊕

The beginning of the sail back down the Pungo was picture-perfect. As Sarah steered the *Phoenix* through the entrance to the Belhaven breakwater, a huge orange moon was rising over the pine forest on the east bank. With its sails full, the sleek yacht sliced ahead through the moon-sparkled waters.

Moments later, the Fountain 30 that had been lurking in the darkness behind the breakwater fell stealthily in behind them at a distance of 150 yards. Seconds later, Kurt began looking around the river, as the old haunting feeling that he was being watched crept over him again. Seeing no running lights from another vessel, he settled back and tried to return his thoughts to the *Phoenix*, its crew, and the beauty of the river under a full moon.

An hour later, they were back at the turn point for their approach to the channel entrance of Jordan Creek. At the helm, Sarah spotted sails heading downwind directly toward them.

"Jason, who's that coming out of the creek?" she asked.

Jason peered through binoculars at the approaching vessel. "Oh hell, that's our friends on the *Jester*. They knew about when we would be coming back. Those guys have had a good dinner and a few drinks, and now they're ready for their favorite sport, a good old-fashioned water balloon fight."

"All right, we're on!" yelled Sarah gleefully.

"I'll take the helm," said Jason, as he stepped behind the wheel. "You go get the ammo."

Sarah scampered down the companionway into the cabin below. Moments later, she reappeared with a bucket of water balloons and a large rubber slingshot.

"I haven't had a water balloon fight since college," said Kurt.

"Well, you're about to have one," said Sarah excitedly. "Help me load up the slingshot before they're on top of us."

Kurt quickly attached the slingshot between the starboard and port stays and pulled the sling back for Sarah to load their first shot. As their first balloon was released, a loud splat came from the deck two feet in front of Kurt. In rapid fire they released another eight balloons, and just as many came hailing down on top of them.

Watching the two boats come closer, Kurt noticed Jason tightening the sails, heading the *Phoenix* closer on the wind. Seconds later, the port side of the *Phoenix* was approaching the *Jester* at a distance of thirty feet. Kurt, Sarah, and Jason hurled as many balloons as possible during the few seconds the boats were passing. After hearty laughter and good-natured insults to their opponents, the crew on both boats quickly loaded up a fresh batch of balloons to reengage the battle.

After coming about, Jason maneuvered the *Phoenix* to approach the *Jester* within less than ten feet. On this pass, Sarah had a surprise for the *Jester*'s crew. She had pulled from the port lazarette the water hose and pump used to wash down the deck with sea water. As the balloon barrage began, Sarah pulled the trigger on the nozzle and proceeded to drench their opponents with a strong stream of cold water being pumped up from the Pungo. Shrieks of laughter and profanity issued from both boats as they sailed off in opposite directions.

⊕ ⊕ ⊕

On the Fountain, through his binoculars Haydar watched the spectacle unfolding.

"What are they doing?" he asked, and passed the binoculars to Jeremy.

As Jeremy studied the moonlit scene in front of him, he chuckled and returned the binoculars to Haydar.

"It's like I told you earlier, they're good sailors and know how to have a good time."

CHAPTER

16

The day began misty, with cool rain showers drifting across the Pamlico River from the southwest. As the morning progressed, the clouds began to dissipate, allowing bursts of sunlight to spike through and sparkle on the waters of the Pamlico. By the time the Battses arrived at noon, it was a picture-perfect day. The clouds were gone, and a warm southwesterly breeze flowed across the river. After greeting their guests, Sarah invited Jennifer to join her for some kayaking on the river. George found his way to a hammock strung between an old holly tree on one end and a large sassafras on the other. Moments later, he drifted off to a sound sleep. The smell of charcoal from the grill behind the cottage soon permeated the air.

Jennifer paddled her kayak clumsily beside Sarah's along the north shore of the Pamlico. Under Sarah's instruction, she soon caught on to the paddling rhythm needed to balance and control the course of a kayak. When they were a half mile upriver from the cottage, Sarah stopped paddling and drifted to a stop. Jennifer followed suit and coasted up beside her.

Sarah turned to Jennifer and said hesitantly, "May I ask you something about Kurt?"

"Sure," said Jennifer, suspecting she knew the question, having noticed the chemistry between the two.

"Kurt is an attractive, smart, and very nice man. So why isn't he married? He doesn't even seem to have a girlfriend."

Jennifer thought about the question and nodded, wondering how much she should reveal. *Why not tell it all?* she quickly concluded. "Sarah, Kurt was an only child, raised by a single mother after his alcoholic father drank himself to death. His mother died during his senior year of high school. With his brains, wits, and intuition, Kurt has made himself who he is today. Several years ago, he and his fiancée were CIA operatives assigned to State Department positions in one of the more volatile countries of the Middle East. A month before the wedding, she was killed in a terrorist attack on the embassy to which they were assigned. In his mind, he still thinks he could have saved her had he been present. To this day he has trouble putting that part of his life behind him. Then he took the job at the USOCO Department of Alternative Energy. That was probably in an effort to find some meaning again in his life, and you know where that ended."

As Sarah thought about what Jennifer had said, a tear trickled down her left cheek. "Oh my," she finally said softly, wiping away the tear. "No wonder he avoids involvement, with what he's been through."

"But, Sarah, he's obviously worth waiting for, and I sense you are attracted to him, and he is to you. Just let him go at his own pace."

An hour later, George was awakened by the voices of Jennifer and Sarah as they came up the walkway from the river below. Still groggy from his nap, he followed the women into the cottage, where Jason and Kurt were in the final stages of preparations for lunch.

"I'm going out to get the ribs. They should be ready to go," said Jason. "Great," replied Sarah. "Jennifer and I will set the table."

During lunch, Sarah tried to keep the conversation light, which was usually no problem for her, especially with this lively group. But she noticed Kurt seemed reserved, as if preoccupied with something.

Jennifer noticed it, too. As George was finishing his second helping of ribs, Jennifer, never known to be anything but direct, looked at Kurt and said, "Okay, handsome. What's on your mind? You always had seconds at our house, and you've only nibbled at these fantastic ribs. And you've said hardly a word."

Kurt sighed and put down the rib he had been playing with. "Jason," he said, "do you remember the conversation we had last spring after dinner at the Beef Barn in Greenville?"

"Um, not really," responded Jason, as he munched on a rib. "What were we talking about?"

"We ended up in your study and you told me about an ancestor of yours, an Indian woman whose name I think you said was Selu. She lived in a village called Secotan. There was also an ancestor of yours named Tobias Knight who was one of the governing officials of the Bath colony. He and Selu had a daughter. And you talked about a legend passed down in your family about the Indians that inhabited the banks of the Pamlico River many years ago."

"Okay. Yes, I do remember that. It's the legend of how their Great Spirit revealed to our ancestor, a Secotan shaman, how to make a salve from something they called swamp green. It supposedly had magical healing abilities for open wounds."

"Yes, Jason, but didn't you mention this legend also referring to some sort of oil?"

Jason glanced at Sarah before responding. "Yes, of course. The legend also speaks of a substance called pocosin, being converted by the shaman's magic into oil that the villagers of Secotan burned in pottery lamps."

"Yes," said Sarah. "It is part of the legend. But more importantly, it's supported by excerpts of the diary of Tobias Knight that we have. His writings also reveal that the Pamouik Indians of that era were far more advanced than what is commonly reported in today's textbooks."

"Absolutely," replied Jason.

Knowing how Kurt's mind worked with questions like this, Jennifer asked, "So, Kurt, what's going on in that restless brain of yours?"

"I'm not sure. I think it was Sherry Anne using the name Sarah Selu when she spoke to Sarah last night. Jason, do you remember showing me an urn that has never been opened, which has been passed down through the generations and now belongs to Sarah?"

"Yes, of course I remember that," said Jason.

"Well then," continued Kurt, "if they burned this mysterious pocosin in their lamps, do you suppose the urn could contain something about what it was and how they made it?"

George, who had been listening intently, finally interrupted. "Well, that begs an obvious question, folks. Why has no one ever opened this urn?"

After a long silence, Jason addressed his question. "Our research shows that Tobias Knight was the secretary to the council that governed the Bath colony in the early 1700s. To add some intrigue to this, from what we can piece together from his diary, Tobias was the father of Selu's only daughter. While most of the diary disappeared, the part we have refers to a secret formula used by Hatteras, the shaman and father of Selu, to produce something called pocosin."

Jason paused, looking across the table at Sarah.

Sarah nodded, signaling her approval for him to continue.

"The diary also states that the oil was made by Hatteras. His name came from an Indian tribe that once lived on one of North Carolina's barrier islands. The diary gets really interesting when it instructs that the urn is to be passed to the oldest or only daughter of each descendant generation of Selu and Tobias. According to the diary, someday one of these descendant daughters will come to know that it is time to open the urn."

"Where did you say the Secotan village was located?" asked Kurt.

"The diary is vague about that. But from what Sarah and I have read of Indian legends, there was a village on the north side of the Pamouik, now known as the Pamlico, near a creek the Indians called Big Bear. Do you want to know our personal theory about its location?"

"Absolutely. Let's hear it," said Kurt.

"One day when Sarah was a child, she and I walked from here up the southern shore of the Pamlico River to a beautiful sandy beach near North Creek. Along the way, we came upon a high, sandy knoll that overlooked the Pamlico to the south and North Creek to the west. Behind this high knoll to the north is a small creek now known as Chambers Creek. This fits with what legends say about the location of the village of Secotan. It is said to have been on a high knoll overlooking the Pamouik to the south, Big Bear to the west, and Little Bear to the north. What clinches it for me is that as Sarah and I walked along this sandy knoll above the beach, she stopped, leaned down, and picked up a very hard piece of clay that was blackened on one side. It had a decorative pattern of corncob rows imprinted on the other. The true test of ancient pottery is to try to break it with your fingers. If you can't, it's the real thing. And guess what? This piece would not break. We then started looking around the sand below us and found all kinds of

182

similar pieces of old clay pottery and small tubes that were probably clay pipes. Almost as interesting was the abundance of oyster shells scattered throughout this high ground."

Jennifer's eyes met Kurt's as she slowly leaned forward, and then she looked sternly at Sarah. "Dear child," Jennifer said softly, "isn't it obvious to you? Your name is Sarah Selu. You are a descendant daughter of Selu and Tobias. We know that Selu's father was the medicine man and shaman who made something called swamp green that was burned as oil by the Secotan. The village was just across the Pamlico River from where we're conducting our research."

Sarah studied Jennifer in silence, considering all that she had just heard.

Jennifer continued, "Sarah, don't you remember our recent discussion about my frustrations and years of work with algae with no clear results? For years I have believed that I was close to unlocking its secrets as a biofuel. My intuition is yelling at me that you are the descendant daughter of Selu and Tobias who is to open the urn. It may have the secret which I and many others have searched for in vain."

Everyone at the table turned and stared intently at Sarah.

Jason finally broke the silence. "Sarah, all of this leads to you. But you alone must decide if you are the descendant daughter who is to open the urn." He studied those present, but wisely refrained from saying what he had suspected for some time now. Sarah was the descendant daughter referred to in the diary of Tobias.

Sarah sat thoughtfully for several minutes before speaking. "For some reason, the question of whether I am the descendant daughter who is to open the urn has haunted me for the past few weeks. I have had a recurring dream for years where I see a fleeting glimpse of an Indian woman next to a distant fire. This strange dream came again several weeks ago, but was much more vivid. I found myself in an Indian village watching a clay urn being molded by this young Indian woman. The dream somehow carried me here to Bella Vista. The cottage was dark except for an oil lamp on the mantle above the fireplace that burned with a strange purplish glow. After pondering this dream for awhile, I finally called Jason from New York last week and asked him to pull out what remains of the diary of Tobias Knight and read it to me. And then, the other day when Jennifer was describing her work with algae, I felt a strange tingling sensation from my head to my toes."

"Where is this urn?" asked George.

"It's here," replied Jason. "After reading the diary to Sarah last week, I started giving the legend a lot more thought. Before I drove down yesterday, I felt that maybe I should bring the urn with me."

Everyone sat silently for a few moments before Sarah spoke.

"How should I open the urn? The last thing I want to do is damage whatever may be in it."

Jason nodded. "I have studied the urn and given that some consideration. There appears to be a clay seal that was used to join the top to the urn. The best way to open it is probably to gently saw the seal in two. You could then lift the top off the urn."

"Very well, Jason," Sarah sighed cautiously. "Please bring the urn."

Jason nodded again and left the table. Deep in thought, no one spoke until he returned.

While placing the cedar box containing the urn gently on the table in front of them, Jason said, "I suggest we take it out back to the shop to open it. I have a small hacksaw that should be delicate enough to make the cut around the clay seal."

Without speaking, they filed out the back door and across the yard to a large, gray, cinder-block building that doubled as a boat garage and shop. Once inside, Jason flipped a switch, flooding the room with light from overhead fluorescent bulbs. Sarah hesitantly walked across the neat and well-organized shop to a workbench on the opposite wall in front of them and gently placed the cedar box on it.

"So, how fragile is the document that may be inside the urn?" asked Kurt.

"From what is said in the diary of Tobias Knight, my guess is that it will be a small piece of parchment," replied Jason. "If so, I am concerned that it could be very brittle. We'll need to be very gentle with it."

"If it's been sealed without air and light all these years, you may be surprised at its condition," George commented.

"I hope you're right, but we must be very, very careful," replied Sarah.

Kurt watched intently as Jason opened a drawer under the workbench, removed a small hacksaw, and handed it to Sarah. The hinges on the latch of the old cedar box squeaked softly as Sarah slowly opened the lid. After staring at its contents for a few seconds, she reached in and gently removed the light brown clay urn from its ancient resting place.

After studying the urn closely, Sarah exhaled tensely. "You were right, Jason. The clay in the area where the lid meets the urn is a different color from the rest of it. It must have been applied after the urn was made. Could you hold the urn while I work on this area with the saw? God, I am so nervous."

With Jason holding it, Sarah took a deep breath and gingerly began making slow, gentle cuts into the clay at the neck of the urn. Once she had completed a small cut around its circumference, she took the urn from Jason and, holding it in her right hand, applied slow, counterclockwise pressure on the lid with her left hand. It did not budge. Sarah exhaled a deep sigh and placed the urn back on the workbench.

Kurt, George, and Jennifer looked on and didn't speak. They knew something truly special was unfolding in front of them.

"Sarah, let's make another pass at it. Make the cut a little deeper this time," suggested Jason.

Sarah nodded nervously.

With Kurt holding the urn, Sarah again began sawing gently around the neck over the cut she had just made. After completing another circle around the urn, Sarah picked it up carefully in her left hand and, with the lid in her right, once more applied counterclockwise pressure. Gradually increasing the pressure, she almost jumped as she felt the lid move and heard a sudden popping sound. Sarah felt her hands tremble and her heart race as the remainder of the clay seal cracked apart. Pulling upward, she lifted the lid slowly off the urn, revealing what was left of a decayed pouch with the tip of a tubular beige roll protruding slightly from it.

"That is indeed a parchment," said Jason. He reached under the workbench for a small towel and spread it on top of the surface. He then went to a tackle box and removed four one-ounce sinker weights.

"Sarah, if you can open the scroll on this towel, I'll place the sinkers at its four corners to keep it open. The less it's handled, the better."

With a now steady right hand, Sarah gently extended her forefinger and thumb into the urn and pulled out the parchment. With both hands, she gently placed it on the towel and slowly unrolled it by extending her fingers and thumbs. Jason deftly placed the sinkers at the document's four corners. Everyone studied it in silence.

George was the first to speak. "It looks like someone's idle doodling on an old parchment. I thought we would find something enlightening in this thing."

"Not so fast, George," replied Jennifer irritably. "Part of this could be a map. But to where, and why?"

Sarah leaned over the counter to look closer. "What I see at the top section looks like a canoe crossing a body of water. But what are those faint words?"

"Try this," said Jason, as he handed her a magnifying glass.

As she studied the parchment again, she gasped. "It says 'Pamouik,' and there's an 'NE' behind the canoe and the word 'Secotan.' In front of it is an 'SW.' The canoe is crossing the Pamouik from Secotan, heading almost due southwest across the river." As Sarah continued to study the map with the magnifying glass, she said in just barely above a whisper, "The words 'Big Bear' are on what appears to be a creek to the west of Secotan, and the words 'Little Bear' are on a creek to the north. Oh yes, the canoe is definitely pointed to the southwest. And on the south shore ahead of it, I see what looks like a lizard in a circular area labeled 'Pocosin.' We all know pocosin is a type of swamp. In the middle of that is a small dot labeled 'Island.'"

No one spoke as they tried to understand the meaning of the words just spoken. Jason straightened slowly and said, "Sarah, tell me if this reminds you of something."

Sarah nodded and set the magnifying glass on the counter. "Isn't the canoe coming from the high ground just east of here on the Pamlico River, where we found the Indian pottery?"

"It sure looks like it to me," he replied.

"And I would also venture to say that the spot surrounded by pocosin is our island, and that lizard-looking thing is meant to be an alligator." Looking at the map again, she asked, "How about the rest of it? Why does the map depict pots labeled 'Pocosin' on a canoe coming back across the Pamouik? And there's a drawing at the bottom depicting a pot on a fire with what looks like a tube running to another one buried underground. They seem to be cooking something."

"May I have a look?" asked Jennifer.

"Please do," said Sarah, and she stepped aside to allow Jennifer to lean forward with the magnifying glass for a closer look.

After scrutinizing the parchment for a few minutes, Jennifer stood and said, "Well, well, what we have here, in my opinion, is an elementary refinery. George, come look at this and tell me that's not what I see."

While George was squinting at the parchment through his wire-rimmed glasses, Jennifer continued, "Doesn't that look like a pipe carrying what's at the top of the pot on a fire down to a pot underground? And look over here on the right edge. Could that be a formula of some kind?"

"Hmm, it may indeed," replied George. "And we all know that oil is lighter than water, and when separated from it will float to the top."

Jennifer's eyes began to water. "Dare I ask the obvious? Could their pocosin simply be algae?"

"What else could it be?" asked Kurt.

"And," Jennifer continued, "if this island is where Sarah and Jason think it is, the algae they were using is the same thing that still surrounds Alligator Island today. It's been right under our noses all the time."

Interrupting the building excitement, Jason asked, "Does it say anything else?"

Using the magnifying glass, Sarah leaned over to study the parchment again. "Yes, there is more. There are faint words at the very bottom of the document."

Kurt watched Sarah intently as she leaned back over the parchment. Moments later, a smile spread across her face as she whispered, "'Hatteras and Selu bestow this knowing to ye, our descendant daughter. Ye time has come. The knowing is for all and for none to keep.'"

CHAPTER

17

Jennifer had been in the lab since four a.m. It was now ten forty p.m. She had been experimenting with the algae from the swamp for two days with nothing to show for it. Tired and frustrated, Jennifer carefully mixed another beaker of the swamp algae with a new variety of fertilizer and placed it under a grow lamp. After exhaling a deep sigh, she stepped back from the beaker and began her rounds to study the progress of other ongoing experiments. When she returned an hour later, she gasped at what she saw.

George was working in his own lab when he received Jennifer's phone call. "George, you won't believe this!" Jennifer said. "You have to come see this. The algae have doubled in size in one hour."

Sarah had been in New York for the last two weeks since the discovery of the urn's message. In her now daily conversations with Kurt, she learned that the focus of the algae research team was almost entirely on algae from the swamp around Alligator Island. Kurt's tone was different; Sarah could almost feel the excitement in his voice.

As Sarah stepped out onto the stairway of the Dutch Phosphate Corporation's Piaggio P180, she saw Kurt standing below beside his Range Rover with a smile on his face. After scampering down the stairs, she gave him a big hug. Kurt responded readily and felt an urge to prolong their embrace.

Once they were in the Range Rover, Kurt called Jennifer to let her know they were on their way. When Sarah and Kurt arrived at the conference room, Jennifer was waiting for them. After exchanging greetings, they settled into chairs around the table.

"Okay, enough of the suspense," said Sarah. "Kurt wouldn't tell me over the phone or on the way here what is going on with the algae research. He just said I'd have to see it to believe it. What is here for me to see that you couldn't tell me on the phone?"

Jennifer gave a tired smile. "The very next day after we saw what was in the urn, which was a Sunday, I had our team members report here to get started. We immediately harvested samples of algae from various locations in the swamp around Alligator Island and started running them in our experiments. The results were absolutely amazing."

"How so?" asked Sarah.

"You have to come see for yourself!" Jennifer replied. "Words can't describe it. Why don't we adjourn to the lab?"

Sarah nodded. "Okay, then. Let's go have a look."

Kurt fell in behind Jennifer and Sarah as they departed the administration building, with George lagging behind.

Stopping outside the algae lab, Jennifer turned to Sarah, extended her arm, and said, "Look at this." She pointed to racks of opaque tubes where the algae were being grown. "We've had to triple the size of our algae growth field in the two weeks since we started experimenting with the algae out there in the swamp. Our refinery can't keep up with this. When we started mixing what we believed was our most potent fertilizer cocktail with this stuff, it almost exploded in growth. It doubles itself every four hours."

Kurt could see the look of disbelief on Sarah's face.

"You have to be kidding me," said Sarah. "Nothing grows that fast."

"But it does," replied Jennifer. "This stuff would take over the island if we didn't limit what we're doing. If we had the space to grow it, and the refinery capacity to process it, our production could be many times over what you see in front of you. The potential for these algae is virtually unlimited. We've been tinkering with some diesel fuel injectors and have found that with a few modifications, we can run the island's diesel engine generators with a fifty-percent mixture of diesel fuel and the refined oil derived from the swamp's algae."

As Jennifer effusively elaborated on recent developments with her project, Kurt couldn't help but notice that George's shoulders seemed slumped and he had added little to the conversation.

Sarah stood looking out over the field of clear plastic tubes in front of her, trying to absorb the implications of what she had just heard. She turned to Kurt and asked, "So the obvious question is, how we can manage this breakthrough? Do we even have the refinery capacity to handle the algae that we can now produce with the space we currently have here on the island?"

"Well, for starters," Kurt said, "we can convert all of our refinery capacity to accommodate just the algae. We can put the corn and the sugarcane experiments on hold."

"Then what?" asked Sarah.

"We need a much larger refinery as soon as possible. There is a remote area of about a hundred acres near the entrance to the causeway that was mined out and restored several years ago. That should be more than enough space to build a refinery." Kurt paused, and then added, "But that's not the problem. We're going to need a big infusion of cash to build a refinery such as that from scratch. We're talking about an enormous amount of money to do it."

Sarah looked at Kurt for a moment, and then asked, "How much?"

"I could only guess right now, but I wouldn't be surprised if it costs us over eighty million dollars, which will clearly break our current budget. But if this stuff is the commercial success we believe it will be, it will quickly pay for itself and further expansions of refinery capacity down the road."

"Before we spend that type of money, we'll need to consult with our board of directors and with our partner in Sharjah. I'll deal with the DPC board. Kurt, you and I need to make a call to Omar. What time is it over there?"

Kurt glanced at his watch. "They're eight hours ahead of us. It's now eleven fifteen here, so it will be seven fifteen p.m. there. Why don't we go back to the office and make the call?"

As they walked back to the administration building, Kurt pulled George to the side, letting Sarah and Jennifer walk ahead.

"George, I know your work is important and you feel passionately about it. But we need for you to put it on the back burner for a while and help with Jennifer's algae project. You can get back to what you're working on later."

"Kurt, that would be a mistake," George protested, with his arms crossed over his chest. "I am very close to a breakthrough myself. I just need to devote more time to it. Why can't we continue work on both?"

"We don't have the time," Kurt responded firmly. "We have something tangible now that can create a return on DPC's investment. You need to put your work aside for a while and assist with the algae project." Waiting for George's response, Kurt could see that he was clearly disappointed.

"This is another bullshit play to corporate America," sighed George. "I can't believe you've fallen into it."

"I understand how you feel. But there will be time later for us to focus on your work."

"I can't tell you how disappointed I am with you, Kurt. Can't you see that corporate profit is again taking precedence over scientific progress?"

Kurt watched George's angry eyes look off across the parking lot. "I'm sorry you feel that way, George, but there really is a bigger picture here."

Without hesitation, George replied, "I need to go shut down my experiments that are under way. Why don't you go ahead with Sarah and Jennifer, and I'll catch up with you later?"

"Sure," Kurt replied. "Thanks for being a team player about this. There will be time for your project later. Just be patient."

George nodded and walked away toward his lab.

Kurt paused for a moment to watch George depart. That uneasy feeling swept over him again. Shrugging it off, Kurt turned and headed back to the administration building for the call to Omar.

⊕ ⊕ ⊕

Once inside his lab, George checked to make sure no one was present. Satisfied that he was alone, he flipped open his cell phone.

Seconds later, a gruff voice answered. "Morton here."

"Jeffrey, this is George Batts."

After a short pause, Morton chuckled. "I wondered how long it would take you to contact me. What's up?"

"I have some information that USOCO needs to know."

"And what is that?" asked Morton.

"The project I mentioned before leaving USOCO is proving to be far more successful than any of us could have dreamed. The Enhanced Maize Project we started there has taken off. But more importantly, the work I'm doing with Tesla's concepts is finally coming together. It's going to turn the world's energy production on its head. USOCO will become a dinosaur." George knew by Morton's silence that he had struck a blow.

"And I assume you must want something from USOCO by making this call."

"Well, well, Jeffrey," replied George sarcastically. "Aren't we perceptive? Here's the deal. I need nine million dollars and safe passage out of here to Panama with my Tesla research." George waited nervously for a response.

Sighing deeply, Morton responded, "You will have to provide a lot more information for me to come up with that kind of money. People way over my head will have to be on board. Let's talk more tomorrow afternoon."

"What time?" asked George.

"I will call you on your cell at three p.m. Central time."

"Okay," replied George, and flipped his cell phone off.

Over the next few weeks, construction work began in order to utilize the sensational new discovery. With all the other construction on Alligator Island, the erection of a huge new fuel tank at the Lee Creek terminal and the pipeline leading to it from Alligator Island went virtually unnoticed. But Kurt had watched it closely. With the completion of this tank and its pipeline, the algae ethanol could be stored near the generators that powered the entire DPC mining operation.

For the past two weeks, Kurt had requested that Gabe run his Suburban using Jennifer's algae ethanol with a 50-percent diesel mix.

If there were no problems, he planned to test the ethanol/diesel mix with the generators that powered the entire DPC mine.

At ten a.m., Kurt, Jennifer, and George met as agreed on the front steps of the administration building. Moments later, Kurt saw Gabe's Suburban pulling into the parking lot.

After the threesome got in, Gabe drove out the Alligator Island front gate onto the causeway. After a few minutes, he turned to Kurt, who was sitting beside him on the front seat. "Am I supposed to notice anything different with the stuff in my fuel tank?"

"Hopefully not."

"Well then, so far so good, because the engine is running fine. But it does seem to be quieter."

"It should," replied Jennifer. "The ethanol added to the diesel fuel allows a much more efficient combustion. A positive side effect is that CO_2 emissions are much less than from pure diesel. We've actually been working on this fuel product for over five years now. Our discoveries were buried by our former superiors at USOCO. Now, with the support of the Dutch Phosphate Corporation, the truth about this breakthrough will see the light of day."

"Indeed it will," added Kurt emphatically. "And Gabe, after today, all you have to do to fill up is drive down to the new tank at the Lee Creek terminal, where we're headed now. As you know, there's one tank of diesel for the tugs. The other tank will have a fifty-percent mix of the island's ethanol and diesel fuel."

"With the price of diesel fuel at almost five dollars per gallon," Gabe said, "I'm happy to oblige."

⊕ ⊕ ⊕

As Gabe turned into the parking lot of the Lee Creek tugboat terminal, he saw the Chevrolet Tahoe with *DPC Security* on the front side doors parked behind the terminal building. After Kurt, Jennifer, and George headed over to the new fuel tank, Gabe walked toward the terminal building. On his way over, Walter, who now wore a Beretta on his hip, stepped from behind the building and started walking slowly toward him.

Earlier that day, Gabe had discussed with Tim Jolley, the chief of security of the DPC phosphate processing facility, the need for heightened security in general, and especially at the Lee Creek terminal. Jolley had agreed to assign Walter full time to the Lee Creek area and to switch him to the second shift, four p.m. to midnight.

"Good evening, Mr. Gabriel. How are you?"

"Very well, Walter. And you?"

"Doin' fine, thanks."

"Have you talked with Tim about keeping an eye on this place?" asked Gabriel.

"Yes. I start tomorrow tonight. Is there anything in particular that I should be looking for?"

"We're not sure. But we are concerned that some uninvited guests may have an interest in what's in our new fuel tank over there. The most probable entrance will be from the Pamlico River into the channel. You should spend most of your time watching for any boat traffic that might try to make its way from the river in toward the Lee Creek channel. If you see or hear anything suspicious, you know how to contact me."

Gabe pulled a set of binoculars from his Suburban and handed them to Walter. "These things have incredible night-vision capability. You should be able to see the eyeballs of anybody out there within half a mile of the channel entrance. We can get over here in ten minutes if you need us. You just need to see them soon enough so we can get here. Once you spot them, stay out of sight and watch. Don't try any heroics."

"Will do," said Walter.

Gabe thanked him, and just as he was about to turn to walk away, he stopped and faced Walter directly. "I need to tell you that this is not an exercise. Please take this assignment very seriously and keep a sharp lookout."

While Gabe and Walter were having their discussion, Jennifer, George, and Kurt were busily inspecting the new tank, its various valves and gauges, the pipeline carrying the refined biofuel from Alligator Island, and the line from the adjacent diesel tank.

"Looks like everything is ready to go," said Jennifer. She picked up her radio phone and called her assistant, Fred Morrison, back on Alligator Island. "Come in, Fred."

Seconds later, a voice said, "I'm here, Jennifer. Are you ready?"

"Yes. Let's get things rolling."

As he had been previously instructed, Jimmy opened the valve leading from the refinery's main tank. With a loud whoosh, its contents began to flow rapidly in the direction of the Lee Creek terminal. Moments later the whooshing could be heard as the flow arrived, and the needle of the pressure gauge George and Jennifer were studying swung over in front of them. Jennifer reached down to place her hand on the valve that controlled the flow of diesel fuel from the adjacent tank as George put his hand on the valve for refined fuel that had just arrived. With Kurt watching closely, George nodded at Jennifer, and they both opened their valves. Pure diesel fuel and the newly refined biofuel from Alligator Island began flowing in equal quantities into the new diesel mix tank.

The threesome had not noticed that Walter and Gabe had walked up and were standing close by, observing what they were doing with quiet interest, saying nothing. Walter's curiosity finally got the better of him.

"May I ask a question? The diesel tank we have contains more than enough fuel for the plant generators and the tugs that come in here three times a week. Why do we need this new tank that looks like it's five times larger than the one we have?"

Gabe, George, and Jennifer looked in Kurt's direction for the answer. Kurt smiled, intrigued by the man's interest.

"Beginning next week, you may see tugboat traffic in here increase dramatically. We will soon have on average three tugs a day with barges getting filled from the contents of this new tank. Your job will be to keep a close eye on everything that's going on. If you see anything suspicious, you need to call Mr. Gabriel immediately."

⊕ ⊕ ⊕

No one noticed that George had walked down to the dock and was talking on his cell phone.

"So, how will I get out of here with all of my work?" George asked.

"We'll have a boat pick up you and your stuff at the Lee Creek terminal after the mayhem starts," Morton replied.

"And the money, when will it be wired?" asked George.

"The next morning," replied Morton gruffly, "unless you screw this up."

CHAPTER 18

SEPTEMBER 10, 2008 — ALLIGATOR ISLAND, NORTH CAROLINA

The sun was setting low in the west when the perimeter guard heard the angry sound of cawing crows echoing across the swamp from the east. He knew the swampy forest that surrounded the island and the habits of its creatures. Something was amiss. Raising his binoculars, he studied the swamp for a few seconds in the direction of the crows' commotion, and then quickly grabbed his radio.

Tom Gabriel was sitting in Kurt's office when his radio crackled to life.

"Got it. I'll be right there."

"What's going on?" asked Kurt.

"Not sure. Let's go see."

After climbing the stairs to the observation tower, they stepped into the small room at the top with darkly tinted windows. Handing his night-vision binoculars to Gabe and an extra set to Kurt, the guard pointed out toward the east.

"The crows out there are making a ruckus. They don't usually sound that annoyed unless they feel threatened, and it's usually by humans. And bingo, look what we have down there to the east, about fifty yards from the edge of the swamp."

Studying the two intruders, Kurt could see they wore camouflage and moved slowly through the thick, low-lying brush. One of the intruders glanced at the GPS on his wrist and at the sun's fading orange glow to the west.

⊕ ⊕ ⊕

"We may have a half hour of light left before we reach the swamp," said the man with the GPS. "We're going to have to go straight into where those crows are sitting. And we need to be in the swamp by dark."

The other intruder responded, "The last thing we need is this kind of racket."

"I know, but if anybody on the island hears them, they will probably think they're just annoyed crows. Crows have always seemed annoyed to me."

When the intruders were within twenty yards of a stand of pine trees near the eastern edge of the swamp, the cawing reached a crescendo. Suddenly, in unison, the crows took flight. After hovering over the two men for a few seconds, they flew off to the west and disappeared into the darkening swamp.

⊕ ⊕ ⊕

With their binoculars, Kurt and Gabe followed the progress of the two intruders as they finally reached the edge of the water. Kurt could see that both men wore a backpack and a pistol holstered over their chests.

⊕ ⊕ ⊕

The man in the lead stopped in waist-high underbrush and showed his companion their position on his wristband GPS. "Here we are," he said, pointing to the navigation instrument on his wrist. "We will follow the straight-line course through the swamp. That should put us on the island in an hour. The water's not that deep, so we should be able to move quickly."

"The infidels on the island will never know what hit them," replied his companion. "Praise be to Allah."

"Praise be to Allah," echoed the man with the GPS. "I will go first. Stay about two meters behind me."

Darkness enveloped them as the two men stepped into the black, waist-deep water. It took only a few minutes of wading for them to realize that the muck on the swamp's bottom was going to make progress slow and difficult.

As they weaved their way around stands of cypress trees through the swamp's black soup, an eerie cacophony of crickets, bullfrogs, and the hoots of a distant owl echoed through the darkness. The man in the lead occasionally checked his GPS for their position.

An hour later, the men were only about a third of the way across the swamp. The lead man stopped and motioned to the man in the rear to come forward. Holding up the GPS, they looked at their progress with frustration. From somewhere ahead of them, the yowl of a bobcat echoed through the swamp. Seconds later, from behind them, another bobcat responded with its eerie yowl. Both men quickly reached down and pulled the pistols from their holsters.

The man with GPS resumed wading forward into the darkness, with his partner close behind. After a half hour, the men stopped again. The GPS showed they were still not halfway to the island. From off to their right, an agitated otter slapped its tail on the swamp's surface with a loud pop, sending chills down the men's spines.

"Maybe we ought to turn back," the man in the rear said nervously.

"No. We are here for a purpose. We cannot fail. Just follow me and you will be fine."

They again resumed their slow progress. The sounds of their legs splashing through the swamp did not go unnoticed by two of its most ancient inhabitants, a breed of giant alligators that had ruled there for eons. Being a third larger than their alligator cousins, these reptilians were big, aggressive, and had enormous appetites. At night, they moved surreptitiously in search of prey, with only their black diamond eyes appearing above the water's surface.

Two pairs of these diamond eyes had been quietly following the intruders in their domain for the past ten minutes. As if on cue, one of the giant gators moved ahead of the other and ghosted to within five feet of the man in the rear. Suddenly, the man heard the surface of the water explode from behind him as the gator's powerful tail rocketed its ten thousand pounds of muscle forward through the water. As the gator's razor-sharp teeth penetrated deep into the right hip of its victim, the intruder let out loud screams of pain and terror that reverberated throughout the swamp. Hearing the commotion, the man in the lead turned around as his partner's screams were being replaced by the crunching sound of bones being shattered under the viselike grip of the gator's huge jaws. As he raised his pistol to fire, he watched in shocked disbelief as the thirty-foot monster disappeared below the now crimson surface of the water with the writhing torso of his companion trapped in its mouth. As quickly as the eruption came, it faded away. The eerie chorus of crickets, bullfrogs, and a great horned owl soon settled back over the swamp.

Bloodcurdling fear now raced through the veins of the victim's companion. After glancing at his GPS, he calculated a course due west for one-tenth of a mile to reach the island. Racing forward, time and again he desperately pulled his feet up from the muck on the bottom of the swamp until he collapsed against a large cypress tree in exhaustion. He gasped for breath for several minutes before his breathing returned to normal.

Suddenly, from the cypress tree directly above him, he heard a heart-stopping scream that echoed through the swamp. The scream came again, but this time even louder, and it was followed by the sound of the fluffing wings of an agitated screech owl taking flight in the darkness. To the intruder, it was as if a hysterical witch had bellowed a piercing cry of terror from a tree limb overhead.

With eyes as big as saucers, the swamp's intruder frantically splashed ahead for several minutes before halting again in exhaustion, gasping heavily to catch his breath.

Then he saw them. There, directly in front of him, were two sparkling black diamonds on the surface of the water, moving quietly toward him. The water exploded. After two bloodcurdling screams, it was over. A moment later, the swamp's remaining intruder lay pinned to the mucky bottom of the swamp, his torso being held under water by the powerful jaws and razor-sharp teeth of another giant gator.

Once his prey died from drowning, the alligator would leisurely consume his meal. As had happened time and again over countless centuries, these two intruders of the swamp joined the ranks of the missing.

⊕ ⊕ ⊕

Gabe and Kurt lowered their binoculars. Both were speechless from the spectacle they had just witnessed. Setting the binoculars on the window ledge, the two men walked down the tower's stairs, saying nothing. At the bottom, they turned and walked to the area where the intruders had apparently been headed. After studying the fenced perimeter and the swamp beyond, Kurt finally spoke.

"That was more effective than all the million dollars we've spent here on security. They didn't even get close enough to set off the motion detectors."

"True," replied Gabe, "but those guys had to really want to get in here to try a stunt like that."

"How could they have gotten into the swamp?" asked Kurt.

"There is an old logging road about a mile to the east. My guess is they took a four-wheeler in and entered the swamp from there. Why don't we check it out first thing in the morning, when we have some light?"

Kurt nodded. "Okay. Let's meet here at the administration building tomorrow at six a.m."

"See you then," replied Gabe, as he turned and headed to his Suburban.

Turning back toward the swamp, Kurt looked out into its forbidding darkness. Suddenly, a wave of questions swept over him. *Who were those guys? Why would they try something that insane? Has Morton found out where we are and what we're doing? But how could he?*

The following morning, Kurt watched the sun rising over the woodlands to the east as Gabe's Suburban bounced along the bumpy dirt road. What remained of an old logging road soon appeared a hundred feet ahead, on the right.

Gabe slowed and turned onto what was now barely a pathway overgrown with shrubs, weeds, and a few small pines. Two lines of freshly crushed foliage from some sort of rugged vehicle trailed off to the southeast along the path. Switching into four-wheel drive, he drove slowly for several hundred feet and stopped. Getting out of the Suburban, Kurt and Gabe quietly closed its doors and studied their surroundings. They observed the tops of a stand of tall pine trees at about two hundred yards to the south, towering over the thick underbrush.

Both spotted a narrow pathway that opened into the thick underbrush, which Kurt surmised had been made by deer on their way to and from the swamp. He pointed it out to Gabe, who nodded his understanding. After strapping on Beretta pistols, the two men stepped onto the pathway and disappeared into the thick foliage. A half mile later, they stopped to study an aerial photo Gabe had removed from his shirt pocket. As Gabe pointed to the trees on the photo, Kurt nodded and pointed to the stand of tall pines ahead of them. Both men guessed that was where the guard first heard the irritated crows. In his mind, Kurt estimated that the trees were about eighty yards ahead to the southeast.

After another half hour of slow, painstaking progress, they reached a clearing. In front of them lay the tall stand of pine trees on a patch of high ground. Underneath the pines was a Ford F250, sitting fifty feet from the edge of the swamp. Between it and the swamp was a thicket of wax myrtle. After another few minutes, they heard the sound of rustling underbrush. A figure appeared, walking slowly through the thick brush toward the truck. As he walked closer, Kurt saw that he had a bushy mustache, dark hair, and olive skin. Reaching the truck, the man pulled out a pack of cigarettes from the driver's side, lit one, and walked slowly toward the back of the truck. Once he was seated on the tailgate, Kurt and Gabe had a clear view of what they recognized as a middle-aged man of Arab descent. Focused on the pistol holstered on the man's right hip, Gabe placed his M16 down in the foliage beside him, pulled his Beretta from its holster, and released the safety.

Turning to Kurt, he whispered, "Why don't you stay here and cover me in case there are others?"

Kurt nodded in agreement.

Seconds later, Gabe jumped from the foliage that had hidden them and raced toward his quarry. When the Arab man finally realized he had company, Gabe was fifteen feet away and pointing his Beretta directly between the man's eyes. As the man reached instinctively for his gun, Gabe commanded, "Stop! Raise your hands! Put them behind your head or die!"

Gabe was now ten feet away, with the barrel of his Beretta pointed directly at the face of the terrified Arab.

"Your friends are dead. Who sent you?" he demanded.

The terror that had first appeared on the Arab's face was now replaced by defiant rage. "Where are they?"

"They are in the belly of the alligators. That's where you're going to be if I don't start getting some answers."

"You lie, infidel. I will tell you nothing. You will die with me."

Kurt watched in disbelief as the man in front of Gabe reached down quickly for his pistol with his right hand.

Gabe commanded again, "Stop, or you die!"

The Arab man's hand was now pulling the pistol up to aim when his eyes met Gabe's.

"Praise be to Allah!" he yelled, as Gabe squeezed the trigger for the last sound the man would ever hear.

For a moment, Gabe stood motionless. Suddenly, from behind him came two shots from what he instantly knew was Kurt's Beretta. Seconds later, a second man holding a rifle fell forward out of a clump of bushes near the swamp.

After ensuring that the two men were no longer a threat, Kurt and Gabe stepped over to the truck and inventoried its contents. In its bed, they found the passports of four male citizens of Abu Dhabi and an assortment of grenades, knives, sawed-off shotguns, and several empty wooden boxes both recognized as containers for electronic explosives.

"Can you believe this shit?" said Gabe. "These guys were obviously not trying to steal research secrets. They wanted to blow us off the face of the earth."

Sitting alone at the desk in Jason's library that evening, Kurt flipped through the passports of the Arab men in the swamp. As he pondered the events of the past two days, no clear answers came to him. After reading until midnight, Kurt walked down the hall to his apartment, lay down, and hoped for restful sleep. It was not to be. After sleeping fitfully for several hours, he looked over at the clock on the bedside table. It was four a.m. With Sharjah being eight hours ahead, it would be noon there. Omar would be up and well into his day. Maybe his friend could make some sense of these recent events.

Moments later, Kurt was dialing the number for Sharjah Oil in Sharjah, United Arab Emirates.

"Sharjah Oil, how can I direct your call?" answered the receptionist.

"This is Kurt Benjamin. I need to speak to my friend Omar."

"Thank you. Please hold."

"Hello, Kurt. How are you? How are things?"

"Omar, I couldn't wait for our weekly call on Monday. We had uninvited visitors yesterday evening. It was not a social visit. They came with some serious explosives."

"Jeez, who were they?"

"All of them had Abu Dhabi passports."

There was a long silence. Both men were asking themselves the same question. Who in Abu Dhabi would know or care about what was going on in a remote swamp in coastal North Carolina?

"Can you give me their names?" asked Omar. "I can have our sources do some checking."

"Before I answer that, Omar, I must ask if there might be someone close to you who might have revealed what we are doing to someone outside of your family."

There was another silence before Omar replied, "Say no more. I will be very careful about my inquiries. Are you okay?"

"Yes."

"How is Sarah? Does she know about this?"

"Not yet. I'll brief her later this morning."

"Be careful, my friend. We obviously have some dangerous people out there with a reason to stop our project."

Setting the phone down slowly, Omar searched his mind, asking, *Who could have known of the project and its location? And more importantly, why would they want to sabotage it?*

He walked over to the windows of his twentieth-floor office and looked out over the city of Sharjah. Thoughts of his brother crept into his head. *He was recently in Dubai with his old friend Massud, the son of the emir of Abu Dhabi. Both of them like to party. Could Naji have gotten drunk enough to reveal a closely held family secret? Could he have done it out of spite or jealousy?*

⊕ ⊕ ⊕

That evening, the emir hastily summoned members of the board of directors of the Abu Dhabi Sovereign Wealth Fund to his palace. It was nine p.m. by the time all the members had arrived in their Mercedes and Cadillac limousines. They settled into large leather chairs in the emir's study. Above them on the domed ceiling were elaborately painted depictions of Arabian history. An ornate old Persian rug covered the center of the room where the board members sat facing the emir's desk.

"We have troubling news from our mission to the Dutch Phosphate project. Haydar and his team are no longer with us. They knew the risks and gave their lives willingly to Allah. Of course, their families will be cared for."

The room was silent for several moments before the emir continued.

"We know that a test run of the phosphate plant's generators using a fifty-percent mix of algae ethanol and diesel fuel will occur soon, and will probably be successful. The phosphate plant uses the equivalent amount of electricity needed to power a city with a population of a hundred thousand."

"If Haydar and his men are dead, how do we know this?" asked Hussein.

"Massud had an opportunity to spend another evening with his friend Naji al Rashid in Dubai recently. As all of you may recall from our last meeting on this subject, Naji is the brother of Omar al Rashid, the one who is so well connected to the Americans at the Dutch Phosphate Corporation. Massud, tell us what you learned from your loose-lipped friend from Sharjah."

"Yes, Father." Clearing his throat, Massud proudly began the details of the evening. "It was quite a weekend. I made sure we had plenty of wine and generous female companionship."

The emir interrupted. "Massud, we do not need to hear the sordid details, just tell us what you learned."

The other men in the room chuckled.

"Yes, Father." Clearing his throat again, and with a sheepish smile, Massud continued. "To make a long story short, on the last night of our weekend, I was able to have dinner alone with Naji. He was clearly excited about news of their venture with the Dutch Phosphate Corporation. Again, his tongue had been loosened with wine. By dinner's end, he had explained in detail how DPC was secretly producing an algae-based ethanol for about forty dollars per barrel. It can be refined to burn very cleanly at a fifty-percent mixture with diesel. He was confident that they will ultimately be able to refine it to the point that it can be mixed at higher percentages than that. The Dutch Phosphate plant in North Carolina is already running its vehicles, research facility, and even tugboats with this mixture. The next experiment will be with the entire mining operation."

"Did Naji speak of the future plans for development of this fuel?" asked Hasad Domani, the minister of finance of the emirate.

"He did. Apparently, the algae used to produce this biofuel can grow prolifically under conditions the researchers have now perfected. The plan is to build an enormous new refinery on the DPC property to mass-produce this fuel. But there is a problem. The cost will be huge, and the Dutch Phosphate Corporation alone cannot foot the entire bill. They are asking for further contributions from Sharjah Oil."

"And will they get it?" inquired Hasad.

"Possibly, but Sharjah Oil is concerned about risking all of its remaining cash reserves on this one project."

"So why don't we get involved in this ourselves?" asked Hussein.

After a few seconds of silence, the emir spoke. "We have. Hasad can report to us on that."

"Yes. After we met last month to discuss this issue, the emir instructed me to cover our bases with discreet purchases of Dutch Phosphate Corporation stock through our affiliate companies. We now own six percent of its outstanding common stock. We are on track to own over ten percent within the next two weeks. Our New York lawyers are preparing to make the necessary disclosure filings with the United States Securities and Exchange Commission. However, we do not want to do this until Sharjah Oil has completed this last infusion of cash. Its holdings will then be at twenty-five percent of all traded Dutch Phosphate Corporation's stock. After that, we will complete our purchases to put us in control of ten percent of its common stock. At that point, a joint venture could be undertaken with our brothers in Sharjah to combine our ten percent with their twenty-five percent. With thirty-five-percent ownership of DPC's stock, we will be in a position to purchase the necessary remaining shares to take control of the company."

"Will they join us?" asked Hussein.

"They will be too far in by then not to join us," the emir pronounced confidently. "Imagine the power we will achieve over the world when the United Arab Emirates control the Dutch Phosphate Corporation. We will own the world's biggest producer of fertilizer, huge oil reserves, as well as the best-known alternative to our oil to date. A large part of the world's food production will directly depend on us. The opportunity to gain such control over the infidels will be too much for our brothers in Sharjah to resist. Massud will stay in close contact with Naji. Once we know their deal is done, we will complete our purchase to acquire our full ten-percent stake."

Sitting confidently behind his desk, the emir watched for any sign of dissent. Instead, he saw smiles and nods of agreement from all the robed men present. At twelve thirty a.m., the emir pronounced the meeting adjourned, and the men filed out to their limousines that were waiting in front of the palace.

CHAPTER

19

Omar had been studying the turmoil in the American financial markets closely for the past several weeks. While at the Wharton School, he had taken a course in Depression era economics. Recalling what he had learned, he was astonished to see the classic signs of a looming deep recession—and possibly worse. In utter disbelief, he saw the leaders of the world's most powerful democracy unable to put aside their petty differences to take the action needed to avoid it. The prescription was there, if they would just take it.

Omar was awakened from his thoughtful trance by the voice of his secretary at his doorway. "You have a call from the emir of Abu Dhabi."

Stunned, Omar sat at his desk and thought, *Why in the world would he want to talk with me? But he is the emir of Abu Dhabi, and they have billions in cash and the lion's share of oil reserves in the United Arab Emirates.*

"Okay, put him through," Omar finally responded. A moment later, in his best diplomatic voice, he gushed, "Sheik Fadil, it is an honor to receive your call."

"Thank you for taking my call, Omar. I have watched your progress and that of your family's businesses with great respect. I am very impressed with what you and your family have achieved."

"Thank you, but our success is dwarfed by the enormous strides being made by Abu Dhabi under your capable leadership."

With the necessary pleasantries out of the way, the emir cut to the chase. "Let me be direct, Omar. We have learned that your family now owns stock and warrants to buy twenty-five percent of the outstanding shares of the Dutch Phosphate Corporation. The Abu Dhabi Sovereign Wealth Fund has completed the purchase today of a ten-percent stake in the outstanding stock of that company. With your shares and ours, we now have the ability, together as brothers of the United Arab Emirates, to purchase the remaining stock necessary to own a controlling interest in the company."

Many questions surged through Omar's mind. *How does he know a closely held secret about my family's involvement with the Dutch Phosphate Corporation? Why does the Sovereign Wealth Fund of Abu Dhabi want to control this particular company? What would this mean for Sharjah Oil?*

Omar responded suspiciously, "Sheik Fadil, why would we want to control the Dutch Phosphate Corporation?"

"We see it as a sound company," replied the emir. "It is the world's largest producer of fertilizer. Regardless of the state of the world's economies, fertilizer, like oil, will always be in demand."

Omar's mind continued to race. He was reminded again that Naji had gone to college with the emir's son. They were still good friends. The two had had another party weekend in Dubai recently, one that Omar suspected was not a weekend his mother would have condoned.

Omar's thoughts were interrupted by the emir. "Omar, let's get our families together to discuss a joint venture to acquire the Dutch Phosphate Corporation. May I suggest that we meet in your office tomorrow? Would ten a.m. be too early?"

Pondering the implications of the emir's call, Omar paused and responded, "Ten o'clock tomorrow morning should be fine. We will see you then."

Hanging up the phone, Omar recalled noticing how the stock of the Dutch Phosphate Corporation had been under significant buying pressure in the past two weeks. This had been curious to him, with the heavy selling activity in the overall U.S. stock market. To Omar, the phone call from Sheik Fadil explained it. The reality of what this meant suddenly rolled through his thoughts. *An unwelcome guest has just arrived at the poker table. Unfortunately, he has the financial clout to take control of the game.*

Omar considered the options. Regardless of what his family decided to do, there was no question that he owed a call to Sarah and Kurt to alert them of these developments. This could not wait for their weekly phone conference. He needed to make this call immediately.

⊕ ⊕ ⊕

Recognizing the number from Sharjah, Sarah quickly picked up the phone.

"Hello, Omar. This is an unexpected surprise. You couldn't wait for us to talk on Monday?"

"Sarah, you have surely noticed the activity in Dutch Phosphate stock over the past few weeks."

"Yes, we have. Someone seems to be interested in our stock."

"Well, I know who that is."

"Who?" she asked.

"It is the Abu Dhabi Sovereign Wealth Fund."

"Why would they want to own a large block of stock in the Dutch Phosphate Corporation?"

"I'm afraid it's a bigger question than that. I just received a call from the emir of Abu Dhabi. He informed me that the Sovereign Wealth Fund now owns a ten-percent stake in the company. Somehow, they found out about Sharjah's relationship with DPC. The emir informed me that he wants us to join them in a joint venture to purchase the remaining shares needed to have a controlling interest in the corporation."

There was a long pause. "How could they possibly have known about your family's interest in DPC? And that begs the question, Omar, what else do they know? Specifically, do they know about our project in North Carolina?"

Both Omar and Sarah had the same question on their minds: *is Abu Dhabi's interest in any way related to the recent effort to destroy the research facility?* But neither of them gave voice to it.

"Sarah, I do not know how they got their information. But I suggest that all of us be very careful going forward."

"Indeed."

After Sarah hung up, she turned and looked out over the New York skyline, pondering what she had just heard. *Why would the Abu Dhabi Sovereign Wealth Fund be so interested in the Dutch Phosphate Corporation? Do they really think they can take over our company? Could they sabotage what we're doing with the alternative energy project? But why would they want to do that?*

⊕ ⊕ ⊕

Mahoney, Sarah, Kurt, and the Battses had been in the conference room for two hours, going over the details for the upcoming test. They would soon know if Jennifer's algae ethanol/diesel mix could power the generators that ran the entire DPC phosphate production plant. This would include the miles of conveyors, the giant electric cranes, and the processing plant itself. During the meeting, Kurt called in various other plant personnel to be briefed and consulted. Once the details and mechanics had been ironed out, Kurt picked up the radio phone to summon Tom Gabriel. Moments later, Gabe knocked on the conference room door and stepped inside, closing the door behind him.

"Gabe, please have a seat and join us," said Kurt. "We're going to try a very important experiment in two days and need your input. The same stuff that you are now running through your Suburban is going to power the entire plant's generators for a while on Thursday night, September eighteenth. We will lose power for a few minutes while we make the switch."

"Wow," said Gabe. "Running my Suburban with this stuff is one thing. But running the generators for the whole plant on it? Are you guys really sure you're ready for this?"

"We are," replied Kurt confidently. "We've tested it many times with different sets of generators. We're confident we've worked out the bugs and are ready to put it to the real test. If we do have a problem, we're simply going to switch back to generators using plain diesel. We don't expect any problems, but if some arise, it could take as much as a half hour to make the switch back to pure diesel and get the plant up and running again."

"That could be rather alarming to the employees. What time do you plan to do this?" asked Gabe.

Mahoney answered, "We're planning on nine p.m. We won't have many management or clerical personnel around at that time of night, so fewer people will be affected. If we did it during the day shift, we could have havoc on our hands. Even so, we plan to issue an advisory to the employees that generator maintenance will be conducted during the evening hours on Thursday which could result in a temporary loss of power."

"Will it affect the power to Alligator Island?" Gabe asked.

"No," replied Kurt. "We've actually been running the island's generators with this biodiesel mix for two weeks now with no problem. Even if we did have a problem, the island has backup generators that are supplied with pure diesel."

The sun was just beginning to rise when Kurt turned his Range Rover onto Highway 33, heading east out of Greenville toward the DPC plant. He could not remember when he had last felt such a rush of adrenaline. The time to test DPC's biodiesel mix had arrived. Kurt mentally went through the necessary preparations again and again to ensure they had not left anything to chance.

The building where George Batts and his team conducted their experiments was quiet. To guarantee his privacy, George had assigned all of his team to assist with the evening's experiment. After meticulously downloading selected data onto a jump drive, he carefully erased all data concerning the Tesla work from each computer in the lab. With that task completed, he filled two large duffel bags with his experiments. After dragging the bags across the building to the back door, he strained under their weight to load them into the back of the Volvo. As he returned to the lab, his cell phone rang. Lifting the phone to his ear, he heard the gruff voice of Jeffrey Morton.

"Okay, Batts. It's one thirty p.m. Is everything ready?"

"Yes. Everything here is ready," replied George. "The power to the entire DPC plant will go off briefly at nine p.m. We will switch the generators to the new biodiesel mix. Everyone around here is totally focused on my experiment. The power to the island is not part of it. Its power is to remain on. When the power to the entire phosphate processing facility goes off at nine, there will be plenty of confusion."

"Excellent. Expect guests on the island tonight around nine oh-five. I would suggest that you and anything you value not be on the island at that time."

"Has the money been wired?" George asked nervously.

"Look, Batts," growled Morton, "it's like I've told you before. The money will be wired tomorrow morning. But for that to happen, you better deliver tonight."

Before Batts could respond, Morton hung up.

George's hands trembled uncontrollably as he placed his cell phone back in its case. Feverishly, he checked the lab once more, making sure he left nothing behind that he would need for his new laboratory in Panama. After locking the lab's front door, he trotted to the Volvo. Twenty minutes later, he pulled into the parking lot in front of the generators at the ferry terminal and backed up to the equipment storage building behind them. Struggling with the weight of the two bags from his lab, he dragged them one at a time to a corner in the back of the storage building and covered them with a plastic tarp. Unnoticed, he drove the Volvo back to Alligator Island.

⊕ ⊕ ⊕

In his office in Houston, Morton had been expecting the call from his men in the field for over an hour. It was now 3:40 p.m. Hearing nothing, he got up and began pacing the floor of his dimly lit office. By the time the phone rang, he was fuming.

Picking it up, he growled, "You were supposed to call me an hour ago."

"I'm sorry, sir," responded the apologetic voice on the line. "We had a little glitch with our helicopter pilot. But we are ready to go. All we need is for you to give us the green light."

"You are a go for nine o'clock tonight," replied Morton, regaining his composure.

"Roger that," said the caller enthusiastically.

"Remember to leave no trace of Batts or who was behind your mission," Morton ordered sternly. "All we want are his duffel bags."

⊕ ⊕ ⊕

At eight p.m., Kurt went over the procedures with George and Jennifer one last time. "You guys will be at the generator compound by eight thirty. You will start the generators with the biodiesel mix at eight forty-five. At nine o'clock you will shut off the power from the generators with the pure diesel mix. At five after nine you will open the main power switch with current from the generators running on the biodiesel mix. If all is running properly, we'll power the plant for an hour with the biodiesel mix. I'll radio you at the generator compound at ten-oh-five to turn the current off and switch back to the generators running on straight diesel. Are there any questions?"

George nodded nervously and Jennifer replied, "Got it."

"Okay, then," said Kurt, "let's get going."

During their meeting, Kurt had noticed that George appeared quiet, as if distracted. *Something is going on with George,* he thought. *Maybe he's just nervous about what is to happen tonight.*

CHAPTER
20

At eight forty-five p.m., Kurt answered Jennifer's call on his radio phone.

"The generators with the biodiesel mix are purring like kittens," she said excitedly. "We are ready to go."

"Okay," Kurt replied calmly. "At nine o'clock, let her rip."

At exactly nine, George closed the main circuit that provided electricity to the entire DPC Plant. At 9:05, Jennifer opened the circuit for electricity from the generators with the 50-percent biodiesel mix.

Gabe, Kurt, and Sarah were in the observation tower looking at the brightly illuminated sky above the mine to the northwest. Exactly at nine p.m., the lights began to flicker, and then dimmed quickly, plunging the DPC plant into darkness. At 9:05, the lights began to flicker and brighten. Two minutes later, the equivalent to a city of a hundred thousand people was brightly illuminated again in front of them.

"Kurt, it's working. We've done it!" shrieked Sarah, as she jumped up and down, clapping her hands.

"Yes, we've done it!" Kurt replied proudly. They exchanged high-fives with Gabe, and then turned and embraced. As their lips met, both were lost in the moment.

Their reverie ended abruptly when the lights on Alligator Island suddenly went dark. Kurt realized that the generators had gone silent. The island had been plunged into complete darkness.

"What the hell?" exclaimed Gabe. "Where are the backup battery lights?"

The silence was soon replaced by the sound of throbbing rotors from a helicopter approaching over the swamp from the east.

Gabe picked up his night-vision binoculars on the ledge in front of him. He quickly recognized a helicopter coming in fast just above the treetops, with no lights on and heading directly toward them.

"Not good." Gabe lowered the binoculars and began barking orders to his guards like he had done many times to his subordinates during his military career.

Sensing trouble as well, Kurt looked at the approaching helicopter and said, "Gabe, we need to get out of this tower. We're sitting ducks up here."

"I agree, but I need to stay up here to make sure my men are properly positioned."

"Not sure that's a good idea. We're heading for ground and will stay in contact by radio."

"Got it," replied Gabe.

Kurt grabbed Sarah's hand and pulled her out of the observation room, and they quickly headed to the bottom of the tower. In the meantime, Gabe was barking into his radiophone, "Code One alert. I repeat, Code One."

Kurt and Sarah ran across the compound to the administration building and then down the hall to his office. Once inside, Kurt pulled her to his desk. "If things get crazy, get under the desk. Stay put until I come back."

"Whoa, where do you think you're going?"

"Please, Sarah, just do it. Lock the door behind me." He unlocked the bottom left drawer of his desk, pulled out a pistol, jammed a clip into it, and handed it to Sarah. He then grabbed another pistol and several clips, turned, and ran out the door. As instructed, Sarah locked it behind him. Before she could get under the desk, the sound of a fifty-caliber machine gun erupted, with a loud explosion coming from just outside the administration building. The building shook violently around her. Once under the desk, she heard the sounds of the building's windows shattering and debris hitting the walls and roof.

Moments after Kurt left Sarah in his office and headed for the front of the building, another blast of fifty-caliber machine gun fire burst from the helicopter. From the front door of the administration building, Kurt watched the gate explode in a fireball, and he dove to the floor behind the reception desk. The windows in the reception area exploded, with glass shards flying across the room. By this time, Gabe had his M2 aimed directly at the black helicopter that was now at eye level with him in the observation tower. After Gabe's initial burst of gunfire on the helicopter, it swung around and directed its fire at the tower. The helicopter was too late. Gabe's aim had been precise, and his bullets hit their target exactly where he had intended. Suddenly, the chopper began circling the watchtower erratically. Gabe could make out the pilot slumped over the controls. Gunfire erupted again from the helicopter.

Damn, thought Gabe, *no pilot, but the gunner is still going.*

Almost simultaneously, he and the gunner made eye contact, and each opened fire. Gabe felt a sharp pain and then the warmth of blood oozing down his right arm. Fortunately, his aim had been the more deadly, and the gunner slumped over the fifty-caliber gun mount for a few seconds before falling out of the helicopter into the darkness below.

In an ever-expanding ball of fire, the chopper spun in wild circles around the tower before plunging to the parking lot in front of the administration building and exploding into an orange fireball. Kurt, from his position behind the reception desk, felt the heat of the red-hot pieces of debris flying into the building and battering the desk and the wall behind him.

When the barrage of flying debris subsided, Kurt raised his head from behind the desk and looked out the shattered windows toward the front gate. Suddenly, more gunfire erupted at the side of the building, and the gate and gatehouse exploded into a ball of fire, sending the remnants skyward.

Those were grenades, thought Kurt.

Almost immediately, he spotted two camouflaged men creeping through the shadows just inside what was once the front gate. At the same time, Kurt saw a figure dressed in the black body suit of the island's security force looking out into the swamp with binoculars, obviously unaware of the two intruders who were moving stealthy toward him. Bracing his pistol on the top of the desk, Kurt's aim was deadly. With two quick, carefully placed shots, the intruders collapsed.

Unseen by Kurt, another invader in camouflage had taken cover behind Gabe's Suburban. Thinking his shot was clear, the intruder set his weapon on the hood and pointed it directly at Kurt.

In the tower, Gabe had a clear view of what was about to happen. He took aim and squeezed the M2's trigger, sending an eruption of automatic gunfire that blew the camouflaged man back ten feet and away from the Suburban.

Another period of silence fell over the island. It was soon interrupted by a blast of automatic gunfire that riddled the watchtower, turning its windows into flying glass that peppered Gabe and rained down into the darkness below. After a brief pause, a second barrage of bullets hit the tower, blowing off its door.

Kurt was finally able to pinpoint the source of the gunfire. It came from near the side of the building where George conducted his research. Kurt could see that from there the gunman had a clear, open shot on the tower, and he knew he had to move fast. Moving stealthily to where the man had been behind the Suburban, Kurt located his automatic weapon. As a third volley began battering the tower, Kurt aimed the AK-47 across the parking lot and opened fire. Silence returned to the island.

Picking up his radio, Kurt whispered, "Are you okay, Gabe?" Fifteen seconds later, Kurt called again. "Come in, Gabe. Are you okay?"

After several seconds, he was relieved to hear Gabe's voice over the radio.

"Roger, Kurt, I've got a scrape on my arm, but I'm okay."

"I just took out the guy who was using you for target practice," responded Kurt. "You're a sitting duck. Get out of the tower. I'll cover you."

For twenty minutes, Sarah had listened to the sounds of automatic weapons and grenades exploding around her. Then, above the uproar came an enormous explosion that shook the building violently, shattering the windows in Kurt's office. An eerie silence followed. Thinking the firefight might be over, Sarah crawled out from under the desk, only to hear an automatic weapon erupt in the hallway. There was another pause, followed by the sound of the doorknob rattling, followed seconds later by the door exploding inward as it was kicked open by a heavy boot. The machine gun wielded by a man in the doorway suddenly erupted, spraying bullets wildly across the room. With the pistol pointed at the man's torso, Sarah quickly squeezed off two shots. The machine gun went silent, and there was a groan and a loud thud as the man collapsed backward onto the hallway floor.

Minutes later, Sarah heard footsteps running toward her down the hall, and Kurt's frantic voice. "Sarah, are you okay?"

"I'm fine, but that guy out in the hall may have a problem."

Shining his flashlight on the man on the hallway floor, Kurt commented flatly, "I didn't know you were a gunslinger."

"Right," replied Sarah sarcastically, "and I suspect your résumé is a bit incomplete as well. You've obviously been around firefights before."

Kurt frowned and responded softly, "I'm afraid so. Let's talk about that later. We need to contact Gabe and secure the island." Speaking into his radio, Kurt asked, "Gabe, where are you?"

"I'm up here looking at what's left of the front gate. Where are you?"

"I'm inside, in my office with Sarah. She's okay. I'm going to call the sheriff's department and request airlift assistance to the ECU medical school. No doubt we have some people who will need it."

"Roger that," replied Gabe. "All quiet now. My men are reporting in from their positions. We will secure the island."

During all the noise and explosions around her, Sarah had not heard the ringing of her cell phone. With the rampage over, she noticed that the phone's message light was blinking. There were four voice mail messages waiting for her. She listened to them; all were frantic calls from Jason. In the last one, she heard, "What the hell is going on over there? Looks like World War III. I'm in the boat, a half mile offshore from you. If I don't hear from you soon, I'm heading into the Lee Creek terminal."

At 9:10 p.m., at the Lee Creek terminal, Jennifer exclaimed, "Can you believe it? Our algae made the biodiesel that is now running the equivalent of a city of a hundred thousand people."

"Six months ago, I certainly wouldn't have believed it," replied George passively. He had barely finished his words when the first explosion thundered from Alligator Island to the southeast. The mine's lights were pale compared to the flash of illumination that followed.

"What the hell was that?" Jennifer gasped.

At that moment, a burst of fire shot from something that was hovering in the air above what Jennifer realized had to be Alligator Island. The sound of automatic gunfire erupted, followed by several loud thuds that shook the earth.

"What do we do, George? All of our work is over there."

"We sure as hell can't go over there right now. We'll certainly be killed. Then where would all of our work be? Regardless of what happens to the island, we can reconstruct our work. In fact, I would suggest we get the hell out of here. Someone really does want to stop what we're doing here. I have a plan."

Ignoring him, Jennifer looked in horror at the explosions to the south. After a moment, she turned and said, "George, are you crazy? Our friends are there. You can stay here if you want. I'm going to the island."

"Don't, Jennifer."

George's last words were drowned out by the explosion that shook the ground beneath him. Seconds later, he turned around to see Jennifer racing out of the parking lot in their Volvo.

George stood watching the explosions coming from the island as his wife of many years drove away. Years of suppressed anger had damped his ability to feel the emotional anxiety he should now be experiencing. In his mind, it really didn't matter what happened on that island or to anyone else now. Nine million dollars would be wired to his Panamanian bank account tomorrow morning. All he had to do was get to Panama and collect it. He could then resume his important research in earnest.

Knowing his agreement with Morton required him to meet his boat with his experiments at 9:50 p.m., George walked briskly to the storage building and dragged the first duffel bag of his work down to the Lee Creek dock. After wrestling the second duffel to the dock, George collapsed onto a bench beside his bags. Looking out over the creek's waters, a wave of excited anticipation swept over him. Morton had assured him that this would be the first leg of his journey—up the Pamlico River to Little Washington. From there, he would rent a car and drive to Raleigh-Durham International Airport for a flight to Miami. The last leg would be the flight to Panama. To George, all the recent focus on Jennifer's algae breakthrough was misplaced. He had no doubt that his experiments with energy from naturally occurring electrical fields far outweighed the importance of the algae work. But to his frustration, neither Jennifer nor anyone else now seemed interested in discussing his work. In George's mind, this was the final straw. His work had been overshadowed by Jennifer's for long enough. He would take his experiments with him and disappear. The nine million dollars waiting for him would be a huge fortune in Panama. He would live like a king and have plenty of money to conduct his experiments.

George glanced at his watch impatiently. It was 9:50 p.m. Looking up toward the entrance to Lee Creek, he saw the silhouette of a light-less boat ghosting into the harbor. It quietly idled over to the dock where George was standing.

"Are you George Batts?" barked the man standing at the boat's stern.

"Yes."

"Then get your ass down here pronto."

"Let me get my bags," George replied.

"We don't give a shit about your bags," barked the man at the helm. "We need to get the hell out of here."

George hastily pushed his bags off the dock into the stern of the boat. As soon as he stepped down from the dock into the boat, he heard the engine roar and felt the boat leap up on a plane. George had to grab the starboard gunwale to keep from being thrown over the stern. Racing through the terminal, the boat cleared the entrance to Lee Creek in seconds and soon disappeared into the darkness of the Pamlico. Moments later, George felt the boat coming to a stop in the middle of the river.

"What are we doing?" asked George nervously.

"We're throwing this shit overboard," growled the man who had been driving.

"The hell you are!" George protested. "All of my life's work is in those bags. They hold the secret to unlimited electrical energy."

"Yeah, sure," laughed the man in the stern. "I guess you have a magic wand, too."

As the boat's operator lifted one of the bags onto the gunwale, he said, "Sorry, weirdo, the bags go."

George clambered forward to try to grab the bag before it went overboard, but stopped short when he saw the barrel of a .357 Magnum pointed at his chest.

"Easy does it, weirdo," said the man at the stern with an evil grin. "Stand back and smile pretty, because this will be your last picture."

Staring terrified at the .357, George's heart sank as he heard the loud splash of his second bag hitting the water. The next sound George heard was his last. With a deafening roar, the .357 propelled two hollow-point bullets into George's chest and out through his back. The gun's two reports reverberated for miles across the still river before finally fading away in the distance. The force of the two shots knocked George backward over the port gunwale and into the river.

"Rest in peace, weirdo," said the boat's operator, as he stepped back to the helm. Pushing the throttle full forward, he turned the boat toward Washington and raced away upriver.

⊕ ⊕ ⊕

Soon after the attack on Alligator Island began, the dispatcher at the sheriff's office began receiving an onslaught of calls from Aurora residents who had seen the night sky afire with the light of large explosions and heard the sound of automatic gunfire. When the commotion subsided, a call came from the island.

"Beaufort County Sheriff's Office. What is the nature of your emergency?"

"This is Kurt Benjamin, out here at Dutch Phosphate. We just had an assault on our facility by a helicopter gunship and heavily armed ground personnel. We have several casualties and need as many ambulances as you can send."

Twenty minutes later, Kurt heard the sirens of approaching police cruisers and ambulances. Their blue and red lights soon appeared on the causeway as they raced toward Alligator Island. One of Gabe's security guards backed the Suburban away from the island's entrance to allow the emergency vehicles to enter.

After hanging up the phone, Kurt said to Sarah, "I'm going to the generator building to try to determine why the emergency battery lights didn't activate. Why don't you meet the sheriff when he arrives?"

"Will do," replied Sarah. Kurt stepped over the body sprawled on the floor and headed down the hall.

Arriving at the generator building, he soon realized why they had no backup battery power. The breaker for the backup lighting system was in the *off* position. Throwing the switch to *on*, the emergency lights on the island flickered to life.

Walking across the room to the generators, he tried to determine why they had gone off. Going over the big diesel engine, he found nothing obvious. On a hunch that it could be a fuel supply problem, he opened the fuel filter. There in front of him, crammed into the filter, was a ball of grease obviously clogging the supply of fuel to the engine. After removing it and flushing the line, he soon had the generators running. Moment later, the lights powered by them flooded the island.

After leaving the generator room, Kurt looked around the island and made a quick assessment of the damage. The gatehouse and barriers were totally destroyed. One of Tom Gabriel's men lay motionless thirty feet away. Another was sitting up, with emergency medical technicians providing attention.

In the parking lot near the entrance were the remains of the helicopter that was still burning vigorously. The mine's fire department had arrived and was pumping water from the swamp onto the blaze.

At the front gate, Kurt spotted an unmarked sheriff's department cruiser pulling in. Sarah stepped over to the vehicle as a plainclothes officer stepped out.

"Are you Sheriff Baker?" asked Sarah.

"I am," replied the sheriff.

"I'm Sarah Carpenter, chief operating officer of the Dutch Phosphate Corporation. Thanks for coming so quickly." Turning to Gabe, who had just walked up, Sarah said, "This is Tom Gabriel, chief of security for our project here on Alligator Island."

"What the hell happened out here?" the sheriff asked with a frown.

"We don't know," Sarah replied.

"Just what is this 'project,' as you call it?" he said suspiciously.

Sarah considered the question for a few seconds before responding. "We're working on some experiments with our crop fertilizers," she said. She knew this was not a complete answer, but at least it was the truth.

"Well, somebody doesn't like what you're doing out here."

Thinking the less said, the better, Sarah chose not to respond.

With a look of skepticism, the sheriff continued, "You sure that's all you folks are doing out here?"

"It's actually a kind of long story," Sarah replied flatly. "We don't have time tonight to go into it. Mr. Gabriel, let's get the injured out of here, and make sure everything is secure for the night."

Turning to Sarah, the sheriff said sternly, "Ms. Carpenter, we need to have a serious talk about why someone would want to do this to you folks and your project."

Gabe's radio suddenly came to life with the tense voice of Walter Brinn. "Alpha One, are you okay? What's going on over there?"

"Alpha One here," Gabe responded. He had heard Walter's earlier calls when he was still up in the tower, but could not return them. "Roger, Delta. We survived. There are casualties and some major damage. What is your status at the terminal?"

"No damage to report. But a boat crept in here at 2150 with two occupants. They left with a third, that weird scientist guy Batts."

"Roger, Delta. Any ID on the boat?"

"No. It was all very strange. They were in one of those low-sided bass boats with a big outboard hung off the back. It cleared out of here like a bat out of hell, going directly out into the middle of the river, and then it suddenly stopped."

There was a pause as Gabe mentally processed this odd turn of events. "Delta, is the boat still out there?"

"No. It sat there for several minutes, and I saw them throw two large bags overboard. Then I heard two shots from what sounded to me like a large-caliber pistol, and one of them was knocked off the boat. Seconds later, it took off up the river toward Little Washington."

"Roger, Delta. Keep a sharp eye out."

With all the confusion on the island, Kurt had not thought about Jason. Now that things were settling down, it occurred to him that Jason had to have seen the fireworks from across the river and would be very concerned. Picking up his cell phone, he pressed the speed dial number for Jason's cell phone.

Jason answered immediately. "Kurt, what the hell is happening over there?"

"Sarah's fine," Kurt said quickly, knowing Jason had to be concerned.

"Thank God. And how about you?"

"I'm okay, but we've had a full-fledged attack here. It seems to be over now. Where are you?"

"I'm a half mile from the creek entrance. I have something you all need to know before I come in."

"Sarah went to survey the damages to the research projects. Hold on a minute, Jason." Kurt turned to Gabe, who was standing nearby, having just finished his radio conversation with Walter Brinn about the mystery boat's visit to Lee Creek. "Jason's half a mile out from the creek. He wants to know if he can come in. He also says there's something he needs to tell us."

Taking the cell phone from Kurt, Gabe said, "Jason, this is Tom Gabriel. I understand there was some peculiar activity on the river a short while ago. What was it?"

"You might say that," replied Jason flatly. "I've got George Batts on board with two holes blown through his chest. Whoever did it took off upriver after they dumped him."

"Okay, Jason. You're clear to come in. I'll alert our man Walter at the dock. He'll meet you there when you get in. I'll send the EMT folks over to assist."

Jason spent a few minutes scrutinizing the river in all directions before flipping on the Grady's running lights, pushing the throttle forward, and heading toward the creek. Once inside the entrance, he proceeded to a spot on the dock just behind the tug *Pfizer*. As he was securing the dock lines, a man appeared from the shadows behind the terminal office and walked briskly toward him.

"You Jason?"

"Yes, and you must be Walter. Mr. Gabriel said you would meet me."

Walter shone his flashlight down into the stern area where the dead man was lying faceup. "Yep, that's the Batts guy."

"Why would anyone want to kill him?"

"All I can tell you is that he was one of the scientists working over on the island. He seemed like kind of a weird duck. A boat came in here just after the fireworks show stopped and picked him up. I watched them through the binoculars out on the river. Did you see it?"

"I'm afraid so," answered Jason. "I dowsed my lights when I saw them coming out of the creek."

Their conversation was interrupted by a vehicle with flashing red lights approaching the terminal gate. Walter waved his flashlight to direct the vehicle to their location. Two emergency medical technicians got out and approached the dock.

"Good evening. Understand you may have a drowning victim down here."

"I suppose a creative pathologist might say that," Jason retorted, "but have a look for yourselves."

Walter directed the beam of his flashlight onto the lifeless figure lying faceup in the bottom of the boat.

"Holy shit!" exclaimed the EMT closest to the boat. "No need to rush this guy anywhere."

CHAPTER

21

When Jennifer reached what was left of the front gate, emergency vehicles had just arrived. Parking the Volvo on the edge of the road, she stepped cautiously through the rubble that remained. In the flashing lights of the emergency vehicles, she saw Sarah talking with Gabe and what she guessed was a law enforcement officer not in uniform. Sarah and Gabe were just finishing their conversation with the officer when Jennifer came up.

"God, what happened here?" asked Jennifer.

Turning, Sarah opened her arms, and the two exchanged hugs of relief.

"Thank God you're okay," Jennifer said. "Where is Kurt?"

"He's fine. Where is George?"

"He stayed back to keep an eye on the generators. Can we see if our research was damaged?" asked Jennifer.

Sarah turned to Gabe, who had just finished a radio call. Having heard their conversation, he nodded. "I don't see a problem. But here, take this flashlight, and be sure to stay away from any downed power lines."

"Thanks, Gabe," responded Sarah, as she took the flashlight in her right hand.

The two walked briskly across the gravel parking lot to what was now known as the algae farm. As they approached, Jennifer saw that a row of plastic containers where the algae was grown had been ripped open in several places, and their supports were broken. Another row lay on the ground, with algae splattered on other rows ten feet away. As they approached the front door of the lab building, they saw a man in camouflage slumped motionless at the left side. The windows and front door were shattered. Stepping on the glass, the two women walked through the lab, surveying the damage.

As they retraced their path from Jennifer's lab building back to the parking lot, Jennifer breathed a huge sigh of relief. "I feared much worse. This can all be repaired. Let's go check on George's building and his experiments. He's sure to ask me as soon as I see him."

The two women walked across the lot to the blue metal prefabricated building where George conducted his experiments.

"George has been such a good sport about all of our recent work with algae," Jennifer commented absently. "I'm afraid his work has been put on the back burner. Once the algae discovery was made, everyone dropped what they were doing and focused their efforts on it."

Jennifer unlocked the front door, stepped inside, and flipped on the light. After looking about for a moment, she gasped, "Oh my God!"

"What is it?" asked Sarah.

"Someone has taken his work."

After surveying the contents of the building, Jennifer made a mental note of what had been where and what was missing. The two women left the building and walked back across the parking lot. Ahead of them were Kurt and Gabe, who were talking with the sheriff in front of the administration building.

Seeing the two women approaching, Kurt broke off the conversation and nodded to them. "Gabe, let me handle this," he said quietly.

"Thanks, Kurt," replied Gabe with a deep sigh.

As Sarah and Jennifer approached, Kurt stepped away from Gabe and the sheriff and walked to meet them. Kurt looked at Jennifer and said, "Jennifer, I'm afraid I have some bad news about George."

"What is it?" she asked. "I just left him a little over an hour ago at the terminal."

"We're not sure, but we are afraid he was killed in the onslaught."

"That can't be. He was fine when I left him, and the attack was over by the time I reached the island. Where is he now?"

"At the terminal," said Kurt.

"Well, let's go," said Jennifer.

Sarah put her arm around Jennifer and they followed Kurt to his Range Rover, and he drove to the terminal. When they arrived, the medical technicians were loading a body into their vehicle. Jason was at the dock talking with Walter.

"Okay, Jennifer, I'm going to ask you to stay here with Sarah for a few minutes while I find out what is going on," Kurt said.

Jennifer, who had ridden over in the backseat with Sarah holding her hand, nodded tearfully and said nothing.

Kurt turned and walked briskly to the emergency vehicle. "Who is he?" he asked.

One of the technicians responded, "The security guard said he was one of the scientists. I think he said his name was Batts."

"Let me see."

The technician pulled the sheet down from over the man's head.

"Yes, it's Batts," acknowledged Kurt. "What happened to him?"

The technician pulled the sheet down farther, to George's belt.

"Those bastards," Kurt muttered to himself.

He walked slowly back to the Range Rover in shocked disbelief. Opening the back door, he suggested they step over to the bench near the terminal building. After Sarah and Jennifer were seated, Kurt sat down on the other side of Jennifer and took her left hand in his, holding it gently.

"Where is he?" Jennifer asked in almost a whisper.

"He's in the ambulance."

"I must see him."

"Jennifer, I don't think that's a good idea right now," replied Kurt.

"No, I must see him. This just doesn't make any sense. Why would anyone want to kill George?"

"Very well. If you must."

When the three reached the ambulance, the EMTs, who were filling out their field report, looked up.

"This is his wife," Kurt said. "She needs to see him."

Kurt was careful to lift only enough of the sheet to expose George's lifeless, ashen face. Jennifer burst into tears immediately.

"Why would anyone do this?" she sobbed. Sarah wrapped her arms around Jennifer gently and did her best to comfort her.

Jason, who had been watching the three, walked over to the ambulance. Sarah released Jennifer and exchanged a silent hug with her uncle. After Jennifer placed a gentle kiss on George's forehead, she stepped away from the ambulance.

Sarah took both of Jennifer's hands in hers and said firmly, "You need to stay with us tonight. There is nothing more we can do here."

The four of them walked slowly over to the Grady. Jason stepped down first and extended a hand to assist Jennifer into the boat. Sarah and Kurt followed. During the trip across the river, Sarah sat beside Jennifer, stroking her back and giving her an occasional hug as she sobbed.

Once the boat was secured at the Bella Vista dock, Sarah took Jennifer to the cottage to find her some fresh clothes and make her comfortable for the night.

Jason and Kurt lingered at the boat with the pretext of fixing some problem that had developed with the engine. Kurt sat on the edge of the dock. After fiddling with the boat for a few minutes, Jason got out and sat down next to Kurt.

"You must have a lot going through your mind right now," Jason said softly.

"None of this makes any sense. First, we have the Arab intruders with explosives coming through the swamp. Then tonight, we have a full-blown paramilitary assault by a group of Caucasians."

"Yeah," answered Jason. "Those guys were obviously profession- als and had a well-planned attack based on very good intelligence. Someone seriously wants to stop what you're doing over there."

"Clearly. But who are they, and why? Where are they getting their information? And why did they kill George?"

"Kurt, I saw it through night-vision binoculars. Cold-blooded mur- der is the only way to describe it."

"Yes, but why? What was he doing on that boat?"

"How well did you know George?"

"I thought very well. He was a brilliant scientist who was devoted to his work and also to Jennifer. Why do you ask?"

"Well, someone went way out of their way to target just him. Was he working on a project for which someone would single him out?"

Kurt considered this. "George was a little secretive about his work."

At that moment, the two heard footsteps on the pier and looked up to see Sarah walking in their direction. She had three glasses in one hand and a wine bottle in the other. "It's been a tough night. I thought we could all use a little something to soothe our nerves." She set the three glasses on the bait table at the end of the pier and poured a generous portion of wine into each.

Kurt and Jason walked over and each picked up a glass.

"Thank you, Sarah," said Kurt. "How is Jennifer?"

"She wanted some time alone to think. I poured her a glass and left her rocking in one of the big rockers on the front porch. She must be in shock."

The three sat quietly for a while. The only sound came from the lapping of waves against the pier pilings below the dock.

"Sarah, we were just talking about how none of this is making any sense to us. Jason was asking me about George. We can't figure out why he was singled out."

Kurt and Jason got up and sat on the bench on one side of the pier, and Sarah sat on the one across from them.

"George never wanted to talk about the details of his work," Kurt said. "Now that I think about it, he said very little about what he was doing during the last couple of months. We were so excited about the algae discovery that his work was overshadowed."

There was another period of silence, finally interrupted by Sarah. "Why would they take him out into the middle of the river to do that? Why didn't they finish him at the dock and leave?"

"Well, I'll add a question to that one," said Jason. "What were the other two objects that were thrown overboard with George's body?"

"I'm sorry. What did you just say?" asked Kurt.

"Oh, I guess I hadn't thought to mention it. Right before the two gunshots, two large objects were thrown overboard."

"Were they bodies, too?" asked Sarah.

"No. It was more like a couple of heavy sacks."

"That's strange," said Kurt. "What could they have been? And why would someone want to throw them into the middle of the Pamlico River?"

"Wait a minute," said Sarah. "When Jennifer and I went to his lab after the attack, she was shocked to see that his primary experimental devices were missing."

A soft voice responded from the darkness a few feet up the dock. "I have a hunch," said Jennifer, startling all of them. They had not heard her quiet, barefooted approach.

Sarah got up to greet her. "Jennifer, I thought you wanted to be alone. We would have included you in this discussion, but I thought tonight was not the time."

Jennifer responded, "There will never be a right time. Something terrible is afoot with our project, and we must deal with it. What we're doing is too important."

Even in the dim lighting of the pier, Sarah could tell that the grief she had seen on Jennifer's face had been replaced by intense determination. "Here, come join us."

As Jennifer took a seat beside her on the bench, Sarah extended the wineglass out to her and said, "Let's share this one."

"Thank you," said Jennifer. She took the glass and, without hesitation, downed a healthy sip.

As was typical for this time of year, the wind had shifted at night, and a gentle land breeze blew from the north out over the river. The occasional hoots of an owl floated with the breeze from the woods behind the cottage.

Kurt broke the silence. "So what is your hunch, Jennifer?"

"Well, it's just that, a hunch. When Sarah and I went into George's lab tonight, I noticed that the experimental energy production devices he had been working on were gone. I didn't take a complete inventory, but the main focus of his work was missing."

"How much are we talking about?"

"Let's just say that you could probably fit it into two large bags."

As the others sat in silence, pondering the implications of what they had just heard, Jennifer continued. "George was frustrated because he felt that he was close to something very big."

"Just what was he working on?" asked Jason.

"His main focus was on some work done in the early 1900s by Nicola Tesla, on what he believed were naturally occurring energy fields. He was also starting to experiment with some work that was done by John Keely in the late 1800s involving what he called sympathetic vibratory physics, or SVP for short. It generally involves harmonics and sound. Somehow, it never really made its way into the mainstream of the research into alternative energy sources. Perhaps it was too much of a long shot. But it shows up in some interesting places. For example, transcripts of some of Edgar Cayce's readings even make reference to it."

"Jason, do you have any idea of where this boat was when all this happened?" asked Kurt.

"Actually, I could probably get us within a hundred feet of it. When I reached the approximate location where I thought the body had been thrown overboard, I hit the waypoint button on the GPS twice. As you know, this is how in an emergency situation you can mark the spot when there's a man overboard. That waypoint is stored on the GPS. It's just a matter of going to it. Also, the boat has sonar to observe the contours of the bottom. This helps me find ledges and reefs where fish sometimes hang out. It may well detect these two sacks on the bottom of the river."

"You're not thinking of going down there and trying to find them, are you?" asked Sarah.

"I am," said Kurt, "but I don't have my dive gear."

"Well, even if you did, you probably wouldn't have much luck," said Sarah. "The visibility on the bottom of the river is probably ten feet or less. You would have to be virtually on top of these bags to see them."

"Kurt, what size wetsuit do you wear?" asked Jason.

"A large."

"Okay, I can fit you. We have tanks in the shop. We'll need to fill them tonight. The underwater flashlights also need to be charged. You'll need all the illumination you can get in that murky water."

"I'm going down with you," said Sarah.

Kurt looked at her and smiled. "I don't think so. Jason will need you up top in case something happens."

"No, and you know as well as I do that a diver should never do something like this alone. Too many things can happen down there. This is not a task for one diver."

Jason piped up, "I think she's right. Besides, Sarah is a very good diver. You're going to need an extra set of hands and eyes down there to find this stuff."

"Very well. What time should we do this?"

"I would suggest that we shoot for late morning, when we'll have the most light," answered Jason.

"One final issue for tonight," said Sarah. "Kurt, we haven't briefed Omar. Should we?"

"Why don't we wait until after we're done with our dive tomorrow?"

Sarah nodded. "I think you're probably right. It's one a.m. Let's all get some sleep."

Jason and Jennifer sat on the dock in silence as Kurt and Sarah walked back to the cottage. Jason remembered the feeling of loss when his wife passed away. He stepped over and sat beside Jennifer.

"Jennifer," he began, "I lost my wife some years ago. We were close, as I know you and George were. I understand the loss you're feeling."

Jennifer turned, put her head against his shoulder, and wept. Jason gently put his arms around her and said softly, "I know. I know."

⊕ ⊕ ⊕

At 12:35 a.m. on the night of the assault, Jeffrey Morton, chief of operations for USOCO, had been pacing his office in Houston for an hour when his cell phone rang. "Yes?" he snapped.

"Mr. Morton, we were told to call you when the operation was complete."

"Is it?"

"Yes."

"Then I assume you were successful."

There was a pause. "I'm afraid we have good news and bad news."

"That is not what I wanted to hear."

"The good news is that Mr. Batts is swimming with the fish in the Pamlico."

"So what's the bad news?"

"Their defenses were much better than we had thought."

"And?"

"We lost the 'copter and all our men."

"What do you mean by lost? Were any of them captured?"

"No, they're all dead. As soon as we dumped Batts and his bags into the river, we hightailed it out of there."

"You what? Did you say you dumped Batts's bags?"

"Well, yes. We didn't want to leave a trail. And if we were stopped, we sure as hell didn't want his personal belongings on our boat."

"You idiots!" yelled Morton. "I gave your boss specific instructions *not* to lose what Batts would have with him. It was to be delivered as an essential part of the bargain."

"Nobody told us that. We just did what made sense at the time."

"Well, make sense of this!" shouted Morton. "You better figure out a way to recover the bags you threw off the boat, or you won't get the final fifty-thousand-dollar payment!"

There was a pause.

"Got it?" asked Morton.

There was another pause before the voice asked, "If we do get these bags, what do we do with them?"

"It's not *if*, it's *when* you get them," barked Morton. "When you get them, call me for instructions. I'll deliver the money when you deliver what you threw away."

No response.

Morton said firmly, "Do you understand?"

"Yes," came the muted reply. "I understand."

"Then good night," growled Morton, and he hung up the phone.

CHAPTER
22

Kurt awoke just after seven o'clock in the morning to hear the faint sound of what he recognized as the NOAA weather report drifting out from somewhere in the living area of the cottage. He quickly pulled on a pair of shorts and a T-shirt, and walked down the hall to find Sarah behind the large counter in the kitchen, slicing a cantaloupe.

"Good morning, Sarah."

She looked up and, with a gentle smile, responded, "Good morning to you, Kurt. I hope you slept well."

"At times. How about you?"

"Same here." She frowned and set the knife on the counter. "Kurt, none of this makes any sense. Who was behind what happened last night, and why?"

Taking a seat on one of the stools, he replied, "I have the same questions. Whoever it is, they seemed pretty determined. The first time involved Arabs. The guys last night were definitely not Arab. Where's Jason? Is he up yet?"

"He's been up for a couple of hours. Right now he's out in the garage putting the dive equipment together. I just listened to the weather forecast. It could be interesting out there today. A low-pressure system will be arriving by late morning. With it will be increasing winds from the southwest, along with afternoon thunderstorms. We'll have twenty-knot winds gusting to thirty by late morning."

"Hmm, sounds as if we need to get out of here pretty soon."

At that moment, Jason came through the back door. Having heard the forecast earlier, he had hastened out to the garage to prepare things so they could leave as soon as possible. Jason gave Kurt a pleasant,

239

"Good morning," and poured his second cup of coffee. "We're going to have our hands full out there today. This is not the weather we wanted."

"I agree," said Sarah, "but if what's out there is as important as Jennifer thinks it is, we really need to find it before someone else does. Otherwise, years of research and perhaps the big breakthrough we've been searching for could be lost forever."

"I understand," said Jason. "We'll just have to make the best of what we're served."

Kurt asked, "Where's Jennifer?"

"She's down on the beach. After making the coffee, she poured a cup and said she needed a little time to think."

"No doubt," reflected Kurt. "If the three of us can't make sense of this, just imagine what kind of questions must be going through her mind right now."

By 8:40 the dive equipment was all loaded onto the Grady White. Although they had encouraged her to stay at the cottage, Jennifer insisted on joining them. Kurt and Sarah cleared and stowed the dock lines as Jason headed out into the river. Jason touched the *Go To* icon on the GPS, and the course to the designated waypoint appeared. A steep chop had already developed, with frequent whitecaps. The Grady's sleek V-hull sliced cleanly through the waves, but Jason held back from putting it on a full plane. There was no need to provide his passengers with a punishing ride this early in the day. Things would get rough enough by late morning.

Forty-five minutes later, the GPS began emitting a steady series of beeps. They were at the waypoint that Jason had marked on the instrument the previous night. He immediately pulled back on the throttle and began a systematic, expanding circling pattern from the waypoint. Sarah's attention was riveted to the sonar screen to see if anything unusual appeared on the bottom. At the same time, Kurt was busily setting up the anchoring gear.

After thirty minutes, there was no trace of any unusual objects appearing on the sonar. The mood was somber. They all knew that unless the sonar picked up something, their dive into the murky waters of the Pamlico would be like searching for the proverbial needle in the haystack. Jason made several more sweeps, to no avail. Sarah let out a deep sigh of frustration.

Jennifer had been seated in the stern trying to get her sea legs. Unlike her companions, she had no boating experience, and had no clue of what to do on a boat in rough conditions such as these. But seeing Sarah's frustration, she stood bravely and inched her way forward, holding tightly to the port gunwale for support. Reaching the center console, she released the gunwale, grabbed the console's handrail next to Jason, and stared down at the sonar screen.

"How do you know what you're looking for?" she asked.

"We should see a bump on the bottom," replied Sarah. "And if those bags were big, we should be able to see them pretty easily." Both stood quietly for several minutes, staring at the screen. "Nothing," said Sarah, looking up as Jason completed another slow sweep. "Getting rougher," she mumbled.

"Yep," her uncle replied tersely.

"What is that?" yelped Jennifer, and pointed to the screen.

Sarah spun around, looked at the sonar screen, and gasped. "Wow! That has to be them!"

At that point, Jason turned the boat into the wind and gave a nod to Kurt at the bow to release the anchor.

With the anchor set, Kurt and Sarah put on their dive gear. After making their safety checks and last-minute inspections of gauges and equipment, they sat on the starboard gunwale with their backs to the water, and then in unison fell backward and disappeared into the cool, dark waters of the Pamlico.

To avoid getting separated, both had their steel diver knives in hand to make periodic raps on their air tanks so each knew the other's position. They slowly moved toward the bow, found the anchor line, and descended to a depth of eighteen feet. They were now near the muddy bottom of the river. As planned, they began a course of thirty degrees to the northeast back under the Grady's hull to the place where they anticipated finding the bags. Jason had tried to position the boat so that the anchor would fall several boat-lengths upwind from the two objects seen on the sonar.

Except for the rhythmic release of air bubbles from their regulators, there was no sound.

Using their underwater lights to scan the murky waters ahead, they slowly made their way forward at a depth of eighteen feet. Suddenly,

Kurt felt Sarah grab his left arm. As she jiggled her light off to the left, he could barely make out the image of some sort of dark blob. Moving closer, through the murky haze they soon saw another similar blob about ten feet behind the first one. Once on top of the objects, they turned to each other and exchanged high-fives. Neither had any doubt that these were George Batts's duffel bags with a lifetime of research stored inside.

They took marker balloon buoys from their dive vests and attached one to each duffel bag, inflating them with their dive regulators.

Jason had been looking off to the stern, following the path of the divers' air bubbles. Suddenly, two small round objects appeared on the choppy surface of the river in front of him.

"Look over there, Jennifer," he said, and pointed to the two balloons bobbing vigorously in the river's waves.

"They've found them," she whispered, letting out a huge sigh of relief. Although she wanted to grab Jason and hug him, she held on to the stern gunwale tightly to keep from being thrown out of the boat.

With their attention focused on the search, Jennifer and Jason had not noticed the presence of a boat positioned a mile to the southwest. In it were two men with binoculars, watching them intently.

Moments later, Kurt and Sarah bobbed to the surface. Each had a line attached to a bag below. Jason first took Sarah's line with the boat hook and tied it to the starboard stern cleat, and then did the same with Kurt's. Sarah and Kurt soon were on board and removing their dive gear. Once the gear was stored, Kurt and Jason began slowly pulling the first bag up to the boat. When the bag broke the surface, its true weight could be felt. With a great deal of effort, they muscled the bag up onto the starboard gunwale and rolled it carefully down onto the deck. As they did so, Kurt suddenly felt the same old eerie feeling of being watched coming over him.

The two men watching the activity on Jason's Grady had not thought to check the NOAA weather forecast before leaving Washington that morning. And being anchored in the protected lee of the south shore of the Pamlico, they had not noticed the ever-increasing height of the waves a mile out into the river.

Their rented boat was the same one they had used the day before. All they had asked the rental company for was a very fast boat, and it was. With a 250-horsepower Yamaha on its stern, the sleek craft with low gunwales could achieve sixty miles per hour on the flat waters of the calm upper reaches of the Pamlico. Little did they know that this speed capability meant nothing in the steep, choppy waters farther down the river. With its scant one foot of freeboard, the boat was ill-suited for the task at hand.

After the second bag came over the transom of Jason's boat, Kurt looked up and saw a boat approaching rapidly from the southwest. "Jason, take a look at that boat over there."

Lifting a set of binoculars to his eyes, Jason studied the approaching craft. "Damn!" he exclaimed, as he lowered the binoculars.

"What is it?" asked Sarah.

"I think it's the same boat I saw out here last night."

As Kurt was hauling the anchor on board, they heard the crack of a gunshot. A bullet whizzed just over Kurt's head.

"Hang on!" yelled Jason. He gunned the engines, brought the Grady onto a plane, and circled off to the northeast and downriver. Studying the water ahead and behind, Jason pushed the throttles to 2,600 rpms, and they began grinding through the steep chop of the Pamlico. A second shot, and then a third whistled past them. Even with its deep V-hull, the Grady pounded violently through the rough waters. A minute later, their pursuers were fifty yards behind them and closing fast, but their boat was pitching and bouncing wildly, making any further shots difficult. When they were within twenty yards of the Grady White, shots erupted again. One hit the starboard engine, which coughed, sputtered, and ground to a stop. Jason had been executing the same weaving maneuvers he had learned years before, during his stint in the Navy, to avoid torpedoes, but this one had not worked. The sound of another shot came, and a bullet slammed through the stern, grazing Sarah's right upper arm and embedding itself into the console between where Jason and Sarah were standing. Sarah let out a short yelp as blood began streaming down her arm onto the deck.

Kurt rushed over to inspect the wound. He quickly removed his shirt and tied it tightly around her arm.

"It's fortunately a surface wound," he said calmly. "This will slow the bleeding until we can do better."

Without showing outward signs of fear, Kurt thought, *With no weapons on board, we're sitting ducks. At this rate, it's only a matter of time.*

Reaching down to the throttle for the remaining engine, Jason yelled, "This is it, folks! Hang on as tight as you can!" Shoving the throttle all the way forward, he focused on keeping the boat from capsizing as it bounced over the tops of the river's steep waves.

Kurt had been facing the stern, studying their attackers. As they continued farther down the river, the height of the waves increased dramatically. The low boat behind them was clearly struggling to deal with the worsening conditions. It was now pitching and pounding violently. The man at the helm obviously did not know how to read the waves ahead of and behind him, and was pushing the vessel far beyond its capability in these conditions. Kurt watched as the man in the bow stood to take another shot, making the ultimate mistake of letting go of the handrail. The boat's bow suddenly slammed down into a wave, which threw him forward and over the bow. Seconds later, the boat's stern bumped upward as it bounced over the man's torso. The engine's prop made a groaning sound as it chewed through flesh. After slowing for a second to look behind him, the man at the controls pushed the throttle forward and resumed the chase.

As Kurt watched the remaining man in the boat trying to steer and aim his weapon, a series of three large waves approached the other craft. The man fired off two more shots, but the bow of his boat lifted abruptly with the first wave and then dove into the trough of the second one, throwing him forward headfirst into the bow. Three feet of water swept quickly over the hapless boat and its now unconscious occupant. Seconds later, the boat and its driver disappeared under the waves and into the murky waters of the Pamlico.

Jason slowed and circled back to where Kurt had last seen the boat. All that remained was a pack of cigarettes, a life jacket, and a package of crackers floating on the river's angry surface. Jason and Kurt exchanged looks and shook their heads. Pushing the throttles forward, Jason turned the boat back to the northeast toward Bella Vista.

Once the boat was moored, Jennifer escorted Sarah down the pier to the cottage to clean and bandage the wound. Jason walked to the base of the pier and returned with a large wheelbarrow. The duffel bags were so big that only one could fit in it at a time. Jason slowly rolled the bags to the garage where their contents could be rinsed with fresh water, dried, and examined. Jennifer and Sarah soon came to help, with Sarah now wearing a gauze bandage around her right arm. Meticulously, they began removing the first bag's contents as Jason went for the second. After rolling it laboriously back to the garage, he returned to the boat to assist Kurt with the dive equipment. Once it was rinsed and hung on lines inside the garage to dry, Kurt and Jason turned their attention to the contents of the duffel bags being inventoried by Jennifer and Sarah.

"We're in luck. His notes and diagrams were in sealed plastic bags. They look fine, but we may not know how the actual equipment fared until we try to use it."

It was five p.m. when they finished examining the bags. As Sarah, Jennifer, and Kurt started to walk back to the cottage, Sarah saw Jason do something she had never seen him do before. He locked the dead-bolts on both garage doors.

Once they were inside the cottage, Jason closed the door and said solemnly, "We need to talk."

Opening the refrigerator, he handed everyone a bottle of water. The four of them took a seat around the kitchen table, saying nothing.

Sarah finally broke the silence, asking, "What happens now?"

There was another moment of silence.

"Jennifer, what exactly did we find in the river today that was worth someone trying to kill us?" asked Jason.

"I really don't know. The duffel bags we just emptied contain what I suspected, along with a project George and I both worked on here and at USOCO before we left. Just like other work we did there, when this project went to management levels for a determination of economic feasibility, it was rejected."

"What exactly was this project?" asked Jason.

"It involved research similar to what we talked about last night. Tesla believed there was an unlimited energy source occurring naturally around us. We think he was close to discovering how to harness it when J. P. Morgan pulled the plug on his funding."

"Yep," Jason said, "I've read about Tesla's work on this. When Morgan figured out there was no way for him to charge the public for it, and that it would be a threat to his oil revenue, he withdrew financial support for the project. This idea has been dead for almost a century. It's pretty amazing that you and George revived it."

"Could someone at USOCO view this project as a threat?" asked Sarah.

The four sat thoughtfully.

"We can't know the answer to that right now," Kurt said evenly. "What we do know is that someone is trying to kill for what we have out there in the garage. It needs to disappear fast."

"How?" asked Sarah.

"I have an idea," said Kurt. "If we can get it to Houston, we can stow it on the *Carpe Diem* and disappear into the Gulf of Mexico, with no trace of our destination."

The others stared intently at Kurt.

"And just where would we go?" asked Jennifer.

Sarah, remembering Kurt once telling her of his favorite scuba diving destinations, smiled. "You think we should hide this in Belize. Am I correct, Kurt?"

Kurt nodded. "No one would ever suspect. Whoever is behind this may be able to trace us to Houston. From there, it would be anyone's guess as to where we went. The Gulf of Mexico is a big place. In fact, we could tell the dock master that our destination is Key West, and then Bermuda. That would send whoever is after us in the opposite direction."

"But we need to think about Jennifer," Sarah said softly, as she reached over to put her hand on Jennifer's.

Jennifer nodded as she looked across the table at Kurt. "George wanted to be cremated, which I can have done tomorrow. His ashes should go with us. I think he would have wanted it that way. When do we leave?"

"Jeez," sighed Jason.

"What choice do we have?" asked Sarah. "I suggest we all make our necessary personal arrangements tomorrow and get the hell out of here. When I explain to my CEO that there were two attempts to kill us in two days, he will insist that Kurt and I disappear for a while. One of the P180s can take us to Houston tomorrow night."

"Very well," said Jason. "I say we meet here tomorrow at six p.m. I'll ask our neighbor down the road, Dallas, to run us over to the DPC terminal in his boat at seven o'clock. Sarah, can you make arrangements for a plane that quickly?"

"I think so," she responded, and then turned to Kurt. "We still haven't talked to Omar. He shouldn't hear about what happened through the DPC or his family."

"I agree, but how much do we tell him? And when?" asked Kurt.

"Why don't you call him tomorrow? Limit the information to the unsuccessful attempt by as yet unknown people to destroy the research facility on Alligator Island. And you will need to say something about George's murder."

"Okay," said Kurt. "It's probably better that he not know that we recovered George's research from the Pamlico River. That way, he can honestly deny knowledge of it. Jennifer, I'll speak with your team tomorrow. They'll accept the fact that you need some time before coming back to your project on the island. I'll tell them to clean up the mess and press on."

Jennifer nodded in agreement. "We've ironed out most of the kinks in the production process. They can carry on production until I get back."

"And there's Gabe," said Kurt. "I'll brief him on what we're doing. He'll be the only one who knows how to reach us, which will be by satellite phone. He knows the number."

⊕ ⊕ ⊕

When Kurt awoke at six o'clock the next morning, he immediately got up and walked out onto the front porch overlooking the Pamlico to place the call to Sharjah. It was 2:05 p.m. there when he finally reached Omar. Cutting short the usual brief pleasantries, Kurt gave Omar a synopsis of what had happened two nights before.

After listening intently, Omar finally asked, "Are you and Sarah safe?"

"That we do not know. Officially, we'll be on a special assignment for DPC for a few weeks, but we'll be in close contact. Jason and Jennifer will be with us."

"What if I need to get in touch with you?"

"It's probably best that you not know where we are. If you need to talk to us, call Tom Gabriel at DPC Security and he'll relay the message. I will then contact you."

"I understand. Be safe, my friend, and take good care of Sarah. She is like a sister to me."

Stepping back into the cottage's living room, Kurt found a beehive of activity as Jason and Sarah went about packing and preparing for an extended time away. Arrangements had to be made for the potential of being out of the country for what they knew could be as long as two months. No one would know where they had taken George's research, exactly what it was, or how far he had gotten with it. Once in Belize, they would find a safe place for Jennifer to decipher George's notes and experiments, to determine exactly what it was that someone was willing to kill for. After things cooled down, they would reappear in the United States, in Houston via the *Carpe Diem*, with no trace of where they had been. At least, that was the plan.

CHAPTER

23

SEPTEMBER 20, 2008 — HOUSTON, TEXAS

At eleven p.m., the wheels of the P180 touched down gently on the runway of Houston's William P. Hobby Airport, a small airport south of the metro area. Being closer to the Houston Yacht Club than George Bush Intercontinental, Kurt liked its convenience. He also expected their pursuers would focus on the major airport and not this smaller airfield if they were trying to track them.

Thirty minutes later, Paul Joyce, Kurt's former next-door neighbor, met them at the terminal with his Suburban. When Paul reached down to help Kurt lift the first duffel bag, he gasped. "What the hell is in here, Kurt? You haulin' gold bullion in this thing?"

Kurt laughed casually. "I wish. It's a bunch of new electronics and navigational equipment. I'm upgrading a lot of the old stuff on board. Since we'll be offshore the entire trip to Key West, we need to be prepared."

When they arrived at the dock, Kurt noticed four wheelbarrows of provisions sitting next to the *Carpe Diem*. Down below, Kurt found the engine room door open and a grease-covered mechanic checking out the engine. After chatting briefly with the mechanic, Kurt joined Sarah, Jason, and Jennifer in the sorting, organizing, and storing of provisions.

When they were finished, Jennifer picked up the urn with George's ashes in it and studied it for a few seconds. "Where can I put George where he'll be safe?"

Kurt pondered the question, knowing how rough seas can rearrange items not properly stored.

"I know," said Sarah. "There's a locker in the bow where Kurt stores blankets. We can wrap the urn in one of the blankets up there. Since we're obviously not going to need blankets on this trip, the ashes won't be disturbed."

Jennifer nodded and followed Sarah to the blanket locker in the bow. When they returned several minutes later, Kurt and Jason were studying the chart of Galveston Bay, plotting their course for tomorrow.

Kurt looked at his watch. "It's three a.m. Let's all get some sleep."

Exhausted, everyone agreed. Moments later, they collapsed into the *Carpe Diem*'s berths and slept soundly.

⊕ ⊕ ⊕

Kurt was the first on deck the next day, followed by Sarah and Jason shortly after. To thoroughly acquaint the *Carpe Diem*'s new crew with her sails and rigging, Kurt led Sarah and Jason on a methodical tour of the yacht. Returning to the galley from their tutorial, they found Jennifer busily preparing breakfast. Knowing she had no nautical experience, Kurt had suggested she run the galley, to which she readily agreed. As Jennifer phrased it, she would have the title of Chief Cook and Bottle Washer.

"I suggest we leave by two p.m. today," said Kurt. "We can get through the ship channel during daylight and be offshore by dark."

All agreed. Jennifer raised her cup of coffee and proposed a toast. "Here's to adventure."

They all chuckled and clinked their cups in unison.

"Well, let's hope not of the variety we've experienced lately," offered Jason. He then raised his cup. "Let's try this. Here's to fair winds and following seas."

⊕ ⊕ ⊕

At two p.m., Sarah and Jason removed the dock lines, coiled, and stowed them as Kurt motored the *Carpe Diem* from her slip out toward the entrance to the channel leading to Galveston Bay. Once out in the bay, he raised the mainsail and unfurled the headsail. With a steady breeze from the west, Kurt felt the *Carpe Diem* surge forward on a brisk broad reach down the bay. Several hours later, they cleared the last marker leading out of the Galveston Bay channel into the Gulf of Mexico. The remnants of the sun's red glow were fading below crimson clouds to the west.

Standing beside Kurt at the helm, Sarah repeated an old sailor's adage, "Red sky at night, sailor's delight, red sky at morning, sailor take warning."

"Yes," replied Kurt thoughtfully. "This is a good sign."

Stepping up the companionway from the navigation station below, Jason announced, "Our course is southeast for the next four hours. If anyone is watching us, this will confirm the official version of our destination being Key West. Once well offshore, we'll change our heading to the south toward the Yucatan Peninsula and then on to Belize."

"Excellent," said Kurt. "Sarah, I believe you drew the first watch. I have the second. We should be out of the Houston shipping lanes in a couple of hours, and the oil tankers will no longer be a threat. Until then, we need to keep our eyes open."

Jason left the cockpit for his berth, and Kurt went forward to ensure everything was secure on the foredeck. Returning to the cockpit a few moments later, he stepped next to Sarah to check their course.

"Everything looks good," he said, putting his arm around Sarah's shoulder and giving it an affectionate squeeze. Sarah turned to face Kurt with a warm smile. To his surprise, she stood on tiptoe and placed her lips gently on his in a warm, affectionate kiss.

"I'll wake you in a few hours," she said.

Slightly taken aback, Kurt smiled faintly, nodded, and stepped down the companionway into the darkened cabin below.

Now alone, Sarah settled into the rhythmic motions of the *Carpe Diem* as the sleek yacht sliced its way gracefully to the southeast through the dark swells of the gulf. The sky was clear and filling with stars, their reflections sparkling on the waters around her. The faint remnants of light from the mainland soon faded away. She felt a sense of quiet peace come over her.

⊕ ⊕ ⊕

Kurt quietly made his way forward through the dimly lit cabin to his berth. As he lay on his back thinking about all that had happened in the past week, he felt the steady movements of the yacht and heard the slosh of waves against the hull as they made their way farther out into the gulf. With the warm sensation of Sarah's lips meeting his, his mind drifted away slowly towards sleep. Suddenly, an old sense of being watched crept over him. At first he tried to push the sensation away thinking it was just fatigue, or an overreaction to the events of the past few days. He tried to focus on their destination, and that they had left no trail. But an inner voice kept telling him that something was amiss. Realizing that sleep was hopeless, he rolled out of his bunk and retraced his steps back through the dark cabin and up the companion-way. There, he found Sarah seated on the port lazarette, gazing off to starboard. Glancing quickly in all directions, he saw nothing except the lights of a giant tanker sliding past them to starboard toward the refinery terminals of Houston.

Sensing a presence, she turned to see Kurt settling onto the port lazarette beside her.

"I couldn't sleep," he said. "Want some company?"

"Yes, I would like that," she said softly.

For the next several hours, they talked. After discussing the events of the past few days, they agreed that whatever the project was that George Batts had lost his life over had to be continued. Once in Belize, they would find a place where Jennifer could resume his work in seclusion and safety. To change the subject from the traumatic past few days, Kurt moved closer and began telling Sarah about San Pedro, Belize, their destination.

"The first thing we need to do is rent a golf cart. That's the primary means of transportation on the island of Ambergris. We'll go to Wild Mango's for our first dinner. It's owned by my good friends Chuck and Amy. The next day, I'll have to take you and Jason scuba diving."

After a while, they sat silently, enjoying the indescribable sensations of sailing under darkness at sea. Sarah eventually leaned back against Kurt's chest, and he put his arms around her. Their conversation drifted to the stars and constellations as they progressed through the night sky above. The sounds of the sea passing under them soon carried Sarah into a peaceful slumber.

In the ensuing hours, Kurt's thoughts wandered back to his decision to leave the CIA and then to his time at USOCO. He recalled his high hopes upon taking the position at USOCO's Department of Alternative Energy, and then his discovery that the department was nothing but a fraudulent public relations ploy. *And here I am in the Gulf of Mexico, running from unknown enemies with secrets that may hold the key to an unlimited energy supply. People are willing to kill for what we have on board. There must be something very special in George's experiments that only Jennifer can unlock. We must find a safe place in Belize for her to continue his work. And in the process, I've once again put the people I love in harm's way.* The memories of the death of his fiancée came sweeping over him again. *What will happen to Sarah? How can I keep her away from the craziness that seems drawn to me? Should I distance myself from her for now?*

Hours later, with the first glimmers of light on the eastern horizon, Kurt heard footsteps coming up the companionway. He looked up to see Jason stepping up into the cockpit. Kurt winked at Jason and raised a finger to his lips, signaling that they would remain silent and let her sleep. After checking their course, Jason nodded with approval. Sarah and Kurt had made the required course change to the south several hours before. Jason quietly retraced his steps back down the companionway. Moments later, Kurt heard the rattling of pans in the galley below.

As the sun pushed its way above the horizon, Sarah awoke to find herself still in Kurt's gentle embrace. Stirring slowly, she sat up and turned to him. Without exchanging words, their lips met for a moment, only to be interrupted by the sound of Jennifer clearing her throat. They looked over toward the companionway and saw her holding two cups of coffee.

"Sorry to interrupt," she said with a knowing smile. "Could I possibly interest you guys in a cup of coffee?"

Epilogue

The financial giants of Wall Street were down on their knees. Bear Stearns was the first to collapse. Merrill Lynch was consumed by Bank of America. Lehman Brothers filed for bankruptcy. AIG received an eighty-five-billion-dollar bailout loan from the Federal Reserve. Wachovia, the country's seventh-largest bank, was facing collapse before it was saved by a shotgun wedding with Wells Fargo forced by the Fed. The country's largest mortgage purchasers, Fannie Mae and Freddie Mac, were taken over by the United States government. The country's financial institutions appeared headed over the cliff, with corporate America not far behind.

The Abu Dhabi registered Gulfstream taxied in the darkness past the tarmac lights that were guiding it to the terminal of the Long Island MacArthur Airport. Each of the Arab men on board wore a conservative, Western-style navy blue suit. But in keeping with the traditions of the United Arab Emirates, each man also wore a kaffiyeh.

Hussein Mubarek, the president of the Abu Dhabi Oil Company, broke the silence. "Are we really sure we want to do this? We will be putting forty percent of our cash reserves into this one American company. I am especially concerned that we are investing this heavily in an economy that may be on the verge of collapse."

The emir responded, "This is a great time for our country. Allah will be proud of what we do over the next few days. America's greed and lust for pleasure, power, and money has now been replaced by panic. Their government leaders cannot agree on how to get themselves out of the mess they are in. The House of Representatives today voted down the emergency legislation the financial institutions needed to stay afloat. This was their last hope. The entire country is in financial gridlock. Like the rest of Americans who own stock in corporate America, the stockholders of the Dutch Phosphate Corporation are desperate and in shock. They have seen even this strong company's share price dragged down by the rest of the stock market. Our timing could not be better. While the U.S. government regulators are distracted with all the turbulence on Wall Street, they will not have time for or interest in our purchase of what they consider to be an obscure fertilizer stock."

Turning to Abdul Ahad, his director of operations, the emir asked, "When will our attorneys make the offer?"

"I am told the formal proposal will be hand-delivered to Mr. Clark, the CEO, at ten o'clock tomorrow morning. Mr. Clark has already received a courtesy notification of our proposal. Once the inevitable sets in, we will have a face-to-face meeting with him."

OCTOBER 6, 2008 — UNITED STATES

In spite of frantic phone calls from major shareholders, members of the board of directors, and senior officers of the Dutch Phosphate Corporation to the Securities and Exchange Commission, Federal Trade Commission, members of Congress, and the White House, no one in government would divert his or her attention from the financial crisis that was upon the nation. They were far more concerned about finding a way to ward off the country's looming financial collapse than being bothered by some Arab sovereign wealth fund's interest in buying a fertilizer company.

At first, many of the largest shareholders of DPC expressed public outrage at the takeover of their company by what they perceived to be a bunch of oil-rich Arabs. However, when the offer for outstanding shares was increased to eighty dollars per share, twice the trading price at the time, resistance quickly disappeared. With their stock portfolios collapsing around them, this windfall came as a touch of salvation for many. At this price, the company's fate was sealed.

www.ingramcontent.com/pod-product-compliance
Lightning Source LLC
Chambersburg PA
CBHW031309170626
46807CB00001B/349